**St. Louis Community
College**

Library

5801 Wilson Avenue
St. Louis, Missouri 63110

THE WORKS OF
W. SOMERSET MAUGHAM

This is a volume in the Arno Press collection

THE WORKS OF
W. SOMERSET MAUGHAM

Introduction by Michael G. Wood

See last pages of this volume for a complete list of titles.

The Magician

by

W. SOMERSET MAUGHAM

ARNO PRESS

A New York Times Company

New York / 1977

Reprint Edition 1977 by Arno Press Inc.

Reprinted by permission of
  Doubleday & Company, Inc.

THE WORKS OF W. SOMERSET MAUGHAM
ISBN for complete set: 0-405-07804-8
See last pages of this volume for titles.

Manufactured in the United States of America

———•———

Library of Congress Cataloging in Publication Data
Maugham, William Somerset, 1874-1965.
    The magician.

    (The works of W. Somerset Maugham)
    Reprint of the 1957 ed. published by Doubleday,
Garden City, N. Y.
    I. Title. II. Series: Maugham, William Somerset,
1874-1965. Works. 1976.
[PZ3.M442Mag16] [PR6025.A86] 823'.9'12   75-25356
ISBN 0-405-07814-5

Introduction

"I have put the whole of my life into my books," Somerset Maugham wrote. The remark suggests a career of confession, and it is true that Maugham is the author of one long, intensely autobiographical novel: *Of Human Bondage*. He himself describes the writing of the book as an act of therapy and exorcism:

> My memories would not let me be. They became such a torment that I determined at last to have done with the theatre until I had released myself from them. My book took two years to write. I was disconcerted by its length, but I was not writing to please: I was writing to free myself from an intolerable obsession. I achieved the result I aimed at, for after I had corrected the proofs, I found all those ghosts were laid, and neither the people nor the incidents ever crossed my mind again.

The ghosts had their small revenge, however. When Maugham began to read *Of Human Bondage* for a recording company, some thirty years after the book was published, he broke down and cried, and the record was never made.

Maugham spoke often of the power of writing to allay a writer's sorrows:

> Whenever he has anything on his mind, whether it be a harassing reflection, grief at the death of a friend, unrequited love, wounded pride, anger at the treachery of someone to whom he has shown kindness, in short any emotion or any perplexing thought, he has only to put it down in black and white, using it as the theme of a story or the decoration of an essay, to forget all about it . . .

> . . . illness, privation, his hopes abandoned, his griefs, humiliations, everything is transformed by his power into material and by writing it he can overcome it . . . Nothing befalls him that he cannot transmute into a stanza, a song or a story, and having done this be rid of it. The artist is the only free man.

We may find the completeness and finality of some of those phrases — he has *only* to put it down to forget *all* about it, *nothing* befalls him that he cannot transmute into art — have a rather wishful ring, and of course we don't need Maugham's returning ghosts to remind us that the accounts of the heart are rarely so thoroughly and so easily settled. As Maugham himself says elsewhere, the imagination compensates us for all the things we have missed or lost in life. But if we hadn't missed or lost them we should not need the compensation: "To imagine is to fail; for it is the acknowledgement of defeat in the encounter with reality."

Still, there is nothing odd in Maugham's insistence on writing as exorcism, since the exorcism, at least once, worked well enough for him. It didn't defeat the ghosts for good, but it kept them quiet for a long spell. What is odd, in the light of Maugham's views, is that apart from *Of Human Bondage* there is scarcely an autobiographical work among all the novels, plays, stories, essays and travel books that Maugham wrote in a long and prolific life. Even his autobiography, he tells us in its opening words, is not an autobiography, and a phrase from the beginning of that book sheds some light on this curious puzzle. "In one way or another," Maugham says, "I have used in my writings whatever has happened to me in the course of my life." He means not that he has confessed all but that he hasn't wasted any of his material. It is in this sense that the whole of his life has gone into his books. His books have said as much about him as he is going to say. Before and after *Of Human Bondage* Maugham is not a writer who consoles himself in fiction for distresses suffered in reality. He is a writer who, in and out of fiction, cultivates a blend of irony and controlled curiosity which keeps reality's distresses at a comfortable distance. The ghosts are not exorcised. Where possible, they are headed off before they get a chance to do any haunting.

In spite of the considerable fame of *Of Human Bondage,* this second, more distant Maugham is undoubtedly the more famous one. This is the writer whose cherished themes, as Graham Greene once said, are usually thought to be adultery in China, murder in Malaya and suicide in the South Seas; whose chief subject is the ragged edge of the British Empire. He is Kipling turned inside out, as V. S. Pritchett suggested, discovering that the white man's burden is as often as not the white woman's infidelity, which is in turn a sort of infection by strange places and loneliness. Maugham writes of England too, of course, of country houses and upper-class London and the more respectable fringes of the literary life, but the constant feature of Maugham's stories and plays and novels, whether they are set in Batavia or in Belgrave Square, is Maugham's own wry, observing presence, the weary, witty, detached intelligence which directs the dialogue of the plays and frequently appears to comment on the goings-on in the novels and stories. It is a portrait of the artist as a man of the world, and it can produce a certain glibness. On the other hand, there is mostly an undercurrent of worry even in the glibness, a nervous streak in the man of the world, and it is the mixture that matters. Maugham speaks of ethics, for example. "It may be that in goodness we may see, not a reason for life nor an explanation, but an extenuation . . ." The idea is familiar enough, but the word *extenuation* gives a disconcerting twist to the tail of the sentence. Or again: "He was developing a sense of humor, and found he had a knack of saying bitter things, which caught people on the raw . . ." Is that what we usually mean by humor? Sometimes Maugham's irony is more carefully and consciously balanced: "I do not think a thought of self ever entered her untidy head. She was a miracle of unselfishness. It was really hardly human." Sometimes it is frankly comic: "Miss Jones was resolutely cheerful. She grimly looked on the bright side of things." Sometimes it conceals a subdued sense of outrage:

> When we went there (a missionary is speaking) they had no sense of sin at all. They broke the commandments one after the other and never knew they were doing wrong. And I think that was the most difficult part of my work, to instill into the natives the sense of sin.

And sometimes it brings off extraordinary, shifting combinations of denunciation and tribute, subtle praise and sharp blame:

> Hypocrisy is the most difficult and nerve-racking vice that any man can pursue; it needs an unceasing vigilance and a rare detachment of spirit. It cannot, like adultery or gluttony, be practised at spare moments; it is a whole-time job.

Maugham is not a difficult or complicated writer, and we can miss all the undercurrents in his prose and still enjoy him a great deal. But the undercurrents are likely to keep Maugham's writing alive when the simpler enjoyment has faded, and in any case I wonder whether anyone misses them entirely. They are like a nameless taste caught up in a taste we know well, a touch of bitterness in a sweet dish — or to be more precise, a touch of genuine bitterness in a bitter-seeming dish, a flavour of real, unnerving acrimony in the midst of a calm and worldly cynicism. Certainly a sense of these undercurrents is what separates Maugham's serious admirers from his serious detractors. Thus Edmund Wilson, seeing nothing of the sceptic within the popular writer, could say Maugham was "a half-trashy novelist, who writes badly, but is patronised by half-serious readers, who do not care much about writing", while Cyril Connolly, who could hardly be called a half-serious reader, saw mainly the scepticism, and insisted on Maugham's continuing dissatisfaction with the things that satisfy too many of us, on his discontent "with the banal routine of self-esteem and habit, with which most of us . . . fidget away our one-and-only lives." Both men are more or less right, because Maugham really had it both ways. He was one of the most successful writers of the century, and yet he seems to peer out at us from the heart of his success with a disappointed, dissenting face, seems to assure us in a whisper that money and fame are merely toys, ways of passing the time, better than most and certainly worth having, but not the secret of eternal life or even, when it comes down to it, of much temporal happiness.

Maugham's friends and family agree in finding him elusive. "I am indebted to him for nearly fifty years of kindness and hospitality," Noel Coward wrote, "but I cannot truthfully say that I really knew him intimately." "Looking back," Maugham's nephew Robin Maugham says, "I realize that though I sometimes feared him, I was fond of him; but I am afraid I never understood him." This is exactly the quality of Maugham's writing. He is present to the reader, an engaging, even a compelling story-teller — it is very hard to put down a Maugham story or novel once you have taken it up — but he is a man who is giving nothing away. Maugham's prose is lucid and musical, but above all it is remarkable for what it *doesn't* say. Consider this little story, one of Maugham's working notes:

> The peacock. We were driving through the jungle. It was not thick and presently we caught sight of a peacock among the trees with its beautiful tail outspread. It walked, a proud, magnificent object, treading the ground with a peculiar delicacy, with a sort of deliberation, and its walk was so elegant, so wonderfully graceful that it recalled to my memory Nijinsky stepping on to the stage at Covent Garden and walking with just such a delicacy, grace and elegance. I have seldom seen a sight more thrilling than that peacock threading its solitary way through the jungle. My companion told the driver to stop and seized his gun.
>
> "I'm going to have a shot at it."
>
> My heart stopped still. He fired, and I hoped he'd miss, but he didn't. The driver jumped out of the car and brought back the dead bird which a moment before had been so exultantly alive. It was a cruel sight.
>
> We ate the breast for dinner that night. The flesh was white, tender and succulent; it was a welcome change from the scraggy chickens which are brought to the table evening after evening in India.

Is there sarcasm there? A comment on the sudden switches of human feeling? A dark warning about the transience of beauty and the lure of food? No, there is just a vivid unsettling sequence: the bird is alive, the bird is dead, the bird is eaten. All interpretation, all attempts to say what such a sequence *means,* are left to us. Maugham merely records the sequence.

In his life and in his writing, Maugham appears to have found a tone which was a perfect disguise, which kept the world away. Even the malice which many often-told stories attribute to him can be seen as part of a role he is playing. "Tra-la-la-la," Maugham is supposed to have sung when he received the news of the death of his wife, divorced from him some twenty years earlier. "No more alimony. Tra-la-, tra-la." Perhaps Maugham's real feelings corresponded closely enough to the feelings he was expressing. But the expression itself still contains a large element of pose: there is a sense of the audience there. Somerset Maugham, seventy years old, is playing at being Somerset Maugham, the shocking, wicked old man. Behind that role, another Maugham, quite unknowable, entertaining who knows what complex configurations of guilt and joy and regret and relief and perfect indifference, lives his entirely private life. "I have put the whole of my life into my books." That innocent-seeming sentence turns into a sly joke. Both books and life for Maugham, apart from *Of Human Bondage* and the painful experiences that went into it, were a system of defences, high walls around a very secret self.

William Somerset Maugham was born in Paris in 1874, the youngest of six sons. His father was solicitor to the British Embassy, and his mother, generally acknowledged to have been a beautiful and charming woman, was well-known in Parisian high society. Maugham spoke only French until he was nine or ten years old. His mother died when he was eight, his father died two years later, and Maugham was sent to live with his uncle and aunt in Whitestable, on the coast of Kent, in England. He spent a number of miserable years there, interspersed in term-time with equally miserable periods at the King's School, Canterbury — all to be recorded with unforgiving anger in *Of Human Bondage*. The young Maugham had a stammer which he felt to be a severe handicap, and which never left him, although in later life he converted it into something of an asset in story-telling. Garson Kanin describes a speech made by Maugham, which began, "There are many . . . virtues in . . . growing old." A long pause followed, which lengthened into an uncomfortable silence. Finally Maugham continued, "I'm just . . . trying . . . to think what they are."

In 1890, Maugham contracted tuberculosis, and underwent a cure at Hyéres in the south of France. A year later he finished his secondary schooling and went to Heidelberg, in Germany, for a year, where he attended lectures at the university and began to take an interest in the theatre. In 1892, he entered St. Thomas' Medical School in London, and in 1897, having served as an intern and delivered some sixty-three babies, he qualified as a doctor, although he was never to practise. Maugham's first novel, *Liza of Lambeth,* based on his medical experiences in the slums and at the hospital, was published in 1897, and on the strength of its moderate success he decided to devote his life to writing. For the next few years he lived in Spain, Italy, London and Paris, published stories and novels, and wrote plays. These were the years of *The Making of a Saint* (1898), *The Hero* (1901), *Mrs. Craddock* (1902), *The Merry-Go-Round* (1904) and *The Magician* (1908) — all novels — and *Orientations* (1899), a collection of short stories. Maugham's first stage success was *Lady Frederick,* produced in London in 1907, and the following year saw two more hits — *Jack Straw* and *Mrs. Dot* — and one near-flop — *The Explorer* — so that four of Maugham's plays were then running in London at one time, and a cartoon published in *Punch* showed Shakespeare biting his nails and brooding in front of the boards which advertised Maugham's four productions. Not all his subsequent plays were to be resounding successes, but many of them were, with long runs both in England and America. Almost overnight, Maugham had become a playwright with a major reputation, and that he remained until *Sheppey,* his last play, was performed in 1933, and for some time afterwards, of course.

When war came to Europe in 1914, Maugham joined a Red Cross unit, and it was in Belgium that he corrected the proofs of *Of Human Bondage,* published the following year. Soon, however, he was transferred to the Intelligence Service, on the grounds that the writer's trade was a good cover for a secret agent. "The work appealed," Maugham wrote later, "both to my sense of romance and my sense of the ridiculous." His missions took him to Switzerland, the South Seas and Russia — this last excursion involving an attempt to halt the Revolution of 1917. Much of his experience at this time found its way into *Ashenden,* a collection of short stories published in 1928, the first (and still one of the best) of the works of anti-romantic spy fiction, a portrait of the grubby, heartless world of espionage which points away from John Buchan's *The Thirty-nine Steps,* for example, and towards John Le Carré's *The Spy Who Came In From The Cold.*

In the midst of his activities as writer and spy, Maugham somehow found time to carry on an affair with, and then to marry Syrie Wellcome in 1916. The marriage was not a happy one; it ended in divorce in 1927. There was one child, Liza.

Towards the end of the war, Maugham's tuberculosis flared up again, and he spent two years in a sanatorium in Scotland. "He enjoyed his illness," Maugham's biographer Richard A. Cordell writes. And Maugham himself later said, "I had a grand time. I discovered for the first time in my life how very delightful it is to lie in bed . . . I delighted in the privacy of my room with the immense window wide open to the starry winter night. It gave me a delicious sense of security, aloofness and freedom."

In 1919, Maugham published *The Moon and Sixpence,* a novel suggested by the life of the painter Gauguin, and in 1925 he published *The Painted Veil,* a novel with a contemporary Chinese setting, but based on an incident in Dante. Several of Maugham's best-known plays — *The Circle* (1921), *East of Suez* (1922), *The Constant Wife* (1926), *The Sacred Flame* (1928) — were produced in the twenties, and there were also three volumes of short stories: *The Trembling of a Leaf* (1921), *The Casuarina Tree* (1926), and as already mentioned, *Ashenden* (1928). Maugham travelled a great deal in these years — to the Far East, the Near East, to America, to North Africa — and wrote two remarkable travel books: *On a Chinese Screen* (1922) and *The Gentleman in the*

Parlour (1930). In 1928 he bought the Villa Mauresque, a house in the south of France, at St. Jean-Cap-Ferrat, between Monaco and Nice, and it was there that he lived for the rest of his life when he wasn't travelling or uprooted by war. He spent the years of the second world war in America, mainly in North Carolina at the house of his publisher, Nelson Doubleday, and returned to the Villa Mauresque in 1946.

In 1930, Maugham published *Cakes and Ale,* a bitter and witty novel about a famous writer and his two successive, contrasting wives, and a work which many people, myself included, regard as Maugham's finest achievement. It was followed by eight more novels, the last of which is *Catalina* (1948) and the most important of which is *The Razor's Edge* (1944). There were five more collections of short stories, some essays and criticism and the literary last will and testament which is called *The Summing Up* (1938). In 1949 Maugham brought out *A Writer's Notebook,* a selection from his working notes taken over nearly sixty years — the first entry is dated 1892 — and in 1952, in a preface to the second volume of his collected short stories, he took his leave as a writer of fiction. If a writer is "so impudent," he wrote, "as to live to a ripe age," then "the time comes at last when, having given what he has to give, his powers fail . . . It is well then if he can bring himself to cease writing stories which might just as well have remained unwritten . . . I have written my last story." Maugham was seventy-eight years old. He continued to write essays, but in 1959 he had most of his remaining papers burned, although some, apparently, did survive the raid. At the age of ninety-one, seriously ill, his memory failing, this man who had once thought of committing suicide at sixty-five, but who now clung to life with the tenacity he had himself described, with some distaste, some fifty years before — "He was set upon one thing indomitably," he wrote of his hero's moribund uncle in *Of Human Bondage,* "and that was living, just living" — had a stroke, lost consciousness and soon died. His ashes were buried in the grounds of the King's School, Canterbury, which was home, of a sort, after all.

"For many years I have been described as a cynic." Maugham's supposed cynicism is partly a matter of his aloofness, of the careful privacy he preserved in his life and his work. This aloofness, as I suggested earlier, is a complicated affair, a game of mischief and masquerade as well as a means of self-protection. But it is also, at times, simply aloofness, absence. Maugham often seems to move his fictional characters around with a chilly, clinical indifference to their feelings, and while the following statement is impressively honest, it doesn't exactly warm the heart:

> I have been interested in men in general not for their own sakes, but for the sake of my work. I have not, as Kant enjoined, regarded each man as an end in himself, but as material that might be useful to me as a writer.

Maugham tended to see people as elements in a pattern, and when he glimpsed, or could invent, a pattern in the lives he observed or encountered, he had a story. One of his notes, for example, describes a successful and much-admired woman who is unhappy until she falls in love with a man much younger than herself, who subsequently dies in an air crash. "Her friends were afraid she would commit suicide. Not at all. She became happy, fat and contented. She had had her tragedy." Obviously there is an interesting human truth in such a reversal of what we would all expect, but above all there is a pattern, a marked neatness of design. Maugham looked for the same thing in his own life, thought of writing a last novel about the London slums because his first novel had been set there, spoke of completing the edifice of his life's works by writing *The Summing Up:*

> If I live I shall write other books, for my amusement and I hope for the amusement of my readers, but I do not think they will add anything essential to my design. The house is built.

There is a striking fidelity here to the philosophy developed by Philip Carey, the young hero of *Of Human Bondage.* Life has no meaning, Philip decides, so the best we can do is to treat life as if it were a rich carpet, and trace out the designs of our doings on it:

> There was one pattern, the most obvious, perfect, and beautiful, in which a man was born, grew to manhood, married, produced children, toiled for his bread, and died; but there were others, intricate and wonderful, in which happiness did not enter and in which success was not attempted; and in them might be discovered a troubling grace. Some lives . . . the blind indifference of chance cut off while the design was still imperfect; and then the solace was comfortable that it did not matter; other lives . . . offered a pattern which was difficult to follow: the point of view had to be shifted and old standards had to be altered before one could understand that such a life was its own justification.

The troubling grace of a life without happiness and without success is a powerful notion, and troubling grace is perhaps the chief quality of Maugham's best work, which creates the sense of a fragile order being rescued from an encroaching confusion. But the rest of the passage has an awkward complacency — "in such a philosophy there is consolation aplenty even for the least consolable of lives," — since everything is bound to make a pattern of some sort and suggests an instinct for tidiness rather than any large depth of sensibility or intellect. Maugham recognized this tendency in himself when he spoke of the "tightness of effect" and the "sensation of airlessness" provoked by fiction that is too well-made, and of course it is present in the remarks I quoted near the beginning of this piece, where literature is seen as too neat a solution to the upsets of life. Interestingly enough, one of the best of all Maugham's stories, *The Lotus Eater,* portrays a man who shapes his life perfectly, only to discover that his nerve is not as good as he thought it was. At the age of thirty-five Thomas Wilson has left England and the bank he worked in, and settled in Capri, where he leads a modest but pleasant and carefree existence. He has just enough money to last him until he is sixty, and then he intends to take his own life. "Don't you think after twenty-five years of perfect happiness one ought to be satisfied to call it a day?" he asks. When he reaches sixty, though, Wilson keeps postponing his final act, subsists on credit as long as his credit lasts, botches an attempt at suicide, and lives out the rest of his life, sick and poor and humiliated, on the charity of his old landlord. The story bears a disturbing, prophetic relation to Maugham's own end, serene at sixty-four ("I look forward to old age without dismay"), prepared for death at seventy-five ("I am on the wing"), but hanging on in angry senility by the time he was eighty-six, quarrelling with his family, and publishing a rancourous memoir about his marriage. As Maugham must have known all along, there are many things more important than patterns.

What seems to be Maugham's cynicism, then, is often merely his aloofness or his tidiness. But a question remains, which is not a question of Maugham's manner but of what he has to *say,* explicitly and implicitly. "I have been accused of making men out worse than they are," he said. "I do not think I have done this. All I have done is to bring into prominence certain traits that many writers shut their eyes to." Perhaps. There is a great deal of cruelty and violence and revenge in Maugham's fiction. Mackintosh, a British administrator in Samoa, so hates his superior that he leaves his gun lying around for a hostile native to use on the hated man. When the native does use it, Mackintosh, in an excess of guilt, walks out into the lagoon and shoots himself. Another administrator, in Borneo, has a subordinate who arouses such anger in the natives that they kill him. The administrator feels a great, quiet exultation: he had disliked the man, and is delighted to be rid of him. A husband finds out about his wife's infidelity, but creates no fuss and causes no trouble. He simply makes sure that she knows he knows. Another husband in the same situation takes his wife off with him to a cholera-infected town. When she asks him, later, whether he meant to kill her that way, he says, after a long hesitation, "At first." He himself dies of cholera, and she survives, to return to England.

Obviously popular fiction feeds on melodrama, which in turn feeds on acts of violence, but there is in Maugham an insistence on retaliation which goes well beyond the needs of the kind of fiction he is writing. There is a recurring pleasure in the sight of an enmity or a rancour which is actively satisfied, which finds a thorough, practical expression. We should not forget, either, that Maugham can take an almost aesthetic delight in random acts of mischief and malice. In the story *A Friend in Need* a kindly, respectable, humorous man sends another, younger man off on a long and dangerous swim, with the promise that he will give him a job when he gets back. The young man drowns in the offshore currents, and when asked whether he knew the young man would drown, the older man says, "Well, I hadn't got a vacancy in my office at the moment." Maugham also tells the story of Elizabeth Russell, who is said to have read out to her sick husband those passages in a book of hers where he appeared in a damaging light. When she finished, he turned his face to the wall and died. Maugham, with obvious relish, asks Mrs. Russell whether this terrible tale is true, and she looks blandly at him and says, "He was very ill. He would have died in any case."

A moralist may frown at all this, and a sentimentalist will be distressed. Maugham himself is being slightly disingenuous when he says he simply tells the truth in such matters, since he is clearly selecting, with great skill, those truths which have an ugly, malevolent glitter to them. Nevertheless, I think there is a genuine, uncompromising vision here, as well as a lot of gratuitous cruelty. At his best Maugham forces us to see that hatred has its own authentic joys and rewards, and I think of a line in Emily Brontë's *Wuthering Heights,* where Heathcliff is admonished to leave his revenge to God, and replies, "No, God won't have the satisfaction that I shall." The real question, perhaps, is not so much whether we have all felt such hatred at any time in our lives as whether we would be able to admit it if we did. There is a kind of courage in Maugham's allowing those grim and terminal revenges to have their day in his fiction.

The ground for most of these revenges in Maugham is humiliation, and Maugham's sourest and most famous contribution to the moral life of our century is probaly his diagnosis of love itself as above all, humiliation. Love in Maugham is either a helpless, unconditional surrender to instinct, an undignified collapse of all our best intentions; or it is a quest for disgrace, an infatuation with a creature we cannot respect and who will bring us only confused and ignoble pain. There is a sequence in *Of Human Bondage* which at first sight appears mismanaged, a clumsy attempt at pathos and suspense, but which then emerges as a strong portrait of love as masochism. Philip Carey introduces Mildred, the girl he loves, to his handsome and lively best friend, and Mildred and the best friend, predictably enough, go off together. It is only when we understand that Philip has not made a mistake, that indeed he has got just what he wanted, that things fall into place. Masochism, Maugham wrote much later, "is a sexual desire in a man to be subjected to ill treatment, physical and mental, by the woman he loves." Philip doesn't seek or receive physical ill treatment from Mildred, but he suffers mental unkindnesses constantly, eagerly. Having brought his friend and his girl together for his own anguish, he is soon offering them money so that they can spend a weekend in Oxford without him. Again, with this view of love as with Maugham's cases of satisfied hatred and cruelty, the question is not whether it is true in any complete sense, whether it is the whole story about human affections. Plainly it is not. The question, as with Proust, for example, is how we are to defend ourselves against a view of love which is obviously true *enough* to shake our most cherished assumptions about our relations with the people we care about.

Maugham was clear, even harsh, about his own limitations. He had some power of invention, he said, but only "small power of imagination."

> I have taken living people and put them into the situations, tragic or comic, that their characters suggested. I might well say that they invented their own stories . . .

> I knew that I had no lyrical quality. I had a small vocabulary and no efforts that I could make to enlarge it much availed me. I had little gift of metaphor; the original and striking simile seldom occurred to me.

The lucidity and simplicity of Maugham's style have often been praised. It is a style which does its job, but it is also the style of a man who has an ear for the flow and fall of a sentence, and occasionally there *is* a metaphor or a simile which stays in the mind. In the cholera epidemic in *The Painted Veil,* death is said to stand round the corner, "taking lives like a gardener digging up potatoes," and the casual, domestic image is perfect, just what is needed. Above all, of course, Maugham is a *readable* writer, a man who knows the art of keeping his audience with him, and the best test of his readability is to read him. A simple illustration of the way he makes himself readable, though, is his knack of suggesting exotic locations without brandishing foreign names or going in for that rather flashy familiarity with strange customs which is characteristic of Lawrence and Hemingway and Durrell and Lowry. A mention of the Pacific, of a Chinese cook, of hot weather, a reef and a lagoon, and we are in Samoa. Sunshine, coolies, rickshaws, a Chinese clerk, an electric fan, and we are in Singapore. These scenes are set with an immaculate discretion. And of course there is always a story being told.

This is true even of Maugham's non-fiction. His travel books are the notes of a man looking for stories. *On a Chinese Screen,* for example, is a set of jottings which Maugham decided to leave as jottings, but some of them were so close to fiction that he could include them, much later, among his *Complete Short Stories.* Similarly, Maugham's essays and criticism are composed mainly of anecdotes. Maugham looks at his favourite writers much as he looks at the people around him, and *The Art of Fiction,* an introduction to ten great novelists and their novels, spends most of its time telling the "stories," as it were, of Fielding and Jane Austen and Stendhal and Balzac and Melville and others. Maugham's criticism is limited by a rather depressing common sense — it may be true that obscurities arise in *Othello* because Shakespeare couldn't think of a better way of doing things, but I think a critic has to do better than that by way of interpretation all the same — and by the taste for tidiness I have already mentioned. I doubt whether many people would agree, for example, that *Wuthering Heights* is "clumsily constructed." Still, he has excellent taste and a gift for making fine and useful distinctions. He is a good companion rather than a provocative critic, and this is perhaps as it should be. Essays, travel books, over a hundred short stories: such works are the natural, continuing expression of the life of a writer who reads a lot and travels a great deal.

The plays and the novels are a slightly different matter, if only because they involve larger and more sustained excursions away from the pose of the casual story-teller. Maugham's plays are skillful and intelligent, but even the best of them — *Our Betters, The Circle, The Constant Wife* — seem rather brittle now, caught in a rather strange zone between nature and artifice. There is an air of elegant clockwork about them, which oddly enough tends to make them seem insufficiently artificial, makes them seem as if they were not quite acting on the strength of their own conventions, so that they have neither the force of naturalism nor the pace and folly of the plays of Congreve, say, or Wilde. Nevertheless, they are consistently playable and entertaining, and full of good lines:

— You have no heart, and you can't imagine that anyone else should have.

— I have plenty of heart, but it beats for people of my own class . . .

— If a man's unfaithful to his wife she's an object of sympathy, whereas if a woman's unfaithful to her husband he's merely an object of ridicule.

— That is one of those conventional prejudices that sensible people must strive to ignore . . .

Among the novels, *Of Human Bondage* is taken by many people to be Maugham's masterpiece, his "one great novel," according to Malcolm Cowley, who speculated on what he called the Somerset Maugham enigma: "Why has he never written another book that was half so good as *Of Human Bondage?*" The short answer, I would say, is that he has, and several of them at that. *Of Human Bondage* is a patient and precise account of a boy's growing up, and the story of Philip Carey's tortured, grovelling love for Mildred is intense and compelling. But otherwise there is a certain blandness about the novel which makes it easy to read but also easy to forget. It is not to be compared with its close contemporaries, Joyce's *Portrait of the Artist as a Young Man* or Lawrence's *Sons and Lovers. Cakes and Ale,* on the other hand, Maugham's own favourite among his novels, escapes blandness because it is so fiercely and unfailingly witty, and because Maugham is on his true home ground, talking not about his personal past but about the business of writing, which is the consuming interest of his present life. The book opens with a cruel portrait of Maugham's friends Hugh Walpole, but the portrait is also a mocking version of Maugham himself as the successful writer who has made a little talent go a very long way. People have been shocked by the book's disrespectful depiction of a figure much resembling Thomas Hardy, who had died only two years before the book appeared. But at this distance in time Maugham's view of Hardy seems extremely affectionate. Hardy is not the lofty and magisterial man of letters he is supposed to be, but he is something better. He is perky and alive and irreverent, the model of a man who has managed to survive his own greatness. Of Maugham's other novels, *The Moon and Sixpence, The Painted Veil* and *The Razor's Edge* are the most successful, although all three of them tend to alternate between masterly scenes and moments of glibness. But then even *Catalina* and *Then and Now*, which Maugham's admirers usually concede to the opposition, seem to me genuinely enjoyable, and that, perhaps, is the truest measure of Maugham's achievement. He never wrote an uninteresting book, and no doubt that is the right reward for knowing your own limitations so well.

Some critics rate Maugham's stories above his novels, but I think that only serves to displace the central question. It is true that the best of Maugham's stories are as good as the best of his novels, but the question is, How good is that? Maugham himself thought he had only "slender baggage" for his journey into posterity, and saw himself as standing "in the very front row of the second-raters." But then that judgement implies a view of who the other second-raters are. Richard A. Cordell puts Maugham alongside Thackeray, Gide, Hardy, Conrad, Bennett and Galsworthy in that category, which I think both subtly inflates Maugham's standing and confuses the issue. On the one hand at least three of those writers are first-rate by any standard, and on the other Maugham is almost certainly more important than Galsworthy, for example. His true peers, perhaps, to take an instance from each of three succeeding generations, are Arnold Bennett, Aldous Huxley and Graham Greene: honourable company, it seems to me. But such games are better not played too long. The names serve only as bearings, means of finding Maugham's domain on the map of modern literature.

Maugham's legacy to other writers is an ideal of perfect craftsmanship, and a reassurance that an author can be extremely popular without sacrificing either his intelligence or his culture. His larger, more general legacy to literature, I think, is the record of a lifelong exploration of a crippling respectability, of a sense of the pressure of opinion which is all the more painful because you know the pressure would vanish if you were brave enough to ignore it. "The Maughams had the intense respectability of the upper middle class," Maugham's nephew Robin writes. Maugham appears never to have felt that being a writer was a respectable profession, and of course his own homosexuality can't have helped much. He told Robin that his greatest mistake was to have persuaded himself that he was "three quarters normal and . . . only a quarter . . . queer — whereas really it was the other way round." Some of Maugham's heroes defeat respectability, flout convention and manage to live a life of their own. But his work contains far more victims than heroes, and most of his characters either succumb to propriety and regret their cowardice for the rest of their days, or they throw over the traces, and then sink further and further into disgrace and degradation, ending all too often in suicide. Maugham plays both roles in these stories, for all his aloofness and cynicism. He is the person who fails and the society which rules on the failure, he is respectability's enemy and the agent of respectability itself. V. S. Pritchett suggested that Maugham's fiction catered to our wish to be worldly and wise in the manner of Maugham's much-travelled, never-ruffled narrators, and that this accounted largely for his huge success. I think the fiction speaks to something more serious than that. It speaks to our profoundly divided social loyalties, to our mixed satisfaction and resentment at the lives we live, to our longing to drop out of it all like Paul Gauguin and to our knowledge that we are really not going to do it. It doesn't ask us to leave the world or change the world, and it doesn't invite us to indulge in regret. It does confront us with the long disappointment which is one of the costs of life in human society, and it reminds us how much of our time, even when we are quite alone, is spent in the confining stare of other people's eyes.

Michael Wood
Columbia University

THE MAGICIAN

The Magician

by

W. SOMERSET MAUGHAM

Together with
A FRAGMENT OF AUTOBIOGRAPHY

DOUBLEDAY & COMPANY, INC.
Garden City, New York, 1957

A FRAGMENT OF AUTOBIOGRAPHY

In 1897, after spending five years at St. Thomas's Hospital I passed the examinations which enabled me to practise medicine. While still a medical student I had published a novel called *Liza of Lambeth* which caused a mild sensation, and on the strength of that I rashly decided to abandon doctoring and earn my living as a writer; so, as soon as I was 'qualified', I set out for Spain and spent the best part of a year in Seville. I amused myself hugely and wrote a bad novel. Then I returned to London and, with a friend of my own age, took and furnished a small flat near Victoria Station. A maid of all work cooked for us and kept the flat neat and tidy. My friend was at the bar, and so I had the day (and the flat) to myself and my work. During the next six years I wrote several novels and a number of plays. Only one of these novels had any success, but even that failed to make the stir that my first one had made. I could get no manager to take my plays. At last, in desperation, I sent one, which I called *A Man of Honour,* to the Stage Society, which gave two performances, one on Sunday night, another on Monday afternoon, of plays which, unsuitable for the commercial theatre, were considered of sufficient merit to please an intellectual audience. As every one knows, it was the Stage Society that produced the early plays of Bernard Shaw. The committee accepted *A Man of Honour,* and W. L. Courtney, who was a member of it, thought well enough of my crude play to publish it in *The Fortnightly Review*, of which he was then editor. It was a feather in my cap.

Though these efforts of mine brought me very little money, they attracted not a little attention, and I made friends. I was looked upon as a promising young writer and, I think I may say it without vanity, was accepted as a member of the intelligentsia, an honourable condition which, some years later, when I became a popular writer of light comedies, I lost; and have never since regained. I was invited to literary parties and to parties given by women of rank and fashion who thought it behoved them to patronise the arts. An unattached and fairly presentable young man is always in demand. I lunched out and dined out. Since I could not afford to take cabs, when I dined out, in tails and a white tie, as was then the custom, I went and came back by bus. I was asked to spend weekends in the country. They were something of a trial on account of the tips you had to give to the butler and to the footman who brought you your morning tea. He unpacked your gladstone bag, and you were uneasily aware that your well-worn pyjamas and modest toilet articles had made an unfavourable impression upon him. For all that, I found life pleasant and I enjoyed myself. There seemed no reason why I should not go on indefinitely in the same way, bringing out a novel once a year (which seldom earned more than the small advance the publisher had given me but which was on the whole respectably reviewed), going to more and more parties, making more and more friends. It was all very nice, but I couldn't see that it was leading me anywhere. I was thirty. I was in a rut. I felt I must get out of it. It did not take me long to make up my mind. I told the friend with whom I shared the flat that I wanted to be rid of it and go abroad. He could not keep it by himself, but we luckily found a middle-aged gentleman who wished to install his mistress in it, and was prepared to take it off our hands. We sold the furniture for what it could fetch, and within a month I was on my way to Paris. I took a room in a cheap hotel on the Left Bank.

A few months before this, I had been fortunate enough to make friends with a young painter who had a studio in the Rue Campagne Première. His name was Gerald Kelly. He had had an upbringing unusual for a painter, for he had been to Eton and to Cambridge. He was highly talented, abundantly loquacious, and immensely enthusiastic. It was he who first made me acquainted with the Impressionists, whose pictures had recently been accepted by the Luxembourg. To my shame, I must admit that I could not make head or tail of them. Without much searching, I found an apartment on the fifth floor of a house near the Lion de Belfort. It had two rooms and a kitchen, and cost seven hundred francs a year, which was then twenty-eight pounds. I bought, second-hand, such furniture and household utensils as were essential, and the *concierge* told me of a woman who would come in for half a day and make my *café au lait* in the morning and my luncheon at noon. I settled down and set to work on still another novel. Soon after my arrival, Gerald Kelly took me to a restaurant called Le Chat Blanc in the Rue d'Odessa, near the Gare Montparnasse, where a number of artists were in the habit of dining; and from then on I dined there every night. I have described the place elsewhere, and in some detail in the novel to which these pages are meant to serve as a preface, so that I need not here say more about it. As a rule, the same people came in every night, but now and then others came, perhaps only once, perhaps two or three times. We were apt to look upon them as interlopers, and I don't think we made them particularly welcome. It was thus that I first met Arnold Bennett and Clive Bell. One of these casual visitors was Aleister Crowley. He was spending the winter in Paris. I took an immediate dislike to him, but he interested and amused me. He was a great talker and he talked uncommonly well. In early youth, I was told, he was extremely handsome, but when I knew him he had put on weight, and his hair was thining. He had fine eyes and a way, whether natural or acquired I do not know, of so focusing them that, when he looked at you, he seemed to look behind you. He was a fake, but not entirely a fake. At Cambridge he had won his chess blue and was esteemed the best whist player of his time. He was a liar and unbecomingly boastful, but the odd thing was that he had actually done some of the things he boasted of. As a mountaineer, he had made an ascent of K.2 in the Hindu Kush, the second highest mountain in India, and he made it without the elaborate equipment, the cylinders of oxygen and so forth, which render the endeavours of the mountaineers of the present day more likely to succeed. He did not reach the top, but got nearer to it than anyone had done before.

Crowley was a voluminous writer of verse, which he published sumptuously at his own expense. He had a gift for rhyming, and his verse is not entirely without merit. He had been greatly influenced by Swinburne and Robert Browning. He was grossly, but not unintelligently, imitative. As you flip through the pages you may well read a stanza which, if you came across it in a volume of Swinburne's, you would accept without question as the work of the master. *"It's rather hard, isn't it, Sir, to make sense of it?"* If you were shown this line and asked what poet had written it, I think you would be inclined to say, Robert Browning. You would be wrong. It was written by Aleister Crowley.

At the time I knew him he was dabbling in Satanism, magic and the occult. There was just then something of a vogue in Paris for that sort of thing, occasioned, I surmise, by the interest that was still taken in a book of Huysmans's, *Là Bas*. Crowley told fantastic stories of his experiences, but it was hard to say whether he was telling the truth or merely pulling your leg. During that winter I saw him several times, but never after I left Paris to return to London. Once, long afterwards, I received a telegram from him which ran as follows: "Please send twenty-five pounds at once. Mother of God and I starving. Aleister Crowley." I did not do so, and he lived on for many disgraceful years.

I was glad to get back to London. My old friend had by then rooms in Pall Mall, and I was able to take a bedroom in the same building and use his sitting-room to work in. *The Magician* was published in 1908, so I suppose it was written during the first six months of 1907. I do not remember how I came to think that Aleister Crowley might serve as the model for the character whom I called Oliver Haddo; nor, indeed, how I came to think of writing that particular novel at all. When, a little while ago, my publisher expressed a wish to re-issue it, I felt that, before consenting to this, I really should read it again. Nearly fifty years had passed since I had done so, and I had completely forgotten it. Some authors enjoy reading their old works; some cannot bear to. Of these I am. When I have corrected the proofs of a book, I have finished with it for good and all. I am impatient when people insist on talking to me about it; I am glad if they like it, but do not much care if they don't. I am no more interested in it than in a worn-out suit of clothes that I have given away. It was thus with disinclination that I began to read *The Magician*. It held my interest, as two of my early novels, which for the same reason I have been obliged to read, did not. One, indeed, I simply could not get through. Another had to my mind some good dramatic scenes, but the humour filled me with mortification, and I should have been ashamed to see it republished. As I read *The Magician*, I wondered how on earth I could have come by all the material concerning the black arts which I wrote of. I must have spent days and days reading in the library of the British Museum. The style is lush and turgid, not at all the sort of style I approve of now, but perhaps not unsuited to the subject; and there are a great many more adverbs and adjectives than I should use to-day. I fancy I must have been impressed by the *écriture artiste* which the French writers of the time had not yet entirely abandoned, and unwisely sought to imitate them.

Though Aleister Crowley served, as I have said, as the model for Oliver Haddo, it is by no means a portrait of him. I made my character more striking in appearance, more sinister and more ruthless than Crowley ever was. I gave him magical powers that Crowley, though he claimed them, certainly never possessed. Crowley, however, recognised himself in the creature of my invention, for such it was, and wrote a full-page review of the novel in *Vanity Fair*, which he signed 'Oliver Haddo'. I did not read it, and wish now that I had. I daresay it was a pretty piece of vituperation, but probably, like his poems, intolerably verbose.

I do not remember what success, if any, my novel had when it was published, and I did not bother about it much, for by then a great change had come into my life. The manager of the Court Theatre, one Otho Stuart, had brought out a play which failed to please, and he could not immediately get the cast he wanted for the next play he had in mind to produce. He had read one of mine, and formed a very poor opinion of it; but he was in a quandary, and it occurred to him that it might just serve to keep his theatre open for a few weeks, by the end of which the actors he wanted for the play he had been obliged to postpone would be at liberty. He put mine on. It was an immediate success. The result of this was that in a very little while other managers accepted the plays they had consistently refused, and I had four running in London at the same time. I, who for ten years had earned an average of one hundred pounds a year, found myself earning several hundred pounds a week. I made up my mind to abandon the writing of novels for the rest of my life. I did not know that this was something out of my control and that when the urge to write a novel seized me, I should be able to do nothing but submit. Five years later, the urge came and, refusing to write any more plays for the time, I started upon the longest of all my novels. I called it *Of Human Bondage*.

THE MAGICIAN

1

Arthur Burdon and Dr. Porhoët walked in silence. They had lunched at a restaurant in the Boulevard Saint Michel, and were sauntering now in the gardens of the Luxembourg. Dr. Porhoët walked with stooping shoulders, his hands behind him. He beheld the scene with the eyes of the many painters who have sought by means of the most charming garden in Paris to express their sense of beauty. The grass was scattered with the fallen leaves, but their wan decay little served to give a touch of nature to the artifice of all besides. The trees were neatly surrounded by bushes, and the bushes by trim beds of flowers. But the trees grew without abandonment, as though conscious of the decorative scheme they helped to form. It was autumn, and some were leafless already. Many of the flowers were withered. The formal garden reminded one of a light woman, no longer young, who sought, with faded finery, with powder and paint, to make a brave show of despair. It had those false, difficult smiles of uneasy gaiety, and the pitiful graces which attempt a fascination that the hurrying years have rendered vain.

Dr. Porhoët drew more closely round his fragile body the heavy cloak which even in summer he could not persuade himself to discard. The best part of his life had been spent in Egypt, in the practice of medicine, and the frigid summers of Europe scarcely warmed his blood. His memory flashed for an instant upon those multi-coloured streets of Alexandria; and then, like a homing bird, it flew to the green woods and the storm-beaten coasts of his native Brittany. His brown eyes were veiled with sudden melancholy.

"Let us wait here for a moment," he said.

They took two straw-bottomed chairs and sat near the octagonal water which completes with its fountain of Cupids the enchanting artificiality of the Luxembourg. The sun shone more kindly now, and the trees which framed the scene were golden and lovely. A balustrade of stone gracefully enclosed the space, and the flowers, freshly bedded, were very gay. In one corner they could see the squat, quaint towers of Saint Sulpice, and on the other side the uneven roofs of the Boulevard Saint Michel.

The palace was grey and solid. Nurses, some in the white caps of their native province, others with the satin streamers of the *nounou*, marched, sedately two by two, wheeling perambulators and talking. Brightly dressed children trundled hoops or whipped a stubborn top. As he watched them, Dr. Porhoët's lips broke into a smile, and it was so tender that his thin face, sallow from long exposure to subtropical suns, was transfigured. He no longer struck you merely as an insignificant little man with hollow cheeks and a thin grey beard; for the weariness of expression which was habitual to him vanished before the charming sympathy of his smile. His sunken eyes glittered with a kindly but ironic good-humour. Now passed a guard in the romantic cloak of a brigand in comic opera and a peaked cap like that of an *alguacil*. A group of telegraph boys in blue stood round a painter, who was making a sketch—notwithstanding half-frozen fingers. Here and there, in baggy corduroys, tight jackets, and wide-brimmed hats, strolled students who might have stepped from the page of Murger's immortal romance. But the students now are uneasy with the fear of ridicule, and more often they walk in bowler hats and the neat coats of the *boulevardier*.

Dr. Prohoët spoke English fluently, with scarcely a trace of foreign accent, but with an elaboration which suggested that he had learned the language as much from study of the English classics as from conversation.

"And how is Miss Dauncey?" he asked, turning to his friend.

Arthur Burdon smiled.

"Oh, I expect she's all right. I've not seen her to-day, but I'm going to tea at the studio this afternoon, and we want you to dine with us at the Chien Noir."

"I shall be much pleased. But do you not wish to be by yourselves?"

"She met me at the station yesterday, and we dined together. We talked steadily from half-past six till midnight."

"Or, rather, she talked and you listened with the delighted attention of a happy lover."

Arthur Burdon had just arrived in Paris. He was a surgeon on the staff of St. Luke's, and had come ostensibly to study the methods of the French operators; but his real object was certainly to see Margaret Dauncey. He was furnished with introductions from London surgeons of repute, and had already spent a morning at the Hôtel Dieu, where the operator, warned that his visitor was a bold and skilful surgeon, whose reputation in England was already considerable, had sought to dazzle him by feats that savoured almost of legerdemain. Though the hint of charlatanry in the Frenchman's methods had not escaped Arthur Burdon's shrewd eyes, the audacious sureness of his hand had excited his enthusiasm. During luncheon he talked of nothing else, and Dr. Porhoët, drawing upon his memory, recounted the more extraordinary operations that he had witnessed in Egypt.

He had known Arthur Burdon ever since he was born, and indeed had missed being present at his birth only because the Khedive Ismaïl had summoned him unexpectedly to Cairo. But the Levantine merchant who was Arthur's father had been his most intimate friend, and it was with singular pleasure that Dr. Porhoët saw the young man, on his advice, enter his own profession and achieve a distinction which himself had never won.

Though too much interested in the characters of the persons whom chance threw in his path to have much ambition on his own behalf, it pleased him to see it in others. He observed with satisfaction the pride which Arthur took in his calling and the determination, backed by his confidence and talent, to become a master of his art. Dr. Porhoët knew that a diversity of interests, though it adds charm to a man's personality, tends to weaken him. To excel one's fellows it is needful to be circumscribed. He did not regret, therefore, that Arthur in many ways was narrow. Letters and the arts meant little to him. Nor would he trouble himself with the graceful trivialities which make a man a good talker. In mixed company he was content to listen silently to others, and only something very definite to say could tempt him to join in the general conversation. He worked very hard, operating, dissecting, or lecturing at his hospital, and took pains to read every word, not only in English, but in French and German, which was published concerning his profession. Whenever he could snatch a free day he spent it on the golf-links of Sunningdale, for he was an eager and a fine player.

But at the operating-table Arthur was different. He was no longer the awkward man of social intercourse, who was sufficiently conscious of his limitations not to talk of what he did not understand, and sincere enough not to express admiration for what he did not like. Then, on the other hand, a singular exhilaration filled him; he was conscious of his power, and he rejoiced in it. No unforeseen accident was able to confuse him. He seemed to have a positive instinct for operating, and his hand and his brain worked in a manner that appeared almost automatic. He never hesitated, and he had no fear of failure. His success had been no less than his courage, and it was plain that soon his reputation with the public would equal that which he had already won with the profession.

Dr. Porhoët had been making listless patterns with his stick upon the gravel, and now, with that charming smile of his, turned to Arthur.

"I never cease to be astonished at the unexpectedness of human nature," he remarked. "It is really very surprising that a man like you should fall so deeply in love with a girl like Margaret Dauncey."

Arthur made no reply, and Dr. Porhoët, fearing that his words might offend, hastened to explain.

"You know as well as I do that I think her a very charming young person. She has beauty and grace and sympathy. But your characters are more different than chalk and cheese. Notwithstanding your birth in the East and your boyhood spent amid the very scenes of the *Thousand and One Nights,* you are the most matter-of-fact creature I have ever come across."

"I see no harm in your saying insular," smiled Arthur. "I confess that I have no imagination and no sense of humour. I am a plain, practical man, but I can see to the end of my nose with extreme clearness. Fortunately it is rather a long one."

"One of my cherished ideas is that it is impossible to love without imagination."

Again Arthur Burdon made no reply, but a curious look came into his eyes as he gazed in front of him. It was the look which might fill the passionate eyes of a mystic when he saw in ecstasy the Divine Lady of his constant prayers.

"But Miss Dauncey has none of that narrowness of outlook which, if you forgive my saying so, is perhaps the secret of your strength. She has a delightful enthusiasm for every form of art. Beauty really means as much to her as bread and butter to the more soberly-minded. And she takes a passionate interest in the variety of life."

"It is right that Margaret should care for beauty, since there is beauty in every inch of her," answered Arthur.

He was too reticent to proceed to any analysis of his feelings; but he knew that he had cared for her first on account of that physical perfection which contrasted so astonishingly with the countless deformities in the study of which his life was spent. But one phrase escaped him almost against his will.

"The first time I saw her I felt as though a new world had opened to my ken."

The divine music of Keats's lines rang through Arthur's remark, and to the Frenchman's mind gave his passion a romantic note that foreboded future tragedy. He sought to dispel the cloud which his fancy had cast upon the most satisfactory of love affairs.

"You are very lucky, my friend. Miss Margaret admires you as much as you adore her. She is never tired of listening to my prosy stories of your childhood in Alexandria, and I'm quite sure that she will make you the most admirable of wives."

"You can't be more sure than I am," laughed Arthur.

He looked upon himself as a happy man. He loved Margaret with all his heart, and he was confident in her great affection for him. It was impossible that anything should arise to disturb the pleasant life which they had planned together. His love cast a glamour upon his work, and his work, by contrast, made love the more entrancing.

"We're going to fix the date of our marriage now," he said. "I'm buying furniture already."

"I think only English people could have behaved so oddly as you, in postponing your marriage without reason for two mortal years."

"You see, Margaret was ten when I first saw her, and only seventeen when I asked her to marry me. She thought she had reason to be grateful to me and would have married me there and then. But I knew she hankered after these two years in Paris, and I didn't feel it was fair to bind her to me till she had seen at least something of the world. And she seemed hardly ready for marriage, she was growing still."

"Did I not say that you were a matter-of-fact young man?" smiled Dr. Porhoët.

"And it's not as if there had been any doubt about our knowing our minds. We both cared, and we had a long time before us. We could afford to wait."

At that moment a man strolled past them, a big stout fellow, showily dressed in a check suit; and he gravely took off his hat to Dr. Porhoët. The doctor smiled and returned the salute.

"Who is your fat friend?" asked Arthur.

"That is a compatriot of yours. His name is Oliver Haddo."

"Art-student?" inquired Arthur, with the scornful tone he used when referring to those whose walk in life was not so practical as his own.

"Not exactly. I met him a little while ago by chance. When I was getting together the material for my little book on the old alchemists I read a great deal at the library of the Arsenal, which, you may have heard, is singularly rich in all works dealing with the occult sciences."

Burdon's face assumed an expression of amused disdain. He could not understand why Dr. Porhoët occupied his leisure with studies so profitless. He had read his book, recently published, on the more famous of the alchemists; and, though forced to admire the profound knowledge upon which it was based, he could not forgive the waste of time which his friend might have expended more usefully on topics of pressing moment.

"Not many people study in that library," pursued the doctor, "and I soon knew by sight those who were frequently there. I saw this gentleman every day. He was immersed in strange old books when I arrived early in the morning, and he was reading them still when I left, exhausted. Sometimes it happened that he had the volumes I asked for, and I discovered that he was studying the same subjects as myself. His appearance was extraordinary, but scarcely sympathetic; so, though I fancied that he gave me opportunities to address him, I did not avail myself of them. One day, however, curiously enough, I was looking up some point upon which it seemed impossible to find authorities. The librarian could not help me, and I had given up the search, when this person brought me the very book I needed. I surmised that the librarian had told him of my difficulty. I was very grateful to the stranger. We left together that afternoon, and our kindred studies gave us a common topic of conversation. I found that his reading was extraordinarily wide, and he was able to give me information about works which I had never even heard of. He had the advantage over me that he could apparently read Hebrew as well as Arabic, and he had studied the Kabbalah in the original."

"And much good it did him, I have no doubt," said Arthur. "And what is he by profession?"

Dr. Porhoët gave a deprecating smile.

"My dear fellow, I hardly like to tell you. I tremble in every limb at the thought of your unmitigated scorn."

"Well?"

"You know, Paris is full of queer people. It is the chosen home of every kind of eccentricity. It sounds incredible in this year of grace, but my friend Oliver Haddo claims to be a magician. I think he is quite serious."

"Silly ass!" answered Arthur with emphasis.

II

Margaret Dauncey shared a flat near the Boulevard du Montparnasse with Susie Boyd; and it was to meet her that Arthur had arranged to come to tea that afternoon. The young women waited for him in the studio. The kettle was boiling on the stove; cups and *petits fours* stood in readiness on a model stand. Susie looked forward to the meeting with interest. She had heard a good deal of the young man, and knew that the connection between him and Margaret was not lacking in romance. For years Susie had led the monotonous life of a mistress in a school for young ladies, and had resigned herself to its dreariness for the rest of her life, when a legacy from a distant relation gave her sufficient income to live modestly upon her means. When Margaret, who had been her pupil, came, soon after this, to announce her intention of spending a couple of years in Paris to study art, Susie willingly agreed to accompany her. Since then she had worked industriously at Colarossi's Academy, by no means under the delusion that she had talent, but merely to amuse herself. She refused to surrender the pleasing notion that her environment was slightly wicked. After the toil of many years it relieved her to be earnest in nothing; and she found infinite satisfaction in watching the lives of those around her.

She had a great affection for Margaret, and though her own stock of enthusiasms was run low, she could enjoy thoroughly Margaret's young enchantment in all that was exquisite. She was a plain woman; but there was no envy in her, and she took the keenest pleasure in Margaret's comeliness. It was almost with maternal pride that she watched each year add a new grace to that exceeding beauty. But her common sense was sound, and she took care by good-natured banter to temper the praises which extravagant admirers at the drawing-class lavished upon the handsome girl both for her looks and for her talent. She was proud to think that she would hand over to Arthur Burdon a woman whose character she had helped to form, and whose loveliness she had culti-vated with a delicate care.

Susie knew, partly from fragments of letters which Margaret read to her, partly from her conversation, how passionately he adored his bride; and it pleased her to see that Margaret loved him in return with a grateful devotion. The story of this visit to Paris touched her imagination. Margaret was the daughter of a country barrister, with whom Arthur had been in the habit of staying; and when he died, many years after his wife, Arthur found himself the girl's guardian and executor. He sent her to school; saw that she had everything she could possibly want; and when, at seven-teen, she told him of her wish to go to Paris and learn drawing, he at once consented. But though he never sought to assume authority over her, he suggested that she should not live alone, and it was on this account that she went to Susie. The preparations for the journey were scarcely made when Margaret discovered by chance that her father had died penniless and she had lived ever since at Arthur's entire expense. When she went to see him with tears in her eyes, and told him what she knew, Arthur was so embarrassed that it was quite absurd.

"But why did you do it?" she asked him. "Why didn't you tell me?"

"I didn't think it fair to put you under any obligation to me, and I wanted you to feel quite free."

She cried. She couldn't help it.

"Don't be so silly," he laughed. "You owe me nothing at all. I've done very little for you, and what I have done has given me a great deal of pleasure."

"I don't know how I can ever repay you."

"Oh, don't say that," he cried. "It makes it so much harder for me to say what I want to."

She looked at him quickly and reddened. Her deep blue eyes were veiled with tears.

"Don't you know that I'd do anything in the world for you?" she cried.

"I don't want you to be grateful to me, because I was hoping—I might ask you to marry me some day."

Margaret laughed charmingly as she held out her hands.

"You must know that I've been wanting you to do that ever since I was ten."

She was quite willing to give up her idea of Paris and be married without delay, but Arthur pressed her not to change her plans. At first Margaret vowed it was impossible to go, for she knew now that she had no money, and she could not let her lover pay.

"But what does it matter?" he said. "It'll give me such pleasure to go on with the small allowance I've been making you. After all, I'm pretty well-to-do. My father left me a moderate income, and I'm making a good deal already by operating."

"Yes, but it's different now. I didn't know before. I thought I was spending my own money."

"If I died to-morrow, every penny I have would be yours. We shall be married in two years, and we've known one another much too long to change our minds. I think that our lives are quite irrevocably united."

Margaret wished very much to spend this time in Paris, and Arthur had made up his mind that in fairness to her they could not marry till she was nineteen. She consulted Susie Boyd, whose common sense prevented her from paying much heed to romantic notions of false delicacy.

"My dear, you'd take his money without scruple if you'd signed your names in a church vestry, and as there's not the least doubt that you'll marry, I don't see why you shouldn't now. Besides, you've got nothing whatever to live on, and you're equally unfitted to be a governess or a typewriter. So it's Hobson's choice, and you'd better put your exquisite sentiments in your pocket."

Miss Boyd, by one accident after another, had never seen Arthur, but she had heard so much that she looked upon him already as an old friend. She admired him for his talent and strength of character as much as for his loving tenderness to Margaret. She had seen portraits of him, but Margaret said he did not photograph well. She had asked if he was good-looking.

"No, I don't think he is," answered Margaret, "but he's very paintable."

"That is an answer which has the advantage of sounding well and meaning nothing," smiled Susie.

She believed privately that Margaret's passion for the arts was a not unamiable pose which would disappear when she was happily married. To have half a dozen children was in her mind much more important than to paint pictures. Margaret's gift was by no means despicable, but Susie was not convinced that callous masters would have been so enthusiastic if Margaret had been as plain and as old as herself.

Miss Boyd was thirty. Her busy life had not caused the years to pass easily, and she looked older. But she was one of those plain women whose plainness does not matter. A gallant Frenchman had to her face called her a *belle laide,* and, far from denying the justness of his observation, she had been almost flattered. Her mouth was large and she had little round bright eyes. Her skin was colourless and much disfigured by freckles. Her nose was long and thin. But her face was so kindly, her vivacity so attractive, that no one after ten minutes thought of her ugliness. You noticed then that her hair, though sprinkled with white, was pretty, and that her figure was exceedingly neat. She had good hands, very white and admirably formed, which she waved continually in the fervour of her gesticulation. Now that her means were adequate she took great pains with her dress, and her clothes, though they cost much more than she could afford, were always beautiful. Her taste was so great, her tact so sure, that she was able to make the most of herself. She was determined that if people called her ugly they should be forced in the same breath to confess that she was perfectly gowned. Susie's talent for dress was remarkable, and it was due to her influence that Margaret was arrayed always in the latest mode. The girl's taste inclined to be artistic, and her sense of colour was apt to run away with her discretion. Except for the display of Susie's firmness, she would scarcely have resisted her desire to wear nondescript garments of violent hue. But the older woman expressed herself with decision.

"My dear, you won't draw any the worse for wearing a

well-made corset, and to surround your body with bands of
grey flannel will certainly not increase your talent."

"But the fashion is so hideous," smiled Margaret.

"Fiddlesticks! The fashion is always beautiful. Last year
it was beautiful to wear a hat like a pork-pie tipped over your
nose; and next year, for all I know, it will be beautiful to
wear a bonnet like a sitz-bath at the back of your head. Art
has nothing to do with a smart frock, and whether a high-
heeled pointed shoe commends itself or not to the painters
in the quarter, it's the only thing in which a woman's foot
looks really nice."

Susie Boyd vowed that she would not live with Margaret
at all unless she let her see to the buying of her things.

"And when you're married, for heaven's sake ask me to
stay with you four times a year, so that I can see after your
clothes. You'll never keep your husband's affection if you trust
to your own judgment."

Miss Boyd's reward had come the night before, when
Margaret, coming home from dinner with Arthur, had repeated an observation of his.

"How beautifully you're dressed!" he had said. "I was
rather afraid you'd be wearing art-serges."

"Of course you didn't tell him that I insisted on buying
every stitch you'd got on," cried Susie.

"Yes, I did," answered Margaret simply. "I told him I had
no taste at all, but that you were responsible for everything."

"That was the least you could do," answered Miss Boyd.

But her heart went out to Margaret, for the trivial incident
showed once more how frank the girl was. She knew quite
well that few of her friends, though many took advantage
of her matchless taste, would have made such an admission

to the lover who congratulated them on the success of their costume.

There was a knock at the studio door, and Arthur came in.

"This is the fairy prince," said Margaret, bringing him to her friend.

"I'm glad to see you in order to thank you for all you've done for Margaret," he smiled, taking the proffered hand.

Susie remarked that he looked upon her with friendliness, but with a certain vacancy, as though too much engrossed in his beloved really to notice anyone else; and she wondered how to make conversation with a man who was so manifestly absorbed. While Margaret busied herself with the preparations for tea, his eyes followed her movements with a doglike, touching devotion. They travelled from her smiling mouth to her deft hands. It seemed that he had never seen anything so ravishing as the way in which she bent over the kettle. Margaret felt that he was looking at her, and turned round. Their eyes met, and they stood for an appreciable time gazing at one another silently.

"Don't be a pair of perfect idiots," cried Susie gaily. "I'm dying for my tea."

The lovers laughed and reddened. It struck Arthur that he should say something polite.

"I hope you'll show me your sketches afterwards, Miss Boyd. Margaret says they're awfully good."

"You really needn't think it in the least necessary to show any interest in me," she replied bluntly.

"She draws the most delightful caricatures," said Margaret. "I'll bring you a horror of yourself, which she'll do the moment you leave us."

"Don't be so spiteful, Margaret."

Miss Boyd could not help thinking all the same that

Arthur Burdon would caricature very well. Margaret was right when she said that he was not handsome, but his clean-shaven face was full of interest to so passionate an observer of her kind. The lovers were silent, and Susie had the conversation to herself. She chattered without pause and had the satisfaction presently of capturing their attention. Arthur seemed to become aware of her presence, and laughed heartily at her burlesque account of their fellow-students at Colarossi's. Meanwhile Susie examined him. He was very tall and very thin. His frame had a Yorkshireman's solidity, and his bones were massive. He missed being ungainly only through the serenity of his self-reliance. He had high cheek-bones and a long, lean face. His nose and his mouth were large, and his skin was sallow. But there were two characteristics which fascinated her, an imposing strength of purpose and a singular capacity for suffering. This was a man who knew his mind and was determined to achieve his desire; it refreshed her vastly after the extreme weakness of the young painters with whom of late she had mostly consorted. But those quick dark eyes were able to express an anguish that was hardly tolerable, and the mobile mouth had a nervous intensity which suggested that he might easily suffer the very agonies of woe.

Tea was ready, and Arthur stood up to receive his cup.

"Sit down," said Margaret. "I'll bring you everything you want, and I know exactly how much sugar to put in. It pleases me to wait on you."

With the grace that marked all her movements she walked across the studio, the filled cup in one hand and the plate of cakes in the other. To Susie it seemed that he was overwhelmed with gratitude by Margaret's condescension. His eyes were soft with indescribable tenderness as he took the sweetmeats she gave him. Margaret smiled with happy pride. For all her good-nature, Susie could not prevent the pang that wrung her heart; for she too was capable of love. There was in her a wealth of passionate affection that none had sought to find. None had ever whispered in her ears the charming nonsense that she read in books. She recognised that she had no beauty to help her, but once she had at least the charm of vivacious youth. That was gone now, and the freedom to go into the world had come too late; yet her instinct told her that she was made to be a decent man's wife and the mother of children. She stopped in the middle of her bright chatter, fearing to trust her voice, but Margaret and Arthur were too much occupied to notice that she had ceased to speak. They sat side by side and enjoyed the happiness of one another's company.

"What a fool I am!" thought Susie.

She had learnt long ago that common sense, intelligence, good-nature, and strength of character were unimportant in comparison with a pretty face. She shrugged her shoulders.

"I don't know if you young things realise that it's growing late. If you want us to dine at the Chien Noir, you must leave us now, so that we can make ourselves tidy."

"Very well," said Arthur, getting up. "I'll go back to my hotel and have a wash. We'll meet at half-past seven."

When Margaret had closed the door on him, she turned to her friend.

"Well, what do you think?" she asked, smiling.

"You can't expect me to form a definite opinion of a man whom I've seen for so short a time."

"Nonsense!" said Margaret.

Susie hesitated for a moment.

"I think he has an extraordinarily good face," she said at

last gravely. "I've never seen a man whose honesty of purpose was so transparent."

Susie Boyd was so lazy that she could never be induced to occupy herself with household matters and, while Margaret put the tea things away, she began to draw the caricature which every new face suggested to her. She made a little sketch of Arthur, abnormally lanky, with a colossal nose, with the wings and the bow and arrow of the God of Love, but it was not half done before she thought it silly. She tore it up with impatience. When Margaret came back, she turned round and looked at her steadily.

"Well?" said the girl, smiling under the scrutiny.

She stood in the middle of the lofty studio. Half-finished canvases leaned with their faces against the wall; pieces of stuff were hung here and there, and photographs of well-known pictures. She had fallen unconsciously into a wonderful pose, and her beauty gave her, notwithstanding her youth, a rare dignity. Susie smiled mockingly.

"You look like a Greek goddess in a Paris frock," she said.

"What have you to say to me?" asked Margaret, divining from the searching look that something was in her friend's mind.

Susie stood up and went to her.

"You know, before I'd seen him I hoped with all my heart that he'd made you happy. Notwithstanding all you'd told me of him, I was afraid. I knew he was much older than you. He was the first man you'd ever known. I could scarcely bear to entrust you to him in case you were miserable."

"I don't think you need have any fear."

"But now I hope with all my heart that you'll make *him* happy. It's not you I'm frightened for now, but him."

Margaret did not answer; she could not understand what Susie meant.

"I've never seen anyone with such a capacity for wretchedness as that man has. I don't think you can conceive how desperately he might suffer. Be very careful, Margaret, and be very good to him, for you have the power to make him more unhappy than any human being should be."

"Oh, but I want him to be happy," cried Margaret vehemently. "You know that I owe everything to him. I'd do all I could to make him happy, even if I had to sacrifice myself, because I love him so much that all I do is pure delight."

Her eyes filled with tears and her voice broke. Susie, with a little laugh that was half hysterical, kissed her.

"My dear, for heaven's sake don't cry! You know I can't bear people who weep, and if he sees your eyes red, he'll never forgive me."

III

THE CHIEN NOIR, where Susie Boyd and Margaret generally dined, was the most charming restaurant in the quarter. Downstairs was a public room, where all and sundry devoured their food, for the little place had a reputation for good cooking combined with cheapness; and the *patron,* a retired horse-dealer who had taken to victualling in order to build up a business for his son, was a cheery soul whose loud-voiced friendliness attracted custom. But on the first floor was a narrow room, with three tables arranged in a horse-shoe, which was reserved for a small party of English or American painters and a few Frenchmen with their wives. At least, they were so nearly wives, and their manner had such a matrimonial respectability, that Susie, when first she and Margaret were introduced into this society, judged it would be vulgar to turn up her nose. She held that it was prudish to insist upon the conventions of Notting Hill in the Boulevard du Montparnasse. The young women who had thrown in their lives with these painters were modest in demeanour and quiet in dress. They were model housewives, who had preserved their self-respect notwithstanding a difficult position, and did not look upon their relation with less seriousness because they had not muttered a few words before *Monsieur le Maire.*

The room was full when Arthur Burdon entered, but Margaret had kept him an empty seat between herself and Miss Boyd. Everyone was speaking at once, in French, at the top of his voice, and a furious argument was proceeding on the merit of the later Impressionists. Arthur sat down, and was hurriedly introduced to a lanky youth, who sat on the other side of Margaret. He was very tall, very thin, very fair. He wore a very high collar and very long hair, and held himself like an exhausted lily.

"He always reminds me of an Aubrey Beardsley that's been dreadfully smudged," said Susie in an undertone. "He's a nice, kind creature, but his name is Jagson. He has virtue and industry. I haven't seen any of his work, but he has absolutely no talent."

"How do you know, if you've not seen his pictures?" asked Arthur.

"Oh, it's one of our conventions here that nobody has talent," laughed Susie. "We suffer one another personally, but we have no illusions about the value of our neighbour's work."

"Tell me who everyone is."

"Well, look at that little bald man in the corner. That is Warren."

Arthur looked at the man she pointed out. He was a small person, with a pate as shining as a billiard-ball, and a pointed beard. He had protruding, brilliant eyes.

"Hasn't he had too much to drink?" asked Arthur frigidly.

"Much," answered Susie promptly, "but he's always in that condition, and the further he gets from sobriety the more charming he is. He's the only man in this room of whom you'll never hear a word of evil. The strange thing is that he's very nearly a great painter. He has the most fascinating sense of colour in the world, and the more intoxicated he is, the more delicate and beautiful is his painting. Sometimes, after more than the usual number of *apéritifs*, he will sit down in a café to do a sketch, with his hand so shaky that he can hardly hold a brush; he has to wait for a favourable moment, and then he makes a jab at the panel. And the immoral thing is that each of these little jabs is lovely. He's the most delightful interpreter of Paris I know, and when you've seen his sketches—he's done hundreds, of unimaginable grace and feeling and distinction—you can never see Paris in the same way again."

The little maid who looked busily after the varied wants of the customers stood in front of them to receive Arthur's order. She was a hard-visaged creature of mature age, but she looked neat in her black dress and white cap; and she had a motherly way of attending to these people, with a capacious smile of her large mouth which was full of charm.

"I don't mind what I eat," said Arthur. "Let Margaret order my dinner for me."

"It would have been just as good if I had ordered it," laughed Susie.

They began a lively discussion with Marie as to the merits of the various dishes, and it was only interrupted by Warren's hilarious expostulations.

"Marie, I precipitate myself at your feet, and beg you to bring me a *poule au riz.*"

"Oh, but give me one moment, *monsieur*," said the maid.

"Do not pay any attention to that gentleman. His morals are detestable, and he only seeks to lead you from the narrow path of virtue."

Arthur protested that on the contrary the passion of hunger occupied at that moment his heart to the exclusion of all others.

"Marie, you no longer love me," cried Warren. "There

was a time when you did not look so coldly upon me when I ordered a bottle of white wine."

The rest of the party took up his complaint, and all besought her not to show too hard a heart to the bald and rubicund painter.

"Mais si, je vous aime, Monsieur Warren," she cried, laughing, *"Je vous aime tous, tous."*

She ran downstairs, amid the shouts of men and women, to give her orders.

"The other day the Chien Noir was the scene of a tragedy," said Susie. "Marie broke off relations with her lover, who is a waiter at Lavenue's, and would have no reconciliation. He waited till he had a free evening, and then came to the room downstairs and ordered dinner. Of course, she was obliged to wait on him, and as she brought him each dish he expostulated with her, and they mingled their tears."

"She wept in floods," interrupted a youth with neatly brushed hair and a fat nose. "She wept all over our food, and we ate it salt with tears. We besought her not to yield; except for our encouragement she would have gone back to him; and he beats her."

Marie appeared again, with no signs now that so short a while ago romance had played a game with her, and brought the dishes that had been ordered. Susie seized once more upon Arthur Burdon's attention.

"Now please look at the man who is sitting next to Mr. Warren."

Arthur saw a tall, dark fellow with strongly-marked features, untidy hair, and a ragged black moustache.

"That is Mr. O'Brien, who is an example of the fact that strength of will and an earnest purpose cannot make a painter. He's a failure, and he knows it, and the bitterness has warped his soul. If you listen to him, you'll hear every painter of eminence come under his lash. He can forgive nobody who's successful, and he never acknowledges merit in anyone till he's safely dead and buried."

"He must be a cheerful companion," answered Arthur. "And who is the stout old lady by his side, with the flaunting hat?"

"That is the mother of Madame Rouge, the little pale-faced woman sitting next to her. She is the mistress of Rouge, who does all the illustrations for *La Semaine*. At first it rather tickled me that the old lady should call him *mon gendre*, my son-in-law, and take the irregular union of her daughter with such a noble unconcern for propriety; but now it seems quite natural."

The mother of Madame Rouge had the remains of beauty, and she sat bolt upright, picking the leg of a chicken with a dignified gesture. Arthur looked away quickly, for, catching his eye, she gave him an amorous glance. Rouge had more the appearance of a prosperous tradesman than of an artist; but he carried on with O'Brien, whose French was perfect, an argument on the merits of Cézanne. To one he was a great master and to the other an impudent charlatan. Each hotly repeated his opinion, as though the mere fact of saying the same thing several times made it more convincing.

"Next to me is Madame Meyer," proceeded Susie. "She was a governess in Poland, but she was much too pretty to remain one, and now she lives with the landscape painter who is by her side."

Arthur's eyes followed her words and rested on a clean-shaven man with a large, quantity of grey, curling hair. He had a handsome face of a deliberately æsthetic type and was very elegantly dressed. His manner and his conversation had

the flamboyance of the romantic thirties. He talked in flowing periods with an air of finality, and what he said was no
less just than obvious. The gay little lady who shared his
fortunes listened to his wisdom with an admiration that
plainly flattered him.

Miss Boyd had described everyone to Arthur except young
Raggles, who painted still life with a certain amount of skill,
and Clayson, the American sculptor. Raggles stood for rank
and fashion at the Chien Noir. He was very smartly dressed
in a horsey way, and he walked with bowlegs, as though he
spent most of his time in the saddle. He alone used scented
pomade upon his neat smooth hair. His chief distinction was
a greatcoat he wore, with a scarlet lining; and Warren, whose
memory for names was defective, could only recall him by that
peculiarity. But it was understood that he knew duchesses in
fashionable streets, and occasionally dined with them in
solemn splendour.

Clayson had a vinous nose and a tedious habit of saying
brilliant things. With his twinkling eyes, red cheeks, and
fair, pointed beard, he looked exactly like a Franz Hals; but
he was dressed like the caricature of a Frenchman in a comic
paper. He spoke English with a Parisian accent.

Miss Boyd was beginning to tear him gaily limb from limb,
when the door was flung open, and a large person entered.
He threw off his cloak with a dramatic gesture.

"Marie, disembarrass me of this coat of frieze. Hang my
sombrero upon a convenient peg."

He spoke execrable French, but there was a grandiloquence about his vocabulary which set everyone laughing.

"Here is somebody I don't know," said Susie.

"But I do, at least, by sight," answered Burdon. He leaned
over to Dr. Porhoët, who was sitting opposite, quietly eating

his dinner and enjoying the nonsense which everyone talked.
"Is not that your magician?"

"Oliver Haddo," said Dr. Porhoët, with a little nod of
amusement.

The new arrival stood at the end of the room with all
eyes upon him. He threw himself into an attitude of command and remained for a moment perfectly still.

"You look as if you were posing, Haddo," said Warren
huskily.

"He couldn't help doing that if he tried," laughed Clayson.

Oliver Haddo slowly turned his glance to the painter.

"I grieve to see, O most excellent Warren, that the ripe
juice of the *apéritif* has glazed your sparkling eye."

"Do you mean to say I'm drunk, sir?"

"In one gross, but expressive, word, drunk."

The painter grotesquely flung himself back in his chair as
though he had been struck a blow, and Haddo looked steadily
at Clayson.

"How often have I explained to you, O Clayson, that
your deplorable lack of education precludes you from the
brilliancy to which you aspire?"

For an instant Oliver Haddo resumed his effective pose;
and Susie, smiling, looked at him. He was a man of great
size, two or three inches more than six feet high; but the
most noticeable thing about him was a vast obesity. His
paunch was of imposing dimensions. His face was large and
fleshy. He had thrown himself into the arrogant attitude of
Velasquez's portrait of Del Borro in the Museum of Berlin;
and his countenance bore of set purpose the same contemptu-
ous smile. He advanced and shook hands with Dr. Porhoët.

"Hail, brother wizard! I greet in you, if not a master, at
least a student not unworthy my esteem."

Susie was convulsed with laughter at his pompousness, and he turned to her with the utmost gravity.

"Madam, your laughter is more soft in mine ears than the singing of Bulbul in a Persian garden."

Dr. Porhoët interposed with introductions. The magician bowed solemnly as he was in turn made known to Susie Boyd, and Margaret, and Arthur Burdon. He held out his hand to the grim Irish painter.

"Well, my O'Brien, have you been mixing as usual the waters of bitterness with the thin claret of Bordeaux?"

"Why don't you sit down and eat your dinner?" returned the other, gruffly.

"Ah, my dear fellow, I wish I could drive the fact into this head of yours that rudeness is not synonymous with wit. I shall not have lived in vain if I teach you in time to realise that of the rapier of irony is more effective an instrument than the bludgeon of insolence."

O'Brien reddened with anger, but could not at once find a retort, and Haddo passed on to that faded, harmless youth who sat next to Margaret.

"Do my eyes deceive me, or is this the Jagson whose name in its inanity is so appropriate to the bearer? I am eager to know if you will devote upon the ungrateful arts talents which were more profitably employed upon haberdashery."

The unlucky creature, thus brutally attacked, blushed feebly without answering, and Haddo went on to the Frenchman, Meyer, as more worthy of his mocking.

"I'm afraid my entrance interrupted you in a discourse. Was it the celebrated harangue on the greatness of Michael Angelo, or was it the searching analysis of the art of Wagner?"

"We were just going," said Meyer, getting up with a frown.

"I am desolated to lose the pearls of wisdom that habitually fall from your cultivated lips," returned Haddo, as he politely withdrew Madame Meyer's chair.

He sat down with a smile.

"I saw the place was crowded, and with Napoleonic instinct decided that I could only make room by insulting somebody. It is cause for congratulation that my gibes, which Raggles, a foolish youth, mistakes for wit, have caused the disappearance of a person who lives in open sin; thereby vacating two seats, and allowing me to eat a humble meal with ample room for my elbows."

Marie brought him the bill of fare, and he looked at it gravely.

"I will have a vanilla ice, O well-beloved, and the wing of a tender chicken, a fried sole, and some excellent pea-soup."

"*Bien, un potage, une sole,* one chicken, and an ice."

"But why should you serve them in that order rather than in the order I gave you?"

Marie and the two Frenchwomen who were still in the room broke into exclamations at this extravagance, but Oliver Haddo waved his fat hand.

"I shall start with the ice, O Marie, to cool the passion with which your eyes inflame me, and then without hesitation I will devour the wing of a chicken in order to sustain myself against your smile. I shall then proceed to a fresh sole, and with the pea-soup I will finish a not unsustaining meal."

Having succeeded in capturing the attention of everyone in the room, Oliver Haddo proceeded to eat these dishes in the order he had named. Margaret and Burdon watched him with scornful eyes, but Susie, who was not revolted by the vanity which sought to attract notice, looked at him curiously. He was clearly not old, though his corpulence added to his apparent age. His features were good, his ears small, and his nose delicately shaped. He had big teeth, but they were white and even. His mouth was large, with heavy moist lips. He had the neck of a bullock. His dark, curling hair had retreated from the forehead and temples in such a way as to give his clean-shaven face a disconcerting nudity. The baldness of his crown was vaguely like a tonsure. He had the look of a very wicked, sensual priest. Margaret, stealing a glance at him as he ate, on a sudden violently shuddered; he affected her with an uncontrollable dislike. He lifted his eyes slowly, and she looked away, blushing as though she had been taken in some indiscretion. These eyes were the most curious thing about him. They were not large, but an exceedingly pale blue, and they looked at you in a way that was singularly embarrassing. At first Susie could not discover in what precisely their pecularity lay, but in a moment she found out: the eyes of most persons converge when they look at you, but Oliver Haddo's, naturally or by a habit he had acquired for effect, remained parallel. It gave the impression that he looked straight through you and saw the wall beyond. It was uncanny. But another strange thing about him was the impossibility of telling whether he was serious. There was a mockery in that queer glance, a sardonic smile upon the mouth, which made you hesitate how to take his outrageous utterances. It was irritating to be uncertain whether, while you were laughing at him, he was not really enjoying an elaborate joke at your expense.

His presence cast an unusual chill upon the party. The French members got up and left. Warren reeled out with

O'Brien, whose uncouth sarcasms were no match for Haddo's bitter gibes. Raggles put on his coat with the scarlet lining and went out with the tall Jagson, who smarted still under Haddo's insolence. The American sculptor paid his bill silently. When he was at the door, Haddo stopped him.

"You have modelled lions at the Jardin des Plantes, my dear Clayson. Have you ever hunted them on their native plains?"

"No, I haven't."

Clayson did not know why Haddo asked the question, but he bristled with incipient wrath.

"Then you have not seen the jackals, gnawing at a dead antelope, scamper away in terror when the King of Beasts stalked down to make his meal."

Clayson slammed the door behind him. Haddo was left with Margaret, and Arthur Burdon, Dr. Porhoët, and Susie. He smiled quietly.

"By the way, are *you* a lion-hunter?" asked Susie flippantly.

He turned on her his straight uncanny glance.

"I have no equal with big game. I have shot more lions than any man alive. I think Jules Gérard, whom the French of the nineteenth century called *Le Tueur de Lions*, may have been fit to compare with me, but I can call to mind no other."

This statement, made with the greatest calm, caused a moment of silence. Margaret stared at him with amazement.

"You suffer from no false modesty," said Arthur Burdon.

"False modesty is a sign of ill-breeding, from which my birth amply protects me."

Dr. Porhoët looked up with a smile of irony.

"I wish Mr. Haddo would take this opportunity to disclose to us the mystery of his birth and family. I have a suspicion that, like the immortal Cagliostro, he was born of unknown but noble parents, and educated secretly in Eastern palaces."

"In my origin I am more to be compared with Denis Zachaire or with Raymond Lully. My ancestor, George Haddo, came to Scotland in the suite of Anne of Denmark, and when James I., her consort, ascended the English throne, he was granted the estates in Staffordshire which I still possess. My family has formed alliances with the most noble blood of England, and the Merestons, the Parnabys, the Hollingtons, have been proud to give their daughters to my house."

"Those are facts which can be verified in works of reference," said Arthur dryly.

"They can," said Oliver.

"And the Eastern palaces in which your youth was spent, and the black slaves who waited on you, and the bearded sheikhs who imparted to you secret knowledge?" cried Dr. Porhoët.

"I was educated at Eton, and I left Oxford in 1896."

"Would you mind telling me at what college you were?" said Arthur.

"I was at the House."

"Then you must have been there with Frank Hurrell."

"Now assistant physician at St. Luke's Hospital. He was one of my most intimate friends."

"I'll write and ask him about you."

"I'm dying to know what you did with all the lions you slaughtered," said Susie Boyd.

The man's effrontery did not exasperate her as it obviously exasperated Margaret and Arthur. He amused her, and she was anxious to make him talk.

"They decorate the floors of Skene, which is the name of my place in Staffordshire." He paused for a moment to light a cigar. "I am the only man alive who has killed three lions with three successive shots."

"I should have thought you could have demolished them by the effects of your oratory," said Arthur.

Oliver leaned back and placed his two large hands on the table.

"Burkhardt, a German with whom I was shooting, was down with fever and could not stir from his bed. I was awakened one night by the uneasiness of my oxen, and I heard the roaring of lions close at hand. I took my carbine and came out of my tent. There was only the meagre light of the moon. I walked alone, for I knew natives could be of no use to me. Presently I came upon the carcass of an antelope, half-consumed, and I made up my mind to wait for the return of the lions. I hid myself among the boulders twenty paces from the prey. All about me was the immensity of Africa and the silence. I waited, motionless, hour after hour, till the dawn was nearly at hand. At last three lions appeared over a rock. I had noticed, the day before, spoor of a lion and two females."

"May I ask how you could distinguish the sex?" asked Arthur, incredulously.

"The prints of a lion's fore feet are disproportionately larger than those of the hind feet. The fore feet and hind feet of the lioness are nearly the same size."

"Pray go on," said Susie.

"They came into full view, and in the dim light, as they stood chest on, they appeared as huge as the strange beasts of the Arabian tales. I aimed at the lioness which stood nearest to me and fired. Without a sound, like a bullock felled at one blow, she dropped. The lion gave vent to a sonorous roar. Hastily I slipped another cartridge in my rifle. Then I became conscious that he had seen me. He lowered his head, and his crest was erect. His lifted tail was twitching, his lips were drawn back from the red gums, and I saw his great white fangs. Living fire flashed from his eyes, and he growled incessantly. Then he advanced a few steps, his head held low; and his eyes were fixed on mine with a look of rage. Suddenly he jerked up his tail, and when a lion does this he charges. I got a quick sight on his chest and fired. He reared up on his hind legs, roaring loudly and clawing at the air, and fell back dead. One lioness remained, and through the smoke I saw her spring to her feet and rush towards me. Escape was impossible, for behind me were high boulders that I could not climb. She came on with hoarse, coughing grunts, and with desperate courage I fired my remaining barrel. I missed her clean. I took one step backwards in the hope of getting a cartridge into my rifle, and fell, scarcely two lengths in front of the furious beast. She missed me. I owed my safety to that fall. And then suddenly I found that she had collapsed. I had hit her after all. My bullet went clean through her heart, but the spring had carried her forwards. When I scrambled to my feet I found that she was dying. I walked back to my camp and ate a capital breakfast."

Oliver Haddo's story was received with astonished silence. No one could assert that it was untrue, but he told it with a grandiloquence that carried no conviction. Arthur would have wagered a considerable sum that there was no word of truth in it. He had never met a person of this kind before, and could not understand what pleasure there might be in the elaborate invention of improbable adventures.

"You are evidently very brave," he said.

"To follow a wounded lion into thick cover is probably the most dangerous proceeding in the world," said Haddo calmly. "It calls for the utmost coolness and for iron nerve."

The answer had an odd effect on Arthur. He gave Haddo a rapid glance, and was seized suddenly with uncontrollable laughter. He leaned back in his chair and roared. His hilarity affected the others, and they broke into peal upon peal of laughter. Oliver watched them gravely. He seemed neither disconcerted nor surprised. When Arthur recovered himself, he found Haddo's singular eyes fixed on him.

"Your laughter reminds me of the crackling of thorns under a pot," he said.

Haddo looked round at the others. Though his gaze preserved its fixity, his lips broke into a queer, sardonic smile.

"It must be plain even to the feeblest intelligence that a man can only command the elementary spirits if he is without fear. A capricious mind can never rule the sylphs, nor a fickle disposition the undines."

Arthur stared at him with amazement. He did not know what on earth the man was talking about. Haddo paid no heed.

"But if the adept is active, pliant, and strong, the whole world will be at his command. He will pass through the storm and no rain shall fall upon his head. The wind will not displace a single fold of his garment. He will go through fire and not be burned."

Dr. Porhoët ventured upon an explanation of these cryptic utterances.

"These ladies are unacquainted with the mysterious beings of whom you speak, *cher ami.* They should know that during the Middle Ages imagination peopled the four elements with intelligences, normally unseen, some of which were friendly to man and others hostile. They were thought to be powerful and conscious of their power, though at the same time they were profoundly aware that they possessed no soul. Their life depended upon the continuance of some natural object, and hence for them there could be no immortality. They must return eventually to the abyss of unending night, and the darkness of death afflicted them always. But it was thought that in the same manner as man by his union with God had won a spark of divinity, so might the sylphs, gnomes, undines, and salamanders by an alliance with man partake of his immortality. And many of their women, whose beauty was more than human, gained a human soul by loving one of the race of men. But the reverse occurred also, and often a love-sick youth lost his immortality because he left the haunts of his kind to dwell with the fair, soulless denizens of the running streams or of the forest airs."

"I didn't know that you spoke figuratively," said Arthur to Oliver Haddo.

The other shrugged his shoulders.

"What else is the world than a figure? Life itself is but a symbol. You must be a wise man if you can tell us what is reality."

"When you begin to talk of magic and mysticism I confess that I am out of my depth."

"Yet magic is no more than the art of employing consciously invisible means to produce visible effects. Will, love, and imagination are magic powers that everyone possesses; and whoever knows how to develop them to their fullest extent is a magician. Magic has but one dogma, namely, that the seen is the measure of the unseen."

"Will you tell us what the powers are that the adept possesses?"

"They are enumerated in a Hebrew manuscript of the sixteenth century, which is in my possession. The privileges of him who holds in his right hand the Keys of Solomon and in his left the Branch of the Blossoming Almond are twenty-one. He beholds God face to face without dying, and converses intimately with the Seven Genii who command the celestial army. He is superior to every affliction and to every fear. He reigns with all heaven and is served by all hell. He holds the secret of the resurrection of the dead, and the key of immortality."

"If you possess even these you have evidently the most varied attainments," said Arthur ironically.

"Everyone can make game of the unknown," retorted Haddo, with a shrug of his massive shoulders.

Arthur did not answer. He looked at Haddo curiously. He asked himself whether he believed seriously these preposterous things, or whether he was amusing himself in an elephantine way at their expense. His manner was earnest, but there was an odd expression about the mouth, a hard twinkle of the eyes, which seemed to belie it. Susie was vastly entertained. It diverted her enormously to hear occult matters discussed with apparent gravity in this prosaic tavern. Dr. Porhoët broke the silence.

"Arago, after whom has been named a neighboring boulevard, declared that doubt was a proof of modesty, which has rarely interfered with the progress of science. But one cannot say the same of incredulity, and he that uses the word impossible outside of pure mathematics is lacking in prudence. It should be remembered that Lactantius proclaimed belief in the existence of antipodes inane, and Saint Augustine of Hippo added that in any case there could be no question of inhabited lands."

"That sounds as if you were not quite sceptical, dear doctor," said Miss Boyd.

"In my youth I believed nothing, for science had taught me to distrust even the evidence of my five senses," he replied, with a shrug of the shoulders. "But I have seen many things in the East which are inexplicable by the known processes of science. Mr. Haddo has given you one definition of magic, and I will give you another. It may be described merely as the intelligent utilisation of forces which are unknown, contemned, or misunderstood of the vulgar. The young man who settles in the East sneers at the ideas of magic which surround him, but I know not what there is in the atmosphere that saps his unbelief. When he has sojourned for some years among Orientals, he comes insensibly to share the opinion of many sensible men that perhaps there is something in it after all."

Arthur Burdon made a gesture of impatience.

"I cannot imagine that, however much I lived in Eastern countries, I could believe anything that had the whole weight of science against it. If there were a word of truth in anything Haddo says, we should be unable to form any reasonable theory of the universe."

"For a scientific man you argue with singular fatuity," said Haddo icily, and his manner had an offensiveness which was intensely irritating. "You should be aware that science, dealing only with the general, leaves out of consideration the individual cases that contradict the enormous majority. Occasionally the heart is on the right side of the body, but you would not on that account ever put your stethoscope in any other than the usual spot. It is possible that under certain conditions the law of gravity does not apply, yet you will conduct your life under the conviction that it does so invariably. Now, there are some of us who choose to deal only with these exceptions to the common run. The dull man who plays at Monte Carlo puts his money on the colours, and generally black or red turns up; but now and then zero appears, and he loses. But we, who have backed zero all the time, win many times our stake. Here and there you will find men whose imagination raises them above the humdrum of mankind. They are willing to lose their all if only they have chance of a great prize. Is it nothing not only to know the future, as did the prophets of old, but by making it to force the very gates of the unknown?"

Suddenly the bantering gravity with which he spoke fell away from him. A singular light came into his eyes, and his voice was hoarse. Now at last they saw that he was serious.

"What should you know of that lust for great secrets which consumes me to the bottom of my soul!"

"Anyhow, I'm perfectly delighted to meet a magician," cried Susie gaily.

"Ah, call me not that," he said, with a flouirsh of his fat hands, regaining immediately his portentous flippancy. "I would be known rather as the Brother of the Shadow."

"I should have thought you could be only a very distant relation of anything so unsubstantial," said Arthur, with a laugh.

Oliver's face turned red with furious anger. His strange blue eyes grew cold with hatred, and he thrust out his scarlet lips till he had the ruthless expression of a Nero. The gibe at his obesity had caught him on the raw. Susie feared that he would make so insulting a reply that a quarrel must ensue.

"Well, really, if we want to go to the fair we must start," she said quickly. "And Marie is dying to be rid of us."

They got up, and clattered down the stairs into the street.

IV

THEY came down to the busy, narrow street which led into
the Boulevard du Montparnasse. Electric trams passed
through it with harsh ringing of bells, and people surged along
the pavements.

The fair to which they were going was held at the Lion
de Belfort, not more than a mile away, and Arthur hailed
a cab. Susie told the driver where they wanted to be set
down. She noticed that Haddo, who was waiting for them
to start, put his hand on the horse's neck. On a sudden, for
no apparent reason, it began to tremble. The trembling
passed through the body and down its limbs till it shook
from head to foot as though it had the staggers. The coachman jumped off his box and held the wretched creature's
head. Margaret and Susie got out. It was a horribly painful
sight. The horse seemed not to suffer from actual pain, but
from an extraordinary fear. Though she knew not why, an
idea came to Susie.

"Take your hand away, Mr. Haddo," she said sharply.

He smiled, and did as she bade him. At the same moment
the trembling began to decrease, and in a moment the poor
old cab-horse was in its usual state. It seemed a little frightened still, but otherwise recovered.

"I wonder what the deuce was the matter with it," said
Arthur.

Oliver Haddo looked at him with the blue eyes that seemed
to see right through people, and then, lifting his hat, walked
away. Susie turned suddenly to Dr. Porhoët.

"Do you think he could have made the horse do that? It came immediately he put his hand on its neck, and it stopped as soon as he took it away."

"Nonsense!" said Arthur.

"It occurred to me that he was playing some trick," said Dr. Porhoët gravely. "An odd thing happened once when he came to see me. I have two Persian cats, which are the most properly conducted of all their tribe. They spend their days in front of my fire, meditating on the problems of metaphysics. But as soon as he came in they started up, and their fur stood right on end. Then they began to run madly round and round the room, as though the victims of uncontrollable terror. I opened the door, and they bolted out. I have never been able to understand exactly what took place."

Margaret shuddered.

"I've never met a man who filled me with such loathing," she said. "I don't know what there is about him that frightens me. Even now I feel his eyes fixed strangely upon me. I hope I shall never see him again."

Arthur gave a little laugh and pressed her hand. She would not let his go, and he felt that she was trembling. Personally, he had no doubt about the matter. He would have no trifling with credibility. Either Haddo believed things that none but a lunatic could, or else he was a charlatan who sought to attract attention by his extravagances. In any case he was contemptible. It was certain, at all events, that neither he nor anyone else could work miracles.

"I'll tell you what I'll do," said Arthur. "If he really knows Frank Hurrell I'll find out all about him. I'll drop a note to Hurrell to-night and ask him to tell me anything he can."

"I wish you would," answered Susie, "because he interests me enormously. There's no place like Paris for meeting queer folk. Sooner or later you run across persons who believe in everything. There's no form of religion, there's no eccentricity or enormity, that hasn't its votaries. Just think what it is to come upon a man in the twentieth century who honestly believes in the occult."

"Since I have been occupied with these matters, I have come across strange people," said Dr. Porhoët quietly, "but I agree with Miss Boyd that Oliver Haddo is the most extraordinary. For one thing, it is impossible to know how much he really believes what he says. Is he an impostor or a madman? Does he deceive himself, or is he laughing up his sleeve at the folly of those who take him seriously? I cannot tell. All I know is that he has travelled widely and is acquainted with many tongues. He has a minute knowledge of alchemical literature, and there is no book I have heard of, dealing with the black arts, which he does not seem to know." Dr. Porhoët shook his head slowly. "I should not care to dogmatise about this man. I know I shall outrage the feelings of my friend Arthur, but I am bound to confess it would not surprise me to learn that he possessed powers by which he was able to do things seemingly miraculous."

Arthur was prevented from answering by their arrival at the Lion de Belfort.

The fair was in full swing. The noise was deafening. Steam bands thundered out the popular tunes of the moment, and to their din merry-go-rounds were turning. At the door of booths men vociferously importuned the passers-by to enter. From the shooting saloons came a continual spatter of toy rifles. Linking up these sounds, were the voices of the serried crowd that surged along the central avenue, and the shuffle of their myriad feet. The night was lurid with acetylene torches, which flamed with a dull unceasing roar. It was a curious sight, half gay, half sordid. The throng seemed bent with a kind of savagery upon amusement, as though, resentful of the weary round of daily labour, it sought by a desperate effort to be merry.

The English party with Dr. Porhoët, mildly ironic, had scarcely entered before they were joined by Oliver Haddo. He was indifferent to the plain fact that they did not want his company. He attracted attention, for his appearance and his manner were remarkable, and Susie noticed that he was pleased to see people point him out to one another. He wore a Spanish cloak, the *capa*, and he flung the red and green velvet of its lining gaudily over his shoulder. He had a large soft hat. His height was great, though less noticeable on account of his obesity, and he towered over the puny multitude.

They looked idly at the various shows, resisting the melodramas, the circuses, the exhibitions of eccentricity, which loudly clamoured for their custom. Presently they came to a man who was cutting silhouettes in black paper, and Haddo insisted on posing for him. A little crowd collected and did not spare their jokes at his singular appearance. He threw himself into his favourite attitude of proud command. Margaret wished to take the opportunity of leaving him, but Miss Boyd insisted on staying.

"He's the most ridiculous creature I've ever seen in my life," she whispered. "I wouldn't let him out of my sight for worlds."

When the silhouette was done, he presented it with a low bow to Margaret.

"I implore your acceptance of the only portrait now in existence of Oliver Haddo," he said.

"Thank you," she answered frigidly.

She was unwilling to take it, but had not the presence of mind to put him off by a jest, and would not be frankly rude. As though certain she set much store on it, he placed it carefully in an envelope. They walked on and suddenly came to a canvas booth on which was an Eastern name. Roughly painted on sail-cloth was a picture of an Arab charming snakes, and above were certain words in Arabic. At the entrance, a native sat cross-legged, listlessly beating a drum. When he saw them stop, he addressed them in bad French.

"Does not this remind you of the turbid Nile, Dr. Porhoët?" said Haddo. "Let us go in and see what the fellow has to show."

Dr. Porhoët stepped forward and addressed the charmer, who brightened on hearing the language of his own country.

"He is an Egyptian from Assiut," said the doctor.

"I will buy tickets for you all," said Haddo.

He held up the flap that gave access to the booth, and Susie went in. Margaret and Arthur Burdon, somewhat against their will, were obliged to follow. The native closed the opening behind them. They found themselves in a dirty little tent, ill-lit by two smoking lamps; a dozen stools were placed in a circle on the bare ground. In one corner sat a fellah woman, motionless, in ample robes of dingy black. Her face was hidden by a long veil, which was held in place by a queer ornament of brass in the middle of the forehead, between the eyes. These alone were visible, large and sombre, and the lashes were darkened with kohl: her fingers were brightly stained with henna. She moved slightly as the visitors entered, and the man gave her his drum. She began to rub it with her hands, curiously, and made a droning sound, which was odd and mysterious. There was a peculiar odour in the place, so that Dr. Porhoët was for a moment transported to the evil-smelling streets of Cairo. It was an acrid mixture of incense, of attar of roses, with every imaginable putrescence. It choked the two women, and Susie asked for a cigarette. The native grinned when he heard the English tongue. He showed a row of sparkling and beautiful teeth.

"My name Mohammed," he said. "Me show serpents to Sirdar Lord Kitchener. Wait and see. Serpents very poisonous."

He was dressed in a long blue gabardine, more suited to the sunny banks of the Nile than to a fair in Paris, and its colour could hardly be seen for dirt. On his head was the national tarboosh.

A rug lay at one side of the tent, and from under it he took a goatskin sack. He placed it on the ground in the middle of the circle formed by the seats and crouched down on his haunches. Margaret shuddered, for the uneven surface of the sack moved strangely. He opened the mouth of it. The woman in the corner listlessly droned away on the drum, and occasionally uttered a barbaric cry. With a leer and a flash of his bright teeth, the Arab thrust his hand into the sack and rummaged as a man would rummage in a sack of corn. He drew out a long, writhing snake. He placed it on the ground and for a moment waited, then he passed his hand over it: it became immediately as rigid as a bar of iron. Except that the eyes, the cruel eyes, were open still, there might have been no life in it.

"Look," said Haddo. "That is the miracle which Moses did before Pharaoh."

Then the Arab took a reed instrument, not unlike the pipe which Pan in the hills of Greece played to the dryads, and he piped a weird, monotonous tune. The stiffness broke away from the snake suddenly, and it lifted its head and raised its long body till it stood almost on the tip of its tail, and it swayed slowly to and fro.

Oliver Haddo seemed extraordinarily fascinated. He leaned forward with eager face, and his unnatural eyes were fixed on the charmer with an indescribable expression. Margaret drew back in terror.

"You need not be frightened," said Arthur. "These people only work with animals whose fangs have been extracted."

Oliver Haddo looked at him before answering. He seemed to consider each time what sort of man this was to whom he spoke.

"A man is only a snake-charmer because, without recourse to medicine, he is proof against the fangs of the most venomous serpents."

"Do you think so?" said Arthur.

"I saw the most noted charmer of Madras die two hours after he had been bitten by a cobra," said Haddo. "I had heard many tales of his prowess, and one evening asked a friend to take me to him. He was out when we arrived, but we waited, and presently, accompanied by some friends, he came. We told him what we wanted. He had been at a marriage-feast and was drunk. But he sent for his snakes, and forthwith showed us marvels which this man has never heard of. At last he took a great cobra from his sack and began to handle it. Suddenly it darted at his chin and bit him. It made two marks like pin-points. The juggler started back.

" 'I am a dead man,' he said.

"Those about him would have killed the cobra, but he prevented them.

" 'Let the creature live,' he said. 'It may be of service to others of my trade. To me it can be of no other use. Nothing can save me.'

"His friends and the jugglers, his fellows, gathered round him and placed him in a chair. In two hours he was dead. In his drunkenness he had forgotten a portion of the spell which protected him, and so he died."

"You have a marvellous collection of tall stories," said Arthur. "I'm afraid I should want better proof that these particular snakes are poisonous."

Oliver turned to the charmer and spoke to him in Arabic. Then he answered Arthur.

"The man has a horned viper, *cerastes* is the name under which you gentlemen of science know it, and it is the most deadly of all Egyptian snakes. It is commonly known as Cleopatra's Asp, for that is the serpent which was brought in a basket of figs to the paramour of Cæsar in order that she might not endure the triumph of Augustus."

"What are you going to do?" asked Susie.

He smiled, but did not answer. He stepped forward to the centre of the tent and fell on his knees. He uttered Arabic words, which Dr. Porhoët translated to the others.

"O viper, I adjure you, by the great God who is all-powerful, to come forth. You are but a snake, and God is greater than all snakes. Obey my call and come."

A tremor went through the goatskin bag, and in a moment a head was protruded. A little body wriggled out. It was a snake of light grey colour, and over each eye was a horn. It lay slightly curled.

"Do you recognise it?" said Oliver in a low voice to the doctor.

"I do."

The charmer sat motionless, and the woman in the dim background ceased her weird rubbing of the drum. Haddo seized the snake and opened its mouth. Immediately it fastened on his hand, and the reptile teeth went deep into his flesh. Arthur watched him for signs of pain, but he did not wince. The writhing snake dangled from his hand. He repeated a sentence in Arabic, and, with the peculiar suddenness of a drop of water falling from a roof, the snake fell to the ground. The blood flowed freely. Haddo spat upon the bleeding place three times, muttering words they could not hear, and three times he rubbed the wound with his fingers. The bleeding stopped. He stretched out his hand for Arthur to look at.

"That surely is what a surgeon would call healing by first intention," he said.

Burdon was astonished, but he was irritated, too, and would not allow that there was anything strange in the cessation of the flowing blood.

"You haven't yet shown that the snake was poisonous."

"I have not finished yet," smiled Haddo.

He spoke again to the Egyptian, who gave an order to his wife. Without a word she rose to her feet and from a box took a white rabbit. She lifted it up by the ears, and it struggled with its four quaint legs. Haddo put it in front of the horned viper. Before anyone could have moved, the snake darted forward, and like a flash of lightning struck the rabbit. The wretched little beast gave a slight scream, a shudder went through it, and it fell dead.

Margaret sprang up with a cry.

"Oh, how cruel! How hatefully cruel!"

"Are you convinced now?" asked Haddo coolly.

The two women hurried to the doorway. They were frightened and disgusted. Oliver Haddo was left alone with the snake-charmer.

V

Dr. Porhoët had asked Arthur to bring Margaret and Miss
Boyd to see him on Sunday at his apartment in the Île Saint
Louis; and the lovers arranged to spend an hour on their way
at the Louvre. Susie, invited to accompany them, preferred
independence and her own reflections.

To avoid the crowd which throngs the picture galleries on
holidays, they went to that part of the museum where ancient
sculpture is kept. It was comparatively empty, and the long
halls had the singular restfulness of places where works of
art are gathered together. Margaret was filled with a genuine
emotion; and though she could not analyse it, as Susie, who
loved to dissect her state of mind, would have done, it
strangely exhilarated her. Her heart was uplifted from the
sordidness of earth, and she had a sensation of freedom which
was as delightful as it was indescribable. Arthur had never
troubled himself with art till Margaret's enthusiasm taught
him that there was a side of life he did not realise. Though
beauty meant little to his practical nature, he sought, in his
great love for Margaret, to appreciate the works which excited
her to such charming ecstasy. He walked by her side with
docility and listened, not without deference, to her outbursts.
He admired the correctness of Greek anatomy, and there was
one statue of an athlete which attracted his prolonged attention, because the muscles were indicated with the precision
of a plate in a surgical text-book. When Margaret talked of
the Greeks' divine repose and of their blitheness, he thought

it very clever because she said it; but in a man it would have aroused his impatience.

Yet there was one piece, the charming statue known as *La Diane de Gabies,* which moved him differently, and to this presently he insisted on going. With a laugh Margaret remonstrated, but secretly she was not displeased. She was aware that his passion for this figure was due, not to its intrinsic beauty, but to a likeness he had discovered in it to herself.

It stood in that fair wide gallery where is the mocking faun, with his inhuman savour of fellowship with the earth which is divine, and the sightless Homer. The goddess had not the arrogance of the huntress who loved Endymion, nor the majesty of the cold mistress of the skies. She was in the likeness of a young girl, and with collected gesture fastened her cloak. There was nothing divine in her save a sweet strange spirit of virginity. A lover in ancient Greece, who offered sacrifice before this fair image, might forget easily that it was a goddess to whom he knelt, and see only an earthly maid fresh with youth and chastity and loveliness. In Arthur's eyes Margaret had all the exquisite grace of that statue, and the same unconscious composure; and in her also breathed the spring odours of ineffable purity. Her features were chiselled with the clear and divine perfection of this Greek girl's; her ears were as delicate and as finely wrought. The colour of her skin was so tender that it reminded you vaguely of all beautiful soft things, the radiance of sunset and the darkness of the night, the heart of roses and the depth of running water. The goddess's hand was raised to her right shoulder, and Margaret's hand was as small, as dainty, and as white.

"Don't be so foolish," said she, as Arthur looked silently at the statue.

He turned his eyes slowly, and they rested upon her. She saw that they were veiled with tears.

"I wish you weren't so beautiful," he answered, awkwardly, as though he could scarcely bring himself to say such foolish things. "I'm so afraid that something will happen to prevent us from being happy. It seems too much to expect that I should enjoy such extraordinarily good luck."

She had the imagination to see that it meant much for the practical man so to express himself. Love of her drew him out of his character, and, though he could not resist, he resented the effect it had on him. She found nothing to reply, but she took his hand.

"Everything has gone pretty well with me so far," he said, speaking almost to himself. "Whenever I've really wanted anything, I've managed to get it. I don't see why things should go against me now."

He was trying to reassure himself against an instinctive suspicion of the malice of circumstances. But he shook himself and straightened his back.

"It's stupid to be so morbid as that," he muttered.

Margaret laughed. They walked out of the gallery and turned to the quay. By crossing the bridge and following the river, they must come eventually to Dr. Porhoët's house.

Meanwhile Susie wandered down the Boulevard Saint Michel, alert with the Sunday crowd, to that part of Paris which was dearest to her heart. L'Ile Saint Louis to her mind offered a synthesis of the French spirit, and it pleased her far more than the garish boulevards in which the English as a rule seek for the country's fascination. Its position on an island in the Seine gave it a compact charm. The narrow streets, with their array of dainty comestibles, had the look of streets in a provincial town. They had a quaintness which appealed to the fancy, and they were very restful. The names of the streets recalled the monarchy that passed away in bloodshed, and in *poudre de riz*. The very plane trees had a greater sobriety than elsewhere, as though conscious they stood in a Paris where progress was not. In front was the turbid Seine, and below, the twin towers of Notre Dame. Susie could have kissed the hard paving stones of the quay. Her good-natured, plain face lit up as she realised the delight of the scene upon which her eyes rested; and it was with a little pang, her mind aglow with characters and events from history and from fiction, that she turned away to enter Dr. Porhoët's house.

She was pleased that the approach did not clash with her fantasies. She mounted a broad staircase, dark but roomy, and, at the command of the *concierge,* rang a tinkling bell at one of the doorways that faced her. Dr. Porhoët opened in person.

"Arthur and Mademoiselle are already here," he said, as he led her in.

They went through a prim French dining-room, with much woodwork and heavy scarlet hangings, to the library. This was a large room, but the bookcases that lined the walls, and a large writing-table heaped up with books, much diminished its size. There were books everywhere. They were stacked on the floor and piled on every chair. There was hardly space to move. Susie gave a cry of delight.

"Now you mustn't talk to me. I want to look at all your books."

"You could not please me more," said Dr. Porhoët, "but I am afraid they will disappoint you. They are of many sorts, but I fear there are few that will interest an English young lady."

He looked about his writing-table till he found a packet of cigarettes. He gravely offered one to each of his guests. Susie was enchanted with the strange musty smell of the old books, and she took a first glance at them in general. For the most part they were in paper bindings, some of them neat enough, but more with broken backs and dingy edges; they were set along the shelves in serried rows, untidily, without method or plan. There were many older ones also in bindings of calf and pigskin, treasure from half the bookshops in Europe; and there were huge folios like Prussian grenadiers; and tiny Elzevirs, which had been read by patrician ladies in Venice. Just as Arthur was a different man in the operating theatre, Dr. Porhoët was changed among his books. Though he preserved the amiable serenity which made him always so attractive, he had there a diverting brusqueness of demeanour which contrasted quaintly with his usual calm.

"I was telling these young people, when you came in, of an ancient Korân which I was given in Alexandria by a learned man whom I operated upon for cataract." He showed her a beautifully-written Arabic work, with wonderful capitals and headlines in gold. "You know that it is almost impossible for an infidel to acquire the holy book, and this is a particularly rare copy, for it was written by Kaït Bey, the greatest of the Mameluke Sultans."

He handled the delicate pages as a lover of flowers would handle rose-leaves.

"And have you much literature on the occult sciences?" asked Susie.

Dr. Porhoët smiled.

"I venture to think that no private library contains so complete a collection, but I dare not show it to you in the presence of our friend Arthur. He is too polite to accuse me of foolishness, but his sarcastic smile would betray him."

Susie went to the shelves to which he vaguely waved, and looked with a peculiar excitement at the mysterious array. She ran her eyes along the names. It seemed to her that she was entering upon an unknown region of romance. She felt like an adventurous princess who rode on her palfrey into a forest of great bare trees and mystic silences, where wan, unearthly shapes pressed upon her way.

"I thought once of writing a life of that fantastic and grandiloquent creature, Philippus Aureolus Theophrastus Paracelsus Bombast von Hohenheim," said Dr. Porhoët, "and I have collected many of his books."

He took down a slim volume in duodecimo, printed in the seventeeth century, with queer plates, on which were all manner of cabbalistic signs. The pages had a peculiar, musty odour. They were stained with iron-mould.

"Here is one of the most interesting works concerning the black art. It is the *Grimoire of Honorius,* and is the principal text-book of all those who deal in the darkest ways of the science."

Then he pointed out the *Hexameron* of Torquemada and the *Tableau de l'Inconstance des Démons,* by Delancre; he drew his finger down the leather back of Delrio's *Disquisitiones Magicæ* and set upright the *Pseudomonarchia Dæmonorum* of Wierus; his eyes rested for an instant on Hauber's *Acta et Scripta Magica,* and he blew the dust carefully off the most famous, the most infamous, of them all, Sprenger's *Malleus Maleficorum.*

"Here is one of my greatest treasures. It is the *Clavicula Salomonis;* and I have much reason to believe that it is the

identical copy which belonged to the greatest adventurer of
the eighteenth century, Jacques Casanova. You will see that
the owner's name has been cut out, but enough remains to
indicate the bottom of the letters; and these correspond exactly
with the signature of Casanova which I have found at the
Bibliothèque Nationale. He relates in his memoirs that a
copy of this book was seized among his effects when he was
arrested in Venice for traffic in the black arts; and it was there,
on one of my journeys from Alexandria, that I picked it up."

He replaced the precious work, and his eye fell on a stout
volume bound in vellum.

"I had almost forgotten the most wonderful, the most
mysterious, of all the books that treat of occult science. You
have heard of the Kabbalah, but I doubt if it is more than a
name to you."

"I know nothing about it at all," laughed Susie, "except
that it's all very romantic and extraordinary and ridiculous."

"This, then, is its history. Moses, who was learned in all
the wisdom of Egypt, was first initiated into the Kabbalah
in the land of his birth; but became most proficient in it
during his wanderings in the wilderness. Here he not only
devoted the leisure hours of forty years to this mysterious
science, but received lessons in it from an obliging angel.
By aid of it he was able to solve the difficulties which arose
during his management of the Israelites, notwithstanding the
pilgrimages, wars, and miseries of that most unruly nation.
He covertly laid down the principles of the doctrine in the
first four books of the Pentateuch, but withheld them from
Deuteronomy. Moses also initiated the Seventy Elders into
these secrets, and they in turn transmitted them from hand
to hand. Of all who formed the unbroken line of tradition,
David and Solomon were the most deeply learned in the

Kabbalah. No one, however, dared to write it down till Schimeon ben Jochai, who lived in the time of the destruction of Jerusalem; and after his death the Rabbi Eleazar, his son, and the Rabbi Abba, his secretary, collected his manuscripts and from them composed the celebrated treatise called *Zohar*."

"And how much do you believe of this marvellous story?" asked Arthur Burdon.

"Not a word," answered Dr. Porhoët, with a smile. "Criticism has shown that *Zohar* is of modern origin. With singular effrontery, it cites an author who is known to have lived during the eleventh century, mentions the Crusades, and records events which occurred in the year of Our Lord 1264. It was some time before 1291 that copies of *Zohar* began to be circulated by a Spanish Jew named Moses de Leon, who claimed to possess an autograph manuscript by the reputed author Schimeon ben Jochai. But when Moses de Leon was gathered to the bosom of his father Abraham, a wealthy Hebrew, Joseph de Avila, promised the scribe's widow, who had been left destitute, that his son should marry her daughter, to whom he would pay a handsome dowry, if she would give him the original manuscript from which these copies were made. But the widow (one can imagine with what gnashing of teeth) was obliged to confess that she had no such manuscript, for Moses de Leon had composed *Zohar* out of his own head, and written it with his own right hand."

Arthur got up to stretch his legs. He gave a laugh.

"I never know how much you really believe of all these things you tell us. You speak with such gravity that we are all taken in, and then it turns out that you've been laughing at us."

"My dear friend, I never know myself how much I believe," returned Dr. Porhoët.

"I wonder if it is for the same reason that Mr. Haddo puzzles us so much," said Susie.

"Ah, there you have a case that is really interesting," replied the doctor. "I assure you that, though I know him fairly intimately, I have never been able to make up my mind whether he is an elaborate practical joker, or whether he is really convinced he has the wonderful powers to which he lays claim."

"We certainly saw things last night that were not quite normal," said Susie. "Why had that serpent no effect on him though it was able to kill the rabbit instantaneously? And how are you going to explain the violent trembling of that horse, Mr. Burdon?"

"I can't explain it," answered Arthur, irritably, "but I'm not inclined to attribute to the supernatural everything that I can't immediately understand."

"I don't know what there is about him that excites in me a sort of horror," said Margaret. "I've never taken such a sudden dislike to anyone."

She was too reticent to say all she felt, but she had been strangely affected last night by the recollection of Haddo's words and of his acts. She had awaked more than once from a nightmare in which he assumed fantastic and ghastly shapes. His mocking voice rang in her ears, and she seemed still to see that vast bulk and the savage, sensual face. It was like a spirit of evil in her path, and she was curiously alarmed. Only her reliance on Arthur's common sense prevented her from giving way to ridiculous terrors.

"I've written to Frank Hurrell and asked him to tell me

all he knows about him," said Arthur. "I should get an answer very soon."

"I wish we'd never come across him," cried Margaret vehemently. "I feel that he will bring us misfortune."

"You're all of you absurdly prejudiced," answered Susie gaily. "He interests me enormously, and I mean to ask him to tea at the studio."

"I'm sure I shall be delighted to come."

Margaret cried out, for she recognised Oliver Haddo's deep bantering tones; and she turned round quickly. They were all so taken aback that for a moment no one spoke. They were gathered round the window and had not heard him come in. They wondered guiltily how long he had been there and how much he had heard.

"How on earth did you get here?" cried Susie lightly, recovering herself first.

"No well-bred sorcerer is so dead to the finer feelings as to enter a room by the door," he answered, with his puzzling smile. "You were standing round the window, and I thought it would startle you if I chose that mode of ingress, so I descended with incredible skill down the chimney."

"I see a little soot on your left elbow," returned Susie. "I hope you weren't at all burned."

"Not at all, thanks," he answered, gravely brushing his coat.

"In whatever way you came, you are very welcome," said Dr. Porhoët, genially holding out his hand.

But Arthur impatiently turned to his host.

"I wish I knew what made you engage upon these studies," he said. "I should have thought your medical profession protected you from any tenderness towards superstition."

Dr. Porhoët shrugged his shoulders.

"I have always been interested in the oddities of mankind. At one time I read a good deal of philosophy and a good deal of science, and I learned in that way that nothing was certain. Some people, by the pursuit of science, are impressed with the dignity of man, but I was only made conscious of his insignificance. The greatest questions of all have been threshed out since he acquired the beginnings of civilisation and he is as far from a solution as ever. Man can know nothing, for his senses are his only means of knowledge, and they can give no certainty. There is only one subject upon which the individual can speak with authority, and that is his own mind, but even here he is surrounded with darkness. I believe that we shall always be ignorant of the matters which it most behoves us to know, and therefore I cannot occupy myself with them. I prefer to set them all aside, and, since knowledge is unattainable, to occupy myself only with folly."

"It is a point of view I do not sympathise with," said Arthur.

"Yet I cannot be sure that it is all folly," pursued the Frenchman reflectively. He looked at Arthur with a certain ironic gravity. "Do you believe that I should lie to you when I promised to speak the truth?"

"Certainly not."

"I should like to tell you of an experience that I once had in Alexandria. So far as I can see, it can be explained by none of the principles known to science. I ask you only to believe that I am not consciously deceiving you."

He spoke with a seriousness which gave authority to his words. It was plain, even to Arthur, that he narrated the event exactly as it occurred.

"I had heard frequently of a certain sheikh who was able by means of a magic mirror to show the inquirer persons who were absent or dead, and a native friend of mine had often begged me to see him. I had never thought it worth while, but at last a time came when I was greatly troubled in my mind. My poor mother was an old woman, a widow, and I had received no news of her for many weeks. Though I wrote repeatedly, no answer reached me. I was very anxious and very unhappy. I thought no harm could come if I sent for the sorcerer, and perhaps after all he had the power which was attributed to him. My friend, who was interpreter to the French Consulate, brought him to me one evening. He was a fine man, tall and stout, of a fair complexion, but with a dark brown beard. He was shabbily dressed, and, being a descendant of the Prophet, wore a green turban. In his conversation he was affable and unaffected. I asked him what persons he could see in the magic mirror, and he said they were a boy not arrived at puberty, a virgin, a black female slave, and a pregnant woman. In order to make sure that there was no collusion, I despatched my servant to an intimate friend and asked him to send me his son. While we waited, I prepared by the magician's direction frankincense and coriander-seed, and a chafing-dish with live charcoal. Meanwhile, he wrote forms of invocation on six strips of paper. When the boy arrived, the sorcerer threw incense and one of the paper strips into the chafing-dish, then took the boy's right hand and drew a square and certain mystical marks on the palm. In the centre of the square he poured a little ink. This formed the magic mirror. He desired the boy to look steadily into it without raising his head. The fumes of the incense filled the room with smoke. The sorcerer muttered Arabic words, indistinctly, and this he continued to do all the time except when he asked the boy a question.

" 'Do you see anything in the ink?' he said.

" 'No,' the boy answered.

"But a minute later, he began to tremble and seemed very much frightened.

" 'I see a man sweeping the ground,' he said.

" 'When he has done sweeping, tell me,' said the sheikh.

" 'He has done,' said the boy.

"The sorcerer turned to me and asked who it was that I wished the boy should see.

" 'I desire him to see the widow Jeanne-Marie Porhoët.'

"The magician put the second and third of the small strips of paper into the chafing-dish, and fresh frankincense was added. The fumes were painful to my eyes. The boy began to speak.

" 'I see an old woman lying on a bed. She has a black dress, and on her head is a little white cap. She has a wrinkled face and her eyes are closed. There is a band tied round her chin. The bed is in a sort of hole, in the wall, and there are shutters to it.'

"The boy was describing a Breton bed, and the white cap was the *coiffe* that my mother wore. And if she lay there in her black dress, with a band about her chin, I knew that it could mean but one thing.

" 'What else does he see?' I asked the sorcerer.

"He repeated my question, and presently the boy spoke again.

" 'I see four men come in with a long box. And there are women crying. They all wear little white caps and black dresses. And I see a man in a white surplice, with a large cross in his hands, and a little boy in a long red gown. And the men take off their hats. And now everyone is kneeling down."

" 'I will hear no more,' I said. 'It is enough.'

"I knew that my mother was dead.

"In a little while, I received a letter from the priest of the village in which she lived. They had buried her on the very day upon which the boy had seen this sight in the mirror of ink."

Dr. Porhoët passed his hand across his eyes, and for a little while there was silence.

"What have you to say to that?" asked Oliver Haddo, at last.

"Nothing," answered Arthur.

Haddo looked at him for a minute with those queer eyes of his which seemed to stare at the wall behind.

"Have you ever heard of Eliphas Levi?" he inquired. "He is the most celebrated occultist of recent years. He is thought to have known more of the mysteries than any adept since the divine Paracelsus."

"I met him once," interrupted Dr. Porhoët. "You never saw a man who looked less like a magician. His face beamed with good-nature, and he wore a long grey beard, which covered nearly the whole of his breast. He was of a short and very corpulent figure."

"The practice of black arts evidently disposes to obesity." said Arthur, icily.

Susie noticed that this time Oliver Haddo made no sign that the taunt moved him. His unwinking, straight eyes remained upon Arthur without expression.

"Levi's real name was Alphonse-Louis Constant, but he adopted that under which he is generally known for reasons that are plain to the romantic mind. His father was a bootmaker. He was destined for the priesthood, but fell in love with a damsel fair and married her. The union was unhappy. A fate befell him which has been the lot of greater men than he, and his wife presently abandoned the marital roof with her lover. To console himself he began to make serious researches in the occult, and in due course published a vast number of mystical works dealing with magic in all its branches."

"I'm sure Mr. Haddo was going to tell us something very interesting about him," said Susie.

"I wished merely to give you his account of how he raised the spirit of Apollonius of Tyana in London."

Susie settled herself more comfortably in her chair and lit a cigarette.

"He went there in the spring of 1856 to escape from internal disquietude and to devote himself without distraction to his studies. He had letters of introduction to various persons of distinction who concerned themselves with the supernatural, but, finding them trivial and indifferent, he immersed himself in the study of the supreme Kabbalah. One day, on returning to his hotel, he found a note in his room. It contained half a card, transversely divided, on which he at once recognised the character of Solomon's Seal, and a tiny slip of paper on which was written in pencil: *The other half of this card will be given you at three o'clock to-morrow in front of Westminster Abbey.* Next day, going to the appointed spot, with his portion of the card in his hand, he found a baronial equipage waiting for him. A footman approached, and, making a sign to him, opened the carriage door. Within was a lady in black satin, whose face was concealed by a thick veil. She motioned him to a seat beside her, and at the same time displayed the other part of the card he had received. The door was shut, and the carriage rolled away. When the lady raised her veil, Eliphas Levi saw that she was of mature age;

and beneath her grey eyebrows were bright black eyes of preter-natural fixity."

Susie Boyd clapped her hands with delight.

"I think it's delicious, and I'm sure every word of it is true," she cried. "I'm enchanted with the mysterious meeting at Westminster Abbey in the Mid-Victorian era. Can't you see the elderly lady in a huge crinoline and a black poke bonnet, and the wizard in a ridiculous hat, a bottle-green frock-coat, and a flowing tie of black silk?"

"Eliphas remarks that the lady spoke French with a marked English accent," pursued Haddo imperturbably. "She addressed him as follows: 'Sir, I am aware that the law of secrecy is rigorous among adepts; and I know that you have been asked for phenomena, but have declined to gratify a frivolous curiosity. It is possible that you do not possess the necessary materials. I can show you a complete magical cabinet, but I must require of you first the most inviolable silence. If you do not guarantee this on your honour, I will give the order for you to be driven home.'"

Oliver Haddo told his story not ineffectively, but with a comic gravity that prevented one from knowing exactly how to take it.

"Having given the required promise Eliphas Levi was shown a collection of vestments and of magical instruments. The lady lent him certain books of which he was in need; and at last, as a result of many conversations, determined him to attempt at her house the experience of a complete evocation. He prepared himself for twenty-one days, scrupulously observing the rules laid down by the Ritual. At length everything was ready. It was proposed to call forth the phantom of the divine Apollonius, and to question it upon two matters, one of which concerned Eliphas Levi and the other, the lady of the crinoline. She had at first counted on assisting at the evocation with a trustworthy person, but at the last moment her friend drew back; and as the triad or unity is rigorously prescribed in magical rites, Eliphas was left alone. The cabinet prepared for the experiment was situated in a turret. Four concave mirrors were hung within it, and there was an altar of white marble, surrounded by a chain of magnetic iron. On it was engraved the sign of the Pentagram, and this symbol was drawn on the new, white sheepskin which was stretched beneath. A copper brazier stood on the altar, with charcoal of alder and of laurel wood, and in front a second brazier was placed upon a tripod. Eliphas Levi was clothed in a white robe, longer and more ample than the surplice of a priest, and he wore upon his head a chaplet of vervain leaves entwined about a golden chain. In one hand he held a new sword and in the other the Ritual."

Susie's passion for caricature at once asserted itself, and she laughed as she saw in fancy the portly little Frenchman, with his round, red face, thus wonderfully attired.

"He set alight the two fires with the prepared materials, and began, at first in a low voice, but rising by degrees, the invocations of the Ritual. The flames invested every object with a wavering light. Presently they went out. He set more twigs and perfumes on the brazier, and when the flame started up once more, he saw distinctly before the altar a human figure larger than life, which dissolved and disappeared. He began the invocations again and placed himself in a circle, which he had already traced between the altar and the tripod. Then the depth of the mirror which was in front of him grew brighter by degrees, and a pale form arose, and it seemed gradually to approach. He closed his eyes, and called three times upon Apollonius. When he opened them, a man stood before him, wholly enveloped in a winding sheet, which seemed more grey than black. His form was lean, melancholy, and beardless. Eliphas felt an intense cold, and when he sought to ask his questions found it impossible to speak. Thereupon, he placed his hand on the Pentagram, and directed the point of his sword toward the figure, adjuring it mentally by that sign not to terrify, but to obey him. The form suddenly grew indistinct and soon it strangely vanished. He commanded it to return, and then felt, as it were, an air pass by him; and, something having touched the hand which held the sword, his arm was immediately benumbed as far as the shoulder. He supposed that the weapon displeased the spirit, and set it down within the circle. The human figure at once reappeared, but Eliphas experienced such a sudden exhaustion in all his limbs that he was obliged to sit down. He fell into a deep coma, and dreamed strange dreams. But of these, when he recovered, only a vague memory remained to him. His arm continued for several days to be numb and painful. The figure had not spoken, but it seemed to Eliphas Levi that the questions were answered in his own mind. For to each an inner voice replied with one grim word: dead."

"Your friend seems to have had as little fear of spooks as you have of lions," said Burdon. "To my thinking it is plain that all these preparations, and the perfumes, the mirrors, the pentagrams, must have the greatest effect on the imagination. My only surprise is that your magician saw no more."

"Eliphas Levi talked to me himself of this evocation," said Dr. Porhoët. "He told me that its influence on him was very great. He was no longer the same man, for it seemed to him that something from the world beyond had passed into his soul."

"I am astonished that you should never have tried such an interesting experiment yourself," said Arthur to Oliver Haddo.

"I have," answered the other calmly. "My father lost his power of speech shortly before he died, and it was plain that he sought with all his might to tell me something. A year after his death, I called up his phantom from the grave so that I might learn what I took to be a dying wish. The circumstances of the apparition are so similar to those I have just told you that it would only bore you if I repeated them. The only difference was that my father actually spoke."

"What did he say?" asked Susie.

"He said solemnly: *'Buy Ashantis, they are bound to go up.'* I did as he told me; but my father was always unlucky in speculation, and they went down steadily. I sold out at considerable loss, and concluded that in the world beyond they are as ignorant of the tendency of the Stock Exchange as we are in this vale of sorrow."

Susie could not help laughing. But Arthur shrugged his shoulders impatiently. It disturbed his practical mind never to be certain if Haddo was serious, or if, as now, he was plainly making game of them.

VI

Two DAYS later, Arthur received Frank Hurrell's answer to his letter. It was characteristic of Frank that he should take such pains to reply at length to the inquiry, and it was clear that he had lost none of his old interest in odd personalities. He analysed Oliver Haddo's character with the patience of a scientific man studying a new species in which he is passionately concerned.

"My dear Burdon:
"It is singular that you should write just now to ask what I know of Oliver Haddo, since by chance I met the other night at dinner at Queen Anne's Gate a man who had much to tell me of him. I am curious to know why he excites your interest, for I am sure his peculiarities make him repugnant to a person of your robust common sense. I can with difficulty imagine two men less capable of getting on together. Though I have not seen Haddo now for years, I can tell you, in one way and another, a good deal about him. He erred when he described me as his intimate friend. It is true that at one time I saw much of him, but I never ceased cordially to dislike him. He came up to Oxford from Eton with a reputation for athletics and eccentricity. But you know that there is nothing that arouses the ill-will of boys more than the latter, and he achieved an unpopularity which was remarkable. It turned out that he played football admirably, and except for his rather scornful indolence he might easily have got his blue. He sneered at the popular enthusiasm for games, and was used to say that cricket was all very well for boys but not fit for the pastime of men. (He was then eighteen!) He talked grandiloquently of big-game shooting and of mountain climbing

as sports which demanded courage and self-reliance. He seemed, indeed, to like football, but he played it with a brutal savagery which the other persons concerned naturally resented. It became current opinion in other pursuits that he did not play the game. He did nothing that was manifestly unfair, but was capable of taking advantages which most people would have thought mean; and he made defeat more hard to bear because he exulted over the vanquished with the coarse banter that youths find so difficult to endure.

"What you would hardly believe is that, when he first came up, he was a person of great physical attractions. He is now grown fat, but in those days was extremely handsome. He reminded one of those colossal statues of Apollo in which the god is represented with a feminine roundness and delicacy. He was very tall and had a magnificent figure. It was so well-formed for his age that one might have foretold his precocious corpulence. He held himself with a dashing erectness. Many called it an insolent swagger. His features were regular and fine. He had a great quantity of curling hair, which was worn long, with a sort of poetic grace: I am told that now he is very bald; and I can imagine that this must be a great blow to him, for he was always exceedingly vain. I remember a peculiarity of his eyes, which could scarcely have been natural, but how it was acquired I do not know. The eyes of most people converge upon the object at which they look, but his remained parallel. It gave them a singular expression, as though he were scrutinising the inmost thought of the person with whom he talked. He was notorious also for the extravagance of his costume, but, unlike the æsthetes of that day, who clothed themselves with artistic carelessness, he had a taste for outrageous colours. Sometimes, by a queer freak, he dressed himself at unseasonable moments with excessive formality. He is the only undergraduate I have ever seen walk down the High in a tall hat and a closely-buttoned frock-coat.

"I have told you he was very unpopular, but it was not an unpopularity of the sort which ignores a man and leaves him chiefly to his own society. Haddo knew everybody and was to be found in the most unlikely places. Though people disliked him, they showed a curious pleasure in his company, and he was probably entertained more than any man in Oxford. I never saw him but he was surrounded by a little crowd, who abused him behind his back, but could not resist his fascination.

"I often tried to analyse this, for I felt it as much as anyone, and though I honestly could not bear him, I could never resist going to see him whenever opportunity arose. I suppose he offered the charm of the unexpected to that mass of undergraduates who, for all their matter-of-fact breeziness, are curiously alive to the romantic. It was impossible to tell what he would do or say next, and you were kept perpetually on the alert. He was certainly not witty, but he had a coarse humour which excited the rather gross sense of the ludicrous possessed by the young. He had a gift for caricature which was really diverting, and an imperturbable assurance. He had also an ingenious talent for profanity, and his inventiveness in this particular was a power among youths whose imaginations stopped at the commoner sorts of bad language. I have heard him preach a sermon of the most blasphemous sort in the very accents of the late Dean of Christ Church, which outraged and at the same time irresistibly amused everyone who heard it. He had a more varied knowledge than the greater part of undergraduates, and, having at the same time a retentive memory and considerable quickness, he was able to assume an attitude of omniscience which was as impressive as it was irritating. I have never heard him confess that he had not read a book. Often, when I tried to catch him, he confounded me by quoting the identical words of a passage in some work which I could have sworn he had never set eyes on. I daresay it was due only to some juggling, like the conjuror's sleight of hand that apparently lets you choose a card, but in fact forces one on you; and he brought the conversation round cleverly to a point when it was obvious I should mention a definite book. He talked very well, with an entertaining flow of rather pompous language which made the amusing things he said particularly funny. His passion for euphuism contrasted strikingly with the simple speech of those with whom he consorted. It certainly added authority to what he said. He was proud of his family and never hesitated to tell the curious of his distinguished descent. Unless he has much altered, you will already have heard of his relationship with various noble houses. He is, in fact, nearly connected with persons of importance, and his ancestry is no less distinguished than he asserts. His father is dead, and he owns a place in Staffordshire which is almost historic. I have seen photographs of it, and it is certainly very fine. His forebears have been noted in the history of England since the days of the courtier who accompanied Anne of Denmark to Scotland, and, if he is proud of his stock, it is not without cause. So he passed his time at Oxford, cordially disliked, at the same time respected and mistrusted; he had the reputation of a liar and a rogue, but it could not be denied that he had considerable influence over others. He amused, angered, irritated, and interested everyone with whom he came in contact. There was always something mysterious about him, and he loved to wrap himself in a romantic impenetrability. Though he knew so many people, no one knew him, and to the end he remained a stranger in our midst. A legend grew up around him, which he fostered sedulously, and it was reported that he had secret vices which could only be whispered with bated breath. He was said to intoxicate himself with Oriental drugs, and to haunt the vilest opium-dens in the East of London. He kept the greatest surprise for the last, since, though he was never seen to work, he managed, to the universal surprise, to get a first. He went down, and to the best of my belief was never seen in Oxford again.

"I have heard vaguely that he was travelling over the world, and, when I met in town now and then some of the fellows who had known him at the 'Varsity, weird rumours reached me. One told me that he was tramping across America, earning his living as he went; another asserted that he had been seen in a monastery in India; a third assured me that he had married a ballet-girl in Milan; and someone else was positive that he had taken to drink. One opinion, however, was common to all my informants, and this was that he did something out of the common. It was clear that he was not the man to settle down to the tame life of a country gentleman which his position and fortune indicated. At last I met him one day in Piccadilly, and we dined together at the Savoy. I hardly recognised him, for he was become enormously stout, and his hair had already grown thin. Though he could not have been more than twenty-five, he looked considerably older. I tried to find out what he had been up to, but, with the air of mystery he affects, he would go into no details. He gave me to understand that he had sojourned in lands where the white man had never been before, and had learnt esoteric secrets which overthrew the foundations of modern science. It seemed to me that he had coarsened in mind as well as in appearance. I do not know if it was due to my own development since the old days at Oxford, and to my greater knowledge of the world, but he did not seem to me so brilliant as I remembered. His facile banter was rather stupid. In fact he bored me. The pose which had seemed amusing in a lad fresh from Eton now was intolerable, and I was glad to leave him. It was characteristic that, after asking me to dinner, he left me in a lordly way to pay the bill.

"Then I heard nothing of him till the other day, when our friend Miss Ley asked me to meet at dinner the German explorer Burkhardt. I dare say you remember that Burkhardt brought out a book a little while ago on his adventures in Central Asia. I knew that Oliver Haddo was his companion in that journey and had meant to read it on this account, but, having been excessively busy, had omitted to do so. I took the opportunity to ask the German about our common acquaintance, and we had a long talk. Burkhardt had met him by chance at Mombasa in East Africa, where he was arranging an expedition after big game, and they agreed to go together. He told me that Haddo was a marvellous shot and a hunter of exceptional ability. Burkhardt had been rather suspicious of a man who boasted so much of his attainments, but was obliged soon to confess that he had boasted of nothing unjustly. Haddo has had an extraordinary experience, the truth of which Burkhardt can vouch for. He went out alone one night on the trail of three lions and killed them all before morning with one shot each. I know nothing of these things, but from the way in which Burkhardt spoke, I judge it must be a unique occurrence. But, characteristically enough, no one was more conscious than Haddo of the singularity of his feat, and he made life almost insufferable for his fellow-traveller in consequence. Burkhardt assures me that Haddo is really remarkable in pursuit of big game. He has a sort of instinct which leads him to the most likely places, and a wonderful feeling for country, whereby he can cut across, and head off animals whose spoor he has noticed. His courage is very great. To follow a wounded lion into thick cover is the most dangerous proceeding in the world, and demands the utmost coolness. The animal invariably sees the sportsman before he sees it, and in most cases charges. But Haddo never hesitated on these occasions, and Burkhardt could only express entire admiration for his pluck. It appears that he is not what is called a good sportsman. He kills wantonly, when there can be no possible excuse, for the mere pleasure of it; and to Burkhardt's indignation frequently shot beasts whose skins and horns they did not even trouble to take. When antelope were so far off that it was impossible to kill them, and the approach of night made it useless to follow, he would often shoot, and leave a wretched wounded beast to die by inches. His selfishness was extreme, and he never shared any information with his friend that might rob him of an uninterrupted pursuit of game. But notwithstanding all this, Burkhardt had so high an opinion of Haddo's general capacity and of his resourcefulness that, when he was arranging his journey in Asia, he asked him to come also. Haddo consented, and it appears that Burkhardt's book gives further proof, if it is needed, of the man's extraordinary qualities. The German confessed that on more than one occasion he owed his life to Haddo's rare power of seizing opportunities. But they quarrelled at last through Haddo's overbearing treatment of the natives. Burkhardt had vaguely suspected him of cruelty, but at length it was clear that he used them in a manner which could not be defended. Finally he had a desperate quarrel with one of the camp servants, as a result of which the man was shot dead. Haddo swore that he fired in self-defence, but his action caused a general desertion, and the travellers found themselves in a very dangerous predicament. Burkhardt thought that Haddo was clearly to blame and refused to have anything more to do with him. They separated. Burkhardt returned to England; and Haddo, pursued by the friends of the murdered man, had great difficulty in escaping with his life. Nothing has been heard of him since till I got your letter.

"Altogether, an extraordinary man. I confess that I can make nothing of him. I shall never be surprised to hear anything in connection with him. I recommend you to avoid him like the plague. He can be no one's friend. As an acquaintance he is treacherous and insincere; as an enemy, I can well imagine that he would be as merciless as he is unscrupulous.

"An immensely long letter!

"Good-bye, my son. I hope that your studies in French methods of surgery will have added to your wisdom. Your industry edifies me, and I am sure that you will eventually be a baronet and the President of the Royal College of Surgeons; and you shall relieve royal persons of their vermiform appendix.

"Yours ever,

"FRANK HURRELL."

Arthur, having read this letter twice, put it in an envelope and left it without comment for Miss Boyd. Her answer came within a couple of hours: "I've asked him to tea on Wednesday, and I can't put him off. You must come and help us, but please be as polite to him as if, like most of us, he had only taken mental liberties with the Ten Commandments."

VII

ON THE MORNING of the day upon which they had asked him to tea, Oliver Haddo left at Margaret's door vast masses of chrysanthemums. There were so many that the austere studio was changed in aspect. It gained an ephemeral brightness that Margaret, notwithstanding pieces of silk hung here and there on the walls, had never been able to give it. When Arthur arrived, he was dismayed that the thought had not occurred to him.

"I'm so sorry," he said. "You must think me very inconsiderate."

Margaret smiled and held his hand.

"I think I like you because you don't trouble about the common little attentions of lovers."

"Margaret's a wise girl," smiled Susie. "She knows that when a man sends flowers it is a sign that he has admired more women than one."

"I don't suppose that these were sent particularly to me."

Arthur Burdon sat down and observed with pleasure the cheerful fire. The drawn curtains and the lamps gave the place a nice cosiness, and there was the peculiar air of romance which is always in a studio. There is a sense of freedom about it that disposes the mind to diverting speculations. In such an atmosphere it is possible to be serious without pompousness and flippant without inanity.

In the few days of their acquaintance Arthur and Susie had arrived at terms of pleasant familiarity. Susie, from her superior standpoint of an unmarried woman no longer young, used him with the good-natured banter which she affected. To her, he was a foolish young thing in love, and she marvelled that even the cleverest man in that condition could behave like a perfect idiot. But Margaret knew that, if her friend chaffed him, it was because she completely approved of him. As their intimacy increased, Susie learnt to appreciate his solid character. She admired his capacity in dealing with matters that were in his province, and the simplicity with which he left alone those of which he was ignorant. There was no pose in him. She was touched also by an ingenuous candour which gave a persuasive charm to his abruptness. And, though she set a plain woman's value on good looks, his appearance, rough hewn like a statue in porphyry, pleased her singularly. It was an index of his character. The look of him gave you the whole man, strong yet gentle, honest and simple, neither very imaginative nor very brilliant, but immensely reliable and trustworthy to the bottom of his soul. He was seated now with Margaret's terrier on his knees, stroking its ears, and Susie, looking at him, wondered with a little pang why no man like that had ever cared for her. It was evident that he would make a perfect companion, and his love, once won, was of the sort that did not alter.

Dr. Porhoët came in and sat down with the modest quietness which was one of his charms. He was not a great talker and loved most to listen in silence to the chatter of young people. The dog jumped down from Arthur's knee, went up to the doctor, and rubbed itself in friendly fashion against his legs. They began to talk in the soft light and had forgotten almost that another guest was expected. Margaret hoped fervently that he would not come. She had never looked more lovely than on this afternoon, and she busied herself with the preparations for tea with a housewifely grace that added a peculiar delicacy to her comeliness. The dignity which encompassed the perfection of her beauty was delightfully softened, so that you were reminded of those sweet domestic saints who lighten here and there the passionate records of the Golden Book.

"*C'est tellement intime ici*," smiled Dr. Porhoët, breaking into French in the impossibility of expressing in English the exact feeling which that scene gave him.

It might have been a picture of some master of *genre*. It seemed hardly by chance that the colours arranged themselves in such agreeable tones, or that the lines of the wall and the seated persons achieved such a graceful decoration. The atmosphere was extraordinarily peaceful.

There was a knock at the door, and Arthur got up to open. The terrier followed at his heels. Oliver Haddo entered. Susie watched to see what the dog would do and was by this time not surprised to see a change come over it. With its tail between its legs, the friendly little beast slunk along the wall to the furthermost corner. It turned a suspicious, frightened eye upon Haddo and then hid its head. The visitor, intent upon his greetings, had not noticed even that there was an animal in the room. He accepted with a simple courtesy they hardly expected from him the young woman's thanks for his flowers. His behaviour surprised them. He put aside his poses. He seemed genuinely to admire the cosy little studio. He asked Margaret to show him her sketches and looked at them with unassumed interest. His observations were pointed and showed a certain knowledge of what he spoke about. He described himself as an amateur, that object of a painter's derision: the man "who knows what he likes"; but his criticism, though generous, showed that he was no fool. The two women were impressed. Putting the sketches aside, he began to talk, for once not of himself, but gaily and quite naturally, of the many places he had seen. It was evident that he sought to please. Susie began to understand how it was that, notwithstanding his affectations, he had acquired so great an influence over the undergraduates of Oxford. There was romance and laughter in his conversation; and though, as Frank Hurrell had said, lacking in wit, he made up for it with a diverting pleasantry that might very well have passed for humour. But Susie, though amused, felt that this was not the purpose for which she had asked him to come. Dr. Porhoët had lent her his entertaining work on the old alchemists, and this gave her a chance to bring their conversation to matters on which Haddo was expert. She had read the book with delight and, her mind all aflame with those strange histories wherein fact and fancy were so wonderfully mingled, she was eager to know more. The long toil in which so many had engaged, always to lose their fortunes, often to suffer persecution and torture, interested her no less than the accounts, almost authenticated, of those who had succeeded in their extraordinary quest.

She turned to Dr. Porhoët.

"You are a bold man to assert that now and then the old alchemists actually did make gold," she said.

"I have not gone quite so far as that," he smiled. "I assert merely that, if evidence as conclusive were offered of any other historical event, it would be credited beyond doubt. We can disbelieve these circumstantial details only by coming to the conclusion beforehand that it is impossible they should be true."

"I wish you would write that life of Paracelsus which you suggest in your preface."

Dr. Porhoët, smiling, shook his head.

"I don't think I shall ever do that now," he said. "Yet he is the most interesting of all the alchemists, for he offers the fascinating problem of an immensely complex character. It is impossible to know to what extent he was a charlatan and to what a man of serious science."

Susie glanced at Oliver Haddo, who sat in silence, his heavy face in shadow, his eyes fixed steadily on the speaker. The immobility of that vast bulk was peculiar.

"His name is not so ridiculous as later associations have made it seem," proceeded the doctor, "for he belonged to the celebrated family of Bombast, and they were called Hohenheim after their ancient residence, which was a castle near Stuttgart in Würtemberg. The most interesting part of his life is that which the absence of documents makes it impossible accurately to describe. He travelled in Germany, Italy, France, the Netherlands, in Denmark, Sweden, and Russia. He went even to India. He was taken prisoner by the Tartars, and brought to the Great Khan, whose son he afterwards accompanied to Constantinople. The mind must be dull indeed that is not thrilled by the thought of this wandering genius traversing the lands of the earth at the most eventful date of the world's history. It was at Constantinople that, according to a certain *aureum vellus* printed at Rorschach in the sixteenth century, he received the philosopher's stone from Solomon Trismosinus. This person possessed also the *Universal Panacea,* and it is asserted that he was seen still alive by a French traveller at the end of the seventeenth century. Paracelsus then passed through the countries that border the Danube, and so reached Italy, where he served as a surgeon in the imperial army. I see no reason why he should not have been present at the battle of Pavia. He collected information from physicians, surgeons and alchemists; from executioners, barbers, shepherds, Jews, gipsies, midwives, and fortune-tellers; from high and low, from learned and vulgar. In the sketch I have given of his career in that volume you hold, I have copied out a few words of his upon the acquirement of knowledge which affect me with a singular emotion."

Dr. Porhoüt took his book from Miss Boyd and opened it thoughtfully. He read out the fine passage from the preface of the *Paragranum*:

"I went in search of my art, often incurring danger of life. I have not been ashamed to learn that which seemed useful to me even from vagabonds, hangmen, and barbers. We know that a lover will go far to meet the woman he adores; how much more will the lover of Wisdom be tempted to go in search of his divine mistress."

He turned the page to find a few more lines further on:

"We should look for knowledge where we may expect to find it, and why should a man be despised who goes in search of it? Those who remain at home may grow richer and live more comfortably than those who wander; but I desire neither to live comfortably nor to grow rich."

"By Jove, those are fine words," said Arthur, rising to his feet.

Their brave simplicity moved him as no rhetoric could have done, and they made him more eager still to devote his own life to the difficult acquisition of knowledge. Dr. Porhoët gave him his ironic smile.

"Yet the man who could write that was in many ways a mere buffoon, who praised his wares with the vulgar glibness of a quack. He was vain and ostentatious, intemperate and boastful. Listen: '*After me, O Avicenna, Galen, Rhases, and Montagnana! After me, not I after you, ye men of Paris, Montpellier, Meissen, and Cologne; all you that come from the countries along the Danube and the Rhine, and you that come from the islands of the sea. It is not for me to follow you, because mine is the lordship. The time will come when none of you shall remain in his dark corner who will not be an object of contempt to the world, because I shall be the King, and the Monarchy will be mine*'."

Dr. Porhoët closed the book.

"Did you ever hear such gibberish in your life? Yet he did a bold thing. He wrote in German instead of in Latin, and so, by weakening the old belief in authority, brought about the beginning of free thought in science. He continued to travel from place to place, followed by a crowd of disciples, sometimes attracted to a wealthy city by hope of gain, sometimes journeying to a petty court at the invitation of a prince. His folly and the malice of his rivals prevented him from remaining anywhere for long. He wrought many wonderful cures. The physicians of Nuremberg denounced him as a quack, a charlatan, and an impostor. To refute them he asked the city council to put under his care patients that had been pronounced incurable. They sent him several cases of elephantiasis, and he cured them: testimonials to that effect may still be found in the archives of Nuremberg. He died as the result of a tavern brawl and was buried at Salzburg. Tradition says that, his astral body having already during physical existence become self-conscious, he is now a living adept, residing with others of his sort in a certain place in Asia. From there he still influences the minds of his followers and at times even appears to them in visible and tangible substance."

"But look here," said Arthur, "didn't Paracelsus, like most of these old fellows, in the course of his researches make any practical discoveries?"

"I prefer those which were not practical," confessed the doctor, with a smile. "Consider for example the *Tinctura Physicorum,* which neither Pope nor Emperor could buy with all his wealth. It was one of the greatest alchemical mysteries, and, though mentioned under the name of *The Red Lion* in many occult works, was actually known to few before Paracelsus, except Hermes Trismegistus and Albertus Magnus. Its preparation was extremely difficult, for the presence was needed of two perfectly harmonious persons whose skill was equal. It was said to be a red ethereal fluid. The least wonderful of its many properties was its power to transmute all inferior metals into gold. There is an old church in the south of Bavaria where the tincture is said to be still buried in the ground. In the year 1698 some of it penetrated through the soil, and the phenomenon was witnessed by many people, who believed it to be a miracle. The church which was thereupon erected is still a well-known place for pilgrimage. Paracelsus concludes his directions for its manufacture with the words: *But if this be incomprehensible to you, remember that only he who desires with his whole heart will find, and to him only who knocks vehemently shall the door be opened.*"

"I shall never try to make it," smiled Arthur.

"Then there was the *Electrum Magicum,* of which the wise made mirrors wherein they were able to see not only the events of the past and of the present, but the doings of men in daytime and at night. They might see anything that had been written or spoken, and the person who said it, and the causes that made him say it. But I like best the *Primum Ens Melissæ.* An elaborate prescription is given for its manufacture. It was a remedy to prolong life, and not only Paracelsus, but his predecessors Galen, Arnold of Villanova, and Raymond Lulli, had laboured studiously to discover it."

"Will it make me eighteen again?" cried Susie.

"It is guaranteed to do so," answered Dr. Porhoët gravely. "Lesebren, a physician to Louis XIV, gives an account of certain experiments witnessed by himself. It appears that one of his friends prepared the remedy, and his curiosity would not let him rest until he had seen with his own eyes the effect of it."

"That is the true scientific attitude," laughed Arthur.

"He took every morning at sunrise a glass of white wine tinctured with this preparation; and after using it for fourteen days his nails began to fall out, without, however, causing him any pain. His courage failed him at this point, and he gave the same dose to an old female servant. She regained at least one of the characteristics of youth, much to her astonishment, for she did not know that she had been taking a medicine, and, becoming frightened, refused to continue. The experimenter then took some grain, soaked it in the tincture, and gave it to an aged hen. On the sixth day the bird began to lose its feathers, and kept on losing them till it was naked as a new-born babe; but before two weeks had passed other feathers grew, and these were more beautifully coloured than any that fortunate hen had possessed in her first youth. Her comb stood up, and she began again to lay eggs."

Arthur laughed heartily.

"I confess I like that story much better than the others. The *Primum Ens Melissæ* at least offers a less puerile benefit than most magical secrets."

"Do you call the search for gold puerile?" asked Haddo, who had been sitting for a long time in complete silence.

"I venture to call it sordid."

"You are very superior."

"Because I think the aims of mystical persons invariably gross or trivial? To my plain mind, it is inane to raise the dead in order to hear from their phantom lips nothing but commonplaces. And I really cannot see that the alchemist who spent his life in the attempted manufacture of gold was a more respectable object than the outside jobber of modern civilisation."

"But if he sought for gold it was for the power it gave him, and it was power he aimed at when he brooded night and day over dim secrets. Power was the subject of all his dreams, but not a paltry, limited dominion over this or that; power over the whole world, power over all created things, power over the very elements, power over God Himself. His lust was so vast that he could not rest till the stars in their courses were obedient to his will."

For once Haddo lost his enigmatic manner. It was plain now that his words intoxicated him, and his face assumed a new, a strange, expression. A peculiar arrogance flashed in his shining eyes.

"And what else is it that men seek in life but power? If they want money, it is but for the power that attends it, and it is power again that they strive for in all the knowledge they acquire. Fools and sots aim at happiness, but men aim only at power. The magus, the sorcerer, the alchemist, are seized with the fascination of the unknown; and they desire a greatness that is inaccessible to mankind. They think by the science they study so patiently, by endurance and strength, by force of will and by imagination, for these are the great weapons of the magician, they may achieve at last a power with which they can face the God of Heaven Himself."

Oliver Haddo lifted his huge bulk from the low chair in which he had been sitting. He began to walk up and down the studio. It was curious to see this heavy man, whose seriousness was always problematical, caught up by a curious excitement.

"You've been talking of Paracelsus," he said. "There is one of his experiments which the doctor has withheld from you. You will find it neither mean nor mercenary, but it is very terrible. I do not know whether the account of it is true, but it would be of extraordinary interest to test it for oneself."

He looked round at the four persons who watched him intently. There was a singular agitation in his manner, as though the thing of which he spoke was very near his heart.

"The old alchemists believed in the possibility of spontaneous generation. By the combination of psychical powers and of strange essences, they claim to have created forms in which life became manifest. Of these, the most marvellous were those strange beings, male and female, which were called *homunculi*. The old philosophers doubted the possibility of this operation, but Paracelsus asserts positively that it can be done. I picked up once for a song on a barrow at London Bridge a little book in German. It was dirty and thumbed, many of the pages were torn, and the binding scarcely held the leaves together. It was called *Die Sphinx* and was edited by a certain Dr. Emil Besetzny. It contained the most extraordinary account I have ever read of certain spirits generated by Johann-Ferdinand, Count von Küffstein, in the Tyrol, in 1775. The sources from which this account is taken consist of masonic manuscripts, but more especially of a diary kept by a certain James Kammerer, who acted in the capacity of butler and famulus to the Count. The evidence is ten times stronger than any upon which men believe the articles of their religion. If it related to less wonderful subjects, you would not hesitate to believe implicity every word you read. There were ten *homunculi*—James Kammerer calls them prophesying spirits—kept in strong bottles, such as are used to preserve fruit, and these were filled with water. They were made in five weeks, by the Count von Küffstein and an Italian mystic and rosicrucian, the Abbé Geloni. The bottles were closed with a magic seal. The spirits were about a span long, and the Count was anxious that they should grow. They were therefore buried under two cart-loads of manure, and the pile daily sprinkled with a certain liquor prepared with great trouble by the adepts. The pile after such sprinklings began to ferment and steam, as if heated by a subterranean fire. When the bottles were removed, it was found that the spirits had grown to about a span and a half each; the male *homunculi* were come into possession of heavy beards, and the nails of the fingers had grown. In two of the bottles there was nothing to be seen save clear water, but when the Abbé knocked thrice at the seal upon the mouth, uttering at the same time certain Hebrew words, the water turned a mysterious colour, and the spirits showed their faces, very small at first, but growing in size till they attained that of a human countenance. And this countenance was horrible and fiendish."

Haddo spoke in a low voice that was hardly steady, and it was plain that he was much moved. It appeared as if his story affected him so that he could scarcely preserve his composure. He went on.

"These beings were fed every three days by the Count with a rose-coloured substance which was kept in a silver box. Once a week the bottles were emptied and filled again with pure rain-water. The change had to be made rapidly, because while the *homunculi* were exposed to the air they closed their eyes and seemed to grow weak and unconscious, as though they were about to die. But with the spirits that were invisible, at certain intervals blood was poured into the water; and it disappeared at once, inexplicably, without colouring or troubling it. By some accident one of the bottles fell one day and was broken. The *homunculus* within died after a few painful respirations in spite of all efforts to save him, and the body was buried in the garden. An attempt to generate another, made by the Count without the assistance of the Abbé, who had left, failed; it produced only a small thing like a leech, which had little vitality and soon died."

Haddo ceased speaking, and Arthur looked at him with amazement. "But taking for granted that the thing is possible, what on earth is the use of manufacturing these strange beasts?" he exclaimed.

"Use!" cried Haddo passionately. "What do you think would be man's sensations when he had solved the great mystery of existence, when he saw living before him the substance which was dead? These *homunculi* were seen by historical persons, by Count Max Lemberg, by Count Franz-Josef von Thun, and by many others. I have no doubt that they were actually generated. But with our modern appliances, with our greater skill, what might it not be possible to do now if we had the courage? There are chemists toiling away in their laboratories to create the primitive protoplasm from matter which is dead, the organic from the inorganic. I have studied their experiments. I know all that they know. Why shouldn't one work on a larger scale, joining to the knowledge of the old adepts the scientific discovery of the moderns? I don't know what would be the result. It might be very strange and very wonderful. Sometimes my mind is verily haunted by the desire to see a lifeless substance move under my spells, by the desire to be as God."

He gave a low weird laugh, half cruel, half voluptuous. It made Margaret shudder with sudden fright. He had thrown himself down in the chair, and he sat in complete shadow. By a singular effect his eyes appeared blood-red, and they stared into space, strangely parallel, with an intensity that was terrifying. Arthur started a little and gave him a searching glance. The laugh and that uncanny glance, the unaccountable emotion, were extraordinarily significant. The whole thing was explained if Oliver Haddo was mad.

There was an uncomfortable silence. Haddo's words were out of tune with the rest of the conversation. Dr. Porhoët had spoken of magical things with a sceptical irony that gave a certain humour to the subject, and Susie was resolutely flippant. But Haddo's vehemence put these incredulous people out of countenance. Dr. Porhoët got up to go. He shook hands with Susie and with Margaret. Arthur opened the door for him. The kindly scholar looked round for Margaret's terrier.

"I must bid my farewells to your little dog."

He had been so quiet that they had forgotten his presence.

"Come here, Copper," said Margaret.

The dog slowly slunk up to them, and with a terrified expression crouched at Margaret's feet.

"What on earth's the matter with you?" she asked.

"He's frightened of me," said Haddo, with that harsh laugh of his which gave such an unpleasant impression.

"Nonsense!"

Dr. Porhoët bent down, stroked the dog's back, and shook its paw. Margaret lifted it up and set it on a table.

"Now, be good," she said, with lifted finger.

Dr. Porhoët with a smile went out, and Arthur shut the door behind him. Suddenly, as though evil had entered into it, the terrier sprang at Oliver Haddo and fixed its teeth in his hand. Haddo uttered a cry, and, shaking it off, gave it a savage kick. The dog rolled over with a loud bark that was almost a scream of pain, and lay still for a moment as if it were desperately hurt. Margaret cried out with horror and indignation. A fierce rage on a sudden seized Arthur so that he scarcely knew what he was about. The wretched brute's suffering, Margaret's terror, his own instinctive hatred of the man, were joined together in frenzied passion.

"You brute," he muttered.

He hit Haddo in the face with his clenched fist. The man collapsed bulkily to the floor, and Arthur, furiously seizing his collar, began to kick him with all his might. He shook him as a dog would shake a rat and then violently flung him down. For some reason Haddo made no resistance. He remained where he fell in utter helplessness. Arthur turned to Margaret. She was holding the poor hurt dog in her hands, crying over it, and trying to comfort it in its pain. Very gently he examined it to see if Haddo's brutal kick had broken a bone. They sat down beside the fire. Susie, to steady her nerves, lit a cigarette. She was horribly, acutely conscious of that man who lay in a mass on the floor behind them. She wondered what he would do. She wondered why he did not go. And she was ashamed of his humiliation. Then her heart stood still; for she realised that he was raising himself to his feet, slowly, with the difficulty of a very fat person. He leaned against the wall and stared at them. He remained there quite motionless. His stillness got on her nerves, and she could have screamed as she felt him look at them, look with those unnatural eyes, whose expression now she dare not even imagine.

At last she could no longer resist the temptation to turn round just enough to see him. Haddo's eyes were fixed upon Margaret so intently that he did not see he was himself observed. His face, distorted by passion, was horrible to look upon. That vast mass of flesh had a malignancy that was inhuman, and it was terrible to see the satanic hatred which hideously deformed it. But it changed. The redness gave way to a ghastly pallor. The revengeful scowl disappeared; and a torpid smile spread over the features, a smile that was even more terrifying than the frown of malice. What did it mean? Susie could have cried out, but her tongue cleaved to her throat. The smile passed away, and the face became once more impassive. It seemed that Margaret and Arthur realised at last the power of those inhuman eyes, and they became quite still. The dog ceased its sobbing. The silence was so great that each one heard the beating of his heart. It was intolerable.

Then Oliver Haddo moved. He came forward slowly.

"I want to ask you to forgive me for what I did," he said. "The pain of the dog's bite was so keen that I lost my temper. I deeply regret that I kicked it. Mr. Burdon was very right to thrash me. I feel that I deserved no less."

He spoke in a low voice, but with great distinctness. Susie was astounded. An abject apology was the last thing she expected.

He paused for Margaret's answer. But she could not bear to look at him. When she spoke, her words were scarcely audible. She did not know why his request to be forgiven made him seem more detestable.

"I think, if you don't mind, you had better go away."

Haddo bowed slightly. He looked at Burdon.

"I wish to tell you that I bear no malice for what you did. I recognise the justice of your anger."

Arthur did not answer at all. Haddo hesitated a moment, while his eyes rested on them quietly. To Susie it seemed that they flickered with the shadow of a smile. She watched him with bewildered astonishment.

He reached for his hat, bowed again, and went.

VIII

Susie could not persuade herself that Haddo's regret was sincere. The humility of it aroused her suspicion. She could not get out of her mind the ugly slyness of that smile which succeeded on his face the first passionate look of deadly hatred. Her fancy suggested various dark means whereby Oliver Haddo might take vengeance on his enemy, and she was at pains to warn Arthur. But he only laughed.

"The man's a funk," he said. "Do you think if he'd had anything in him at all he would have let me kick him without trying to defend himself?"

Haddo's cowardice increased the disgust with which Arthur regarded him. He was amused by Susie's trepidation.

"What on earth do you suppose he can do? He can't drop a brickbat on my head. If he shoots me he'll get his head cut off, and he won't be such an ass as to risk that!"

Margaret was glad that the incident had relieved them of Oliver's society. She met him in the street a couple of day's later, and since he took off his hat in the French fashion without waiting for her to acknowledge him, she was able to make her cut more pointed.

She began to discuss with Arthur the date of their marriage. It seemed to her that she had got out of Paris all it could give her, and she wished to begin a new life. Her love for Arthur appeared on a sudden more urgent, and she was filled with delight at the thought of the happiness she would give him.

A day or two later Susie received a telegram. It ran as follows:

"PLEASE MEET ME AT THE GARE DU NORD, 2:40.
NANCY CLERK."

It was an old friend, who was apparently arriving in Paris that afternoon. A photograph of her, with a bold signature, stood on the chimney-piece, and Susie gave it an inquisitive glance. She had not seen Nancy for so long that it surprised her to receive this urgent message.

"What a bore it is!" she said. "I suppose I must go."

They meant to have tea on the other side of the river, but the journey to the station was so long that it would not be worth Susie's while to come back in the interval; and they arranged therefore to meet at the house to which they were invited. Susie started a little before two.

Margaret had a class that afternoon and set out two or three minutes later. As she walked through the courtyard she started nervously, for Oliver Haddo passed slowly by. He did not seem to see her. Suddenly he stopped, put his hand to his heart, and fell heavily to the ground. The *concierge*, the only person at hand, ran forward with a cry. She knelt down and, looking round with terror, caught sight of Margaret.

"Oh, *mademoiselle, venez vite!*" she cried.

Margaret was obliged to go. Her heart beat horribly. She looked down at Oliver, and he seemed to be dead. She forgot that she loathed him. Instinctively she knelt down by his side and loosened his collar. He opened his eyes. An expression of terrible anguish came into his face.

"For the love of God, take me in for one moment," he sobbed. "I shall die in the street."

Her heart was moved towards him. He could not go into the poky den, evil-smelling and airless, of the *concierge*. But with her help Margaret raised him to his feet, and together they brought him to the studio. He sank painfully into a chair.

"Shall I fetch you some water?" asked Margaret.

"Can you get a pastille out of my pocket?"

He swallowed a white tabloid, which she took out of a case attached to his watch-chain.

"I'm very sorry to cause you this trouble," he gasped. "I suffer from a disease of the heart, and sometimes I am very near death."

"I'm glad that I was able to help you," she said.

He seemed able to breathe more easily. She left him to himself for a while, so that he might regain his strength. She took up a book and began to read. Presently, without moving from his chair, he spoke.

"You must hate me for intruding on you."

His voice was stronger, and her pity waned as he seemed to recover. She answered with freezing indifference.

"I couldn't do any less for you than I did. I would have brought a dog into my room if it seemed hurt."

"I see that you wish me to go."

He got up and moved towards the door, but he staggered and with a groan tumbled to his knees. Margaret sprang forward to help him. She reproached herself bitterly for those scornful words. The man had barely escaped death, and she was merciless.

"Oh, please stay as long as you like," she cried. "I'm sorry, I didn't mean to hurt you."

He dragged himself with difficulty back to the chair, and she, conscience-stricken, stood over him helplessly. She poured out a glass of water, but he motioned it away as though he would not be beholden to her even for that.

"Is there nothing I can do for you at all?" she exclaimed, painfully.

"Nothing, except allow me to sit in this chair," he gasped. "I hope you'll remain as long as you choose."

He did not reply. She sat down again and pretended to read. In a little while he began to speak. His voice reached her as if from a long way off.

"Will you never forgive me for what I did the other day?"

She answered without looking at him, her back still turned.

"Can it matter to you if I forgive or not?"

"You have no pity. I told you then how sorry I was that a sudden uncontrollable pain drove me to do a thing which immediately I bitterly regretted. Don't you think it must have been hard for me, under the actual circumstances, to confess my fault?"

"I wish you not to speak of it. I don't want to think of that horrible scene."

"If you knew how lonely I was and how unhappy, you would have a little mercy."

His voice was strangely moved. She could not doubt now that he was sincere.

"You think me a charlatan because I aim at things that are unknown to you. You won't try to understand. You won't give me any credit for striving with all my soul to a very great end."

She made no reply, and for a time there was silence. His voice was different now and curiously seductive.

"You look upon me with disgust and scorn. You almost persuaded yourself to let me die in the street rather than stretch out to me a helping hand. And if you hadn't been merciful then, almost against your will, I should have died."

"It can make no difference to you how I regard you," she whispered.

She did not know why his soft, low tones mysteriously wrung her heartstrings. Her pulse began to beat more quickly.

"It makes all the difference in the world. It is horrible to think of your contempt. I feel your goodness and your purity. I can hardly bear my own unworthiness. You turn your eyes away from me as though I were unclean."

She turned her chair a little and looked at him. She was astonished at the change in his appearance. His hideous obesity seemed no longer repellent, for his eyes wore a new expression; they were incredibly tender now, and they were moist with tears. His mouth was tortured by a passionate distress. Margaret had never seen so much unhappiness on a man's face, and an overwhelming remorse seized her.

"I don't want to be unkind to you," she said.

"I will go. That is how I can best repay you for what you have done."

The words were so bitter, so humiliated, that the colour rose to her cheeks.

"I ask you to stay. But let us talk of other things."

For a moment he kept silence. He seemed no longer to see Margaret, and she watched him thoughtfully. His eyes rested on a print of *La Gioconda* which hung on the wall. Suddenly he began to speak. He recited the honeyed words with which Walter Pater expressed his admiration for that consummate picture.

"Hers is the head upon which all the ends of the world are come, and the eyelids are a little weary. It is a beauty wrought out from within upon the flesh, the deposit, little

*cell by cell, of strange thoughts and fantastic reveries and
exquisite passions. Set it for a moment beside one of those
white Greek goddesses or beautiful women of antiquity, and
how would they be troubled by this beauty, into which the
soul with all its maladies has passed. All the thoughts and
experience of the world have etched and moulded there, in
that which they have of power to refine and make expressive
the outward form, the animalism of Greece, the lust of Rome,
the mysticism of the Middle Ages, with its spiritual ambition
and imaginative loves, the return of the Pagan world, the sins
of the Borgias."*

His voice, poignant and musical, blended with the suave
music of the words so that Margaret felt she had never before
known their divine significance. She was intoxicated with
their beauty. She wished him to continue, but had not the
strength to speak. As if he guessed her thought, he went on,
and now his voice had a richness in it as of an organ heard
afar off. It was like an overwhelming fragrance and she could
hardly bear it.

*"She is older than the rocks among which she sits; like the
vampire, she has been dead many times, and learned the
secrets of the grave; and has been a diver in deep seas, and
keeps their fallen day about her; and trafficked for strange
evils with Eastern merchants; and, as Leda, was the mother
of Helen of Troy, and, as Saint Anne, the mother of Mary;
and all this has been to her but as the sound of lyres and
flutes, and lives only in the delicacy with which it has moulded
the changing lineaments, and tinged the eyelids and the
hands."*

Oliver Haddo began then to speak of Leonardo da Vinci,
mingling with his own fantasies the perfect words of that
essay which, so wonderful was his memory, he seemed to

know by heart. He found exotic fancies in the likeness between Saint John the Baptist, with his soft flesh and waving
hair, and Bacchus, with his ambiguous smile. Seen through
his eyes, the seashore in the Saint Anne had the airless
lethargy of some damasked chapel in a Spanish nunnery, and
over the landscapes brooded a wan spirit of evil that was very
troubling. He loved the mysterious pictures in which the
painter had sought to express something beyond the limits
of painting, something of unsatisfied desire and of longing
for unhuman passions. Oliver Haddo found this quality in
unlikely places, and his words gave a new meaning to paint-
ings that Margaret had passed thoughtlessly by. There was
the portrait of a statuary by Bronzino in the Long Gallery
of the Louvre. The features were rather large, the face rather
broad. The expression was sombre, almost surly in the repose
of the painted canvas, and the eyes were brown, almond-
shaped like those of an Oriental; the red lips were exquisitely
modelled, and the sensuality was curiously disturbing; the
dark, chestnut hair, cut short, curled over the head with an
infinite grace. The skin was like ivory softened with a delicate
carmine. There was in that beautiful countenance more than
beauty, for what most fascinated the observer was a supreme
and disdainful indifference to the passion of others. It was
a vicious face, except that beauty could never be quite vicious;
it was a cruel face, except that indolence could never be
quite cruel. It was a face that haunted you, and yet your
admiration was alloyed with an unreasoning terror. The
hands were nervous and adroit, with long fashioning fingers;
and you felt that at their touch the clay almost moulded itself
into gracious forms. With Haddo's subtle words the character
of that man rose before her, cruel yet indifferent, indolent
and passionate, cold yet sensual; unnatural secrets dwelt in

his mind, and mysterious crimes, and a lust for the knowledge
that was arcane. Oliver Haddo was attracted by all that was
unusual, deformed, and monstrous, by the pictures that represented the hideousness of man or that reminded you of his
mortality. He summoned before Margaret the whole array of
Ribera's ghoulish dwarfs, with their cunning smile, the insane
light of their eyes, and their malice: he dwelt with a horrible
fascination upon their malformations, the humped backs, the
club feet, the hydrocephalic heads. He described the picture
by Valdes Leal, in a certain place at Seville, which represents
a priest at the altar; and the altar is sumptuous with gilt and
florid carving. He wears a magnificent cope and a surplice of
exquisite lace, but he wears them as though their weight was
more than he could bear; and in the meagre trembling hands,
and in the white, ashen face, in the dark hollowness of the
eyes, there is a bodily corruption that is terrifying. He seems
to hold together with difficulty the bonds of the flesh, but
with no eager yearning of the soul to burst its prison, only
with despair; it is as if the Lord Almighty had forsaken him
and the high heavens were empty of their solace. All the
beauty of life appears forgotten, and there is nothing in the
world but decay. A ghastly putrefaction has attacked already
the living man; the worms of the grave, the piteous horror of
mortality, and the darkness before him offer naught but fear.
Beyond, dark night is seen and a turbulent sea, the dark
night of the soul of which the mystics write, and the troublous
sea of life whereon there is no refuge for the weary and the
sick at heart.

Then, as if in pursuance of a definite plan, he analysed
with a searching, vehement intensity the curious talent of
the modern Frenchman, Gustave Moreau. Margaret had
lately visited the Luxembourg, and his pictures were fresh

in her memory. She had found in them little save a decorative arrangement marred by faulty drawing; but Oliver Haddo gave them at once a new, esoteric import. Those effects as of a Florentine jewel, the clustered colours, emerald and ruby, the deep blue of sapphires, the atmosphere of scented chambers, the mystic persons who seem ever about secret, religious rites, combined in his cunning phrases to create, as it were, a pattern on her soul of morbid and mysterious intricacy. Those pictures were filled with a strange sense of sin, and the mind that contemplated them was burdened with the decadence of Rome and with the passionate vice of the Renaissance; and it was tortured, too, by all the introspections of this later day.

Margaret listened, rather breathlessly, with the excitement of an explorer before whom is spread the plain of an undiscovered continent. The painters she knew spoke of their art technically, and this imaginative appreciation was new to her. She was horribly fascinated by the personality that imbued these elaborate sentences. Haddo's eyes were fixed upon hers, and she responded to his words like a delicate instrument made for recording the beatings of the heart. She felt an extraordinary languor. At last he stopped. Margaret neither moved nor spoke. She might have been under a spell. It seemed to her that she had no power in her limbs.

"I want to do something for you in return for what you have done for me," he said.

He stood up and went to the piano.

"Sit in this chair," he said.

She did not dream of disobeying. He began to play. Margaret was hardly surprised that he played marvellously. Yet it was almost incredible that those fat, large hands should have such a tenderness of touch. His fingers caressed the notes with a peculiar suavity, and he drew out of the piano effects which she had scarcely thought possible. He seemed to put into the notes a troubling, ambiguous passion, and the instrument had the tremulous emotion of a human being. It was strange and terrifying. She was vaguely familiar with the music to which she listened; but there was in it, under his fingers, an exotic savour that made it harmonious with all that he had said that afternoon. His memory was indeed astonishing. He had an infinite tact to know the feeling that occupied Margaret's heart, and what he chose seemed to be exactly that which at the moment she imperatively needed. Then he began to play things she did not know. It was music the like of which she had never heard, barbaric, with a plaintive weirdness that brought to her fancy the moonlit nights of desert places, with palm trees mute in the windless air, and tawny distances. She seemed to know tortuous narrow streets, white houses of silence with strange moon-shadows, and the glow of yellow light within, and the tinkling of uncouth instruments, and the acrid scents of Eastern perfumes. It was like a procession passing through her mind of persons who were not human, yet existed mysteriously, with a life of vampires. Mona Lisa and Saint John the Baptist, Bacchus and the mother of Mary, went with enigmatic motions. But the daughter of Herodias raised her hands as though, engaged for ever in a mystic rite, to invoke outlandish gods. Her face was very pale, and her dark eyes were sleepless; the jewels of her girdle gleamed with sombre fires; and her dress was of colours that have long been lost. The smile, in which was all the sorrow of the world and all its wickedness, beheld the wan head of the Saint, and with a voice that was cold with the coldness of death she murmured the words of the poet:

"*I am amorous of thy body, Iokanaan! Thy body is white*

like the lilies of a field that the mower hath never mowed. Thy body is white like the snows that lie on the mountains of Judæa, and come down into the valleys. The roses in the garden of the Queen of Arabia are not so white as thy body. Neither the roses in the garden of the Queen of Arabia, the garden of spices of the Queen of Arabia, nor the feet of the dawn when they light on the leaves, nor the breast of the moon when she lies on the breast of the sea . . . There is nothing in the world so white as thy body. Suffer me to touch thy body."

Oliver Haddo ceased to play. Neither of them stirred. At last Margaret sought by an effort to regain her self-control.

"I shall begin to think that you really are a magician," she said, lightly.

"I could show you strange things if you cared to see them," he answered, again raising his eyes to hers.

"I don't think you will ever get me to believe in occult philosophy," she laughed.

"Yet it reigned in Persia with the magi, it endowed India with wonderful traditions, it civilised Greece to the sounds of Orpheus' lyre."

He stood before Margaret, towering over her in his huge bulk; and there was a singular fascination in his gaze. It seemed that he spoke only to conceal from her that he was putting forth now all the power that was in him.

"It concealed the first principles of science in the calculations of Pythagoras. It established empires by its oracles, and at its voice tyrants grew pale upon their thrones. It governed the minds of some by curiosity, and others it ruled by fear."

His voice grew very low, and it was so seductive that Margaret's brain reeled. The sound of it was overpowering like too sweet a fragrance.

"I tell you that for this art nothing is impossible. It commands the elements, and knows the language of the stars, and directs the planets in their courses. The moon at its bidding falls blood-red from the sky. The dead rise up and form into ominous words the night wind that moans through their skulls. Heaven and Hell are in its province; and all forms, lovely and hideous; and love and hate. With Circe's wand it can change men into beasts of the field, and to them it can give a monstrous humanity. Life and death are in the right hand and in the left of him who knows its secrets. It confers wealth by the transmutation of metals and immortality by its quintessence."

Margaret could not hear what he said. A gradual lethargy seized her under his baleful glance, and she had not even the strength to wish to free herself. She seemed bound to him already by hidden chains.

"If you have powers, show them," she whispered, hardly conscious that she spoke.

Suddenly he released the enormous tension with which he held her. Like a man who has exerted all his strength to some end, the victory won, he loosened his muscles, with a faint sigh of exhaustion. Margaret did not speak, but she knew that something horrible was about to happen. Her heart beat like a prisoned bird, with helpless flutterings, but it seemed too late now to draw back. Her words by a mystic influence had settled something beyond possibility of recall.

On the stove was a small bowl of polished brass in which water was kept in order to give a certain moisture to the air. Oliver Haddo put his hand in his pocket and drew out a little silver box. He tapped it, with a smile, as a man taps a snuff-box, and it opened. He took an infinitesimal quantity of a blue powder that it contained and threw it on the water in the brass bowl. Immediately a bright flame sprang up, and Margaret gave a cry of alarm. Oliver looked at her quickly and motioned her to remain still. She saw that the water was on fire. It was burning as brilliantly, as hotly, as if it were common gas; and it burned with the same dry, hoarse roar. Suddenly it was extinguished. She leaned forward and saw that the bowl was empty.

The water had been consumed, as though it were straw, and not a drop remained. She passed her hand absently across her forehead.

"But water cannot burn," she muttered to herself.

It seemed that Haddo knew what she thought, for he smiled strangely.

"Do you know that nothing more destructive can be invented than this blue powder, and I have enough to burn up all the water in Paris? Who dreamt that water might burn like chaff?"

He paused, seeming to forget her presence. He looked thoughtfully at the little silver box.

"But it can be made only in trivial quantities, at enormous expense and with exceeding labour; it is so volatile that you cannot keep it for three days. I have sometimes thought that with a little ingenuity I might make it more stable, I might so modify it that, like radium, it lost no strength as it burned; and then I should possess the greatest secret that has ever been in the mind of man. For there would be no end of it. It would continue to burn while there was a drop of water on the earth, and the whole world would be consumed. But it would be a frightful thing to have in one's hands; for once it were cast upon the waters, the doom of all that existed would be sealed beyond repeal."

He took a long breath, and his eyes glittered with a devilish ardour. His voice was hoarse with overwhelming emotion.

"Sometimes I am haunted by the wild desire to have seen that great and final scene when the irrevocable flames poured down the river, hurrying along the streams of the earth, searching out the moisture in all growing things, tearing it even from the eternal rocks; when the flames poured down like the rushing of the wind, and all that lived fled from before them till they came to the sea; and the sea itself was consumed in vehement fire."

Margaret shuddered, but she did not think the man was mad. She had ceased to judge him. He took one more particle of that atrocious powder and put it in the bowl. Again he thrust his hand in his pocket and brought out a handful of some crumbling substance that might have been dried leaves, leaves of different sorts, broken and powdery. There was a trace of moisture in them still, for a low flame sprang up immediately at the bottom of the dish, and a thick vapour filled the room. It had a singular and pungent odour that Margaret did not know. It was difficult to breathe, and she coughed. She wanted to beg Oliver to stop, but could not. He took the bowl in his hands and brought it to her.

"Look," he commanded.

She bent forward, and at the bottom saw a blue fire, of a peculiar solidity, as though it consisted of molten metal. It was not still, but writhed strangely, like serpents of fire tortured by their own unearthly ardour.

"Breathe very deeply."

She did as he told her. A sudden trembling came over her, and darkness fell across her eyes. She tried to cry out, but could utter no sound. Her brain reeled. It seemed to her that Haddo bade her cover her face. She gasped for breath, and it was as if the earth spun under her feet. She appeared to travel at an immeasurable speed. She made a slight movement, and Haddo told her not to look round. An immense terror seized her. She did not know whither she was borne, and still they went quickly, quickly; and the hurricane itself would have lagged behind them. At last their motion ceased, and Oliver was holding her arm.

"Don't be afraid," he said. "Open your eyes and stand up."

The night had fallen; but it was not the comfortable night that soothes the troubled minds of mortal men; it was a night that agitated the soul mysteriously so that each nerve in the body tingled. There was a lurid darkness which displayed and yet distorted the objects that surrounded them. No moon shone in the sky, but small stars appeared to dance on the heather, vague night-fires like spirits of the damned. They stood in a vast and troubled waste, with huge stony boulders and leafless trees, rugged and gnarled like tortured souls in pain. It was as if there had been a devastating storm, and the country reposed after the flood of rain and the tempestuous wind and the lightning. All things about them appeared dumbly to suffer, like a man racked by torments who has not the strength even to realise that his agony has ceased. Margaret heard the flight of monstrous birds, and they seemed to whisper strange things on their passage. Oliver took her hand. He led her steadily to a cross-road, and she did not know if they walked amid rocks or tombs.

She heard the sound of a trumpet, and from all parts, strangely appearing where before was nothing, a turbulent assembly surged about her. That vast empty space was suddenly filled by shadowy forms, and they swept along like the waves of the sea, crowding upon one another's heels. And it seemed that all the mighty dead appeared before her; and she

saw grim tyrants, and painted courtesans, and Roman em-
perors in their purple, and sultans of the East. All those fierce
evil women of olden time passed by her side, and now it was
Mona Lisa and now the subtle daughter of Herodias. And
Jezebel looked out upon her from beneath her painted brows,
and Cleopatra turned away a wan, lewd face; and she saw
the insatiable mouth and the wanton eyes of Messalina, and
Faustine was haggard with the eternal fires of lust. She saw
cardinals in their scarlet, and warriors in their steel, gay gentlemen in periwigs, and ladies in powder and patch. And on
a sudden, like leaves by the wind, all these were driven before the silent throngs of the oppressed; and they were innumerable as the sands of the sea. Their thin faces were
earthy with want and cavernous from disease, and their eyes
were dull with despair. They passed in their tattered motley,
some in the fantastic rags of the beggars of Albrecht Dürer
and some in the grey cerecloths of Le Nain; many wore the
blouses and the caps of the rabble in France, and many the
dingy, smoke-grimed weeds of English poor. And they surged
onward like a riotous crowd in narrow streets flying in terror
before the mounted troops. It seemed as though all the world
were gathered there in strange confusion.

Then all again was void; and Margaret's gaze was riveted
upon a great, ruined tree that stood in that waste place, alone,
in ghastly desolation; and though a dead thing, it seemed to
suffer a more than human pain. The lightning had torn it
asunder, but the wind of centuries had sought in vain to drag
up its roots. The tortured branches, bare of any twig, were
like a Titan's arms, convulsed with intolerable anguish. And
in a moment she grew sick with fear, for a change came into
the tree, and the tremulousness of life was in it; the rough
bark was changed into brutish flesh and the twisted branches

into human arms. It became a monstrous, goat-legged thing, more vast than the creatures of nightmare. She saw the horns and the long beard, the great hairy legs with their hoofs, and the man's rapacious hands. The face was horrible with lust and cruelty, and yet it was divine. It was Pan, playing on his pipes, and the lecherous eyes caressed her with a hideous tenderness. But even while she looked, as the mist of early day, rising, discloses a fair country, the animal part of that ghoulish creature seemed to fall away, and she saw a lovely youth, titanic but sublime, leaning against a massive rock. He was more beautiful than the Adam of Michael Angelo who wakes into life at the call of the Almighty; and, like him freshly created, he had the adorable languor of one who feels still in his limbs the soft rain on the loose brown earth. Naked and full of majesty he lay, the outcast son of the morning; and she dared not look upon his face, for she knew it was impossible to bear the undying pain that darkened it with ruthless shadows. Impelled by a great curiosity, she sought to come nearer, but the vast figure seemed strangely to dissolve into a cloud; and immediately she felt herself again surrounded by a hurrying throng. Then came all legendary monsters and foul beasts of a madman's fancy; in the darkness she saw enormous toads, with paws pressed to their flanks, and huge limping scarabs, shelled creatures the like of which she had never seen, and noisome brutes with horny scales and round crabs' eyes, uncouth primeval things, and winged serpents, and creeping animals begotten of the slime. She heard shrill cries and peals of laughter and the terrifying rattle of men at the point of death. Haggard women, dishevelled and lewd, carried wine; and when they spilt it there were stains like the stains of blood. And it seemed to Margaret that a fire burned in her veins, and her soul fled from her body; but a new soul came in its place, and suddenly she knew all that was obscene. She took part in some festival of hideous lust, and the wickedness of the world was patent to her eyes. She saw things so vile that she screamed in terror, and she heard Oliver laugh in derision by her side. It was a scene of indescribable horror, and she put her hands to her eyes so that she might not see.

She felt Oliver Haddo take her hands. She would not let him drag them away. Then she heard him speak.

"You need not be afraid."

His voice was quite natural once more, and she realised with a start that she was sitting quietly in the studio. She looked around her with frightened eyes. Everything was exactly as it had been. The early night of autumn was fallen, and the only light in the room came from the fire. There was still that vague, acrid scent of the substance which Haddo had burned.

"Shall I light the candles?" he said.

He struck a match and lit those which were on the piano. They threw a strange light. Then Margaret suddenly remembered all that she had seen, and she remembered that Haddo had stood by her side. Shame seized her, intolerable shame, so that the colour, rising to her cheeks, seemed actually to burn them. She hid her face in her hands and burst into tears.

"Go away," she said. "For God's sake, go."

He looked at her for a moment; and the smile came to his lips which Susie had seen after his tussle with Arthur, when last he was in the studio.

"When you want me you will find me in the Rue de Vaugiraud, number 209," he said. "Knock at the second door on the left, on the third floor."

She did not answer. She could only think of her appalling shame.

"I'll write it down for you in case you forget."

He scribbled the address on a sheet of paper that he found on the table. Margaret took no notice, but sobbed as though her heart would break. Suddenly, looking up with a start, she saw that he was gone. She had not heard him open the door or close it. She sank down on her knees and prayed desperately, as though some terrible danger threatened her.

But when she heard Susie's key in the door, Margaret sprang to her feet. She stood with her back to the fireplace, her hands behind her, in the attitude of a prisoner protesting his innocence. Susie was too much annoyed to observe this agitation.

"Why on earth didn't you come to tea?" she asked. "I couldn't make out what had become of you."

"I had a dreadful headache," answered Margaret, trying to control herself.

Susie flung herself down wearily in a chair. Margaret forced herself to speak.

"Had Nancy anything particular to say to you?" she asked.

"She never turned up," answered Susie irritably. "I can't understand it. I waited till the train came in, but there was no sign of her. Then I thought she might have hit upon that time by chance and was not coming from England, so I walked about the station for half an hour."

She went to the chimneypiece, on which had been left the telegram that summoned her to the Gare du Nord, and read it again. She gave a little cry of surprise.

"How stupid of me! I never noticed the postmark. It was sent from the Rue Littré."

This was less than ten minutes' walk from the studio. Susie looked at the message with perplexity.

"I wonder if someone has been playing a silly practical joke on me." She shrugged her shoulders. "But it's too foolish. If I were a suspicious woman," she smiled, "I should think you had sent it yourself to get me out of the way."

The idea flashed through Margaret that Oliver Haddo was the author of it. He might easily have seen Nancy's name on the photograph during his first visit to the studio. She had no time to think before she answered lightly.

"If I wanted to get rid of you, I should have no hesitation in saying so."

"I suppose no one has been here?" asked Susie.

"No one."

The lie slipped from Margaret's lips before she had made up her mind to tell it. Her heart gave a great beat against her chest. She felt herself redden.

Susie got up to light a cigarette. She wished to rest her nerves. The box was on the table and, as she helped herself, her eyes fell carelessly on the address that Haddo had left. She picked it up and read it aloud.

"Who on earth lives there?" she asked.

"I don't know at all," answered Margaret.

She braced herself for further questions, but Susie, without interest, put down the sheet of paper and struck a match.

Margaret was ashamed. Her nature was singularly truthful, and it troubled her extraordinarily that she had lied to her greatest friend. Something stronger than herself seemed to impel her. She would have given much to confess her two falsehoods, but had not the courage. She could not bear that Susie's implicit trust in her straightforwardness should be destroyed; and the admission that Oliver Haddo had been there would entail a further acknowledgement of the nameless horrors she had witnessed. Susie would think her mad.

There was a knock at the door; and Margaret, her nerves shattered by all that she had endured, could hardly restrain a cry of terror. She feared that Haddo had returned. But it was Arthur Burdon. She greeted him with a passionate relief that was unusual, for she was by nature a woman of great self-possession. She felt excessively weak, physically exhausted as though she had gone a long journey, and her mind was highly wrought. Margaret remembered that her state had been the same on her first arrival in Paris, when, in her eagerness to get a preliminary glimpse of its marvels, she had hurried till her bones ached from one celebrated monument to another. They began to speak of trivial things. Margaret tried to join calmly in the conversation, but her voice sounded unnatural, and she fancied that more than once Arthur gave her a curious look. At length she could control herself no longer and burst into a sudden flood of tears. In a moment, uncomprehending but affectionate, he caught her in his arms. He asked tenderly what was the matter. He sought to comfort her. She wept ungovernably, clinging to him for protection.

"Oh, it's nothing," she gasped. "I don't know what is the matter with me. I'm only nervous and frightened."

Arthur had an idea that women were often afflicted with what he described by the old-fashioned name of vapours, and was not disposed to pay much attention to this vehement distress. He soothed her as he would have done a child.

"Oh, take care of me, Arthur. I'm so afraid that some dreadful thing will happen to me. I want all your strength. Promise that you'll never forsake me."

He laughed, as he kissed away her tears, and she tried to smile.

"Why can't we be married at once?" she asked. "I don't want to wait any longer. I shan't feel safe till I'm actually your wife."

He reasoned with her very gently. After all, they were to be married in a few weeks. They could not easily hasten matters, for their house was not yet ready, and she needed time to get her clothes. The date had been fixed by her. She listened sullenly to his words. Their wisdom was plain, and she did not see how she could possibly insist. Even if she told him all that had passed he would not believe her; he would think she was suffering from some trick of her morbid fancy.

"If anything happens to me," she answered, with the dark, anguished eyes of a hunted beast, "you will be to blame."

"I promise you that nothing will happen."

IX

Margaret's night was disturbed, and next day she was unable to go about her work with her usual tranquillity. She tried to reason herself into a natural explanation of the events that had happened. The telegram that Susie had received pointed to a definite scheme on Haddo's part, and suggested that his sudden illness was but a device to get into the studio. Once there, he had used her natural sympathy as a means whereby to exercise his hypnotic power, and all she had seen was merely the creation of his own libidinous fancy. But though she sought to persuade herself that, in playing a vile trick on her, he had taken a shameful advantage of her pity, she could not look upon him with anger. Her contempt for him, her utter loathing, were alloyed with a feeling that aroused in her horror and dismay. She could not get the man out of her thoughts. All that he had said, all that she had seen, seemed, as though it possessed a power of material growth, unaccountably to absorb her. It was as if a rank weed were planted in her heart and slid long poisonous tentacles down every artery, so that each part of her body was enmeshed. Work could not distract her, conversation, exercise, art, left her listless; and between her and all the actions of life stood the flamboyant, bulky form of Oliver Haddo. She was terrified of him now as never before, but curiously had no longer the physical repulsion which hitherto had mastered all other feelings. Although she repeated to herself that she wanted never to see him again, Margaret could scarcely resist an overwhelming desire to go to him. Her will had been taken from her, and she was an automaton. She struggled, like a bird in the fowler's net with useless beating of the wings; but at the bottom of her heart she was dimly conscious that she did not want to resist. If he had given her that address, it was because he knew she would use it. She did not know why she wanted to go to him; she had nothing to say to him; she knew only that it was necessary to go. But a few days before she had seen the *Phèdre* of Racine, and she felt on a sudden all the torments that wrung the heart of that unhappy queen; she, too, struggled aimlessly to escape from the poison that the immortal gods poured in her veins. She asked herself frantically whether a spell had been cast over her, for now she was willing to believe that Haddo's power was all-embracing. Margaret knew that if she yielded to the horrible temptation nothing could save her from destruction. She would have cried for help to Arthur or to Susie, but something, she knew not what, prevented her. At length, dirven almost to distraction, she thought that Dr. Porhoët might do something for her. He, at least, would understand her misery. There seemed not a moment to lose, and she hastened to his house. They told her he was out. Her heart sank, for it seemed that her last hope was gone. She was like a person drowning, who clings to a rock; and the waves dash against him, and beat upon his bleeding hands with a malice all too human, as if to tear them from their refuge.

Instead of going to the sketch-class, which was held at six in the evening, she hurried to the address that Oliver Haddo had given her. She went along the crowded street stealthily, as though afraid that someone would see her, and her heart was in a turmoil. She desired with all her might not to go, and sought vehemently to prevent herself, and yet withal she went. She ran up the stairs and knocked at the door. She remembered his directions distinctly. In a moment Oliver Haddo stood before her. He did not seem astonished that she was there. As she stood on the landing, it occurred to her suddenly that she had no reason to offer for her visit, but his words saved her from any need for explanation.

"I've been waiting for you," he said.

Haddo led her into a sitting-room. He had an apartment in a *maison neublée*, and heavy hangings, the solid furniture of that sort of house in Paris, was unexpected in connection with him. The surroundings were so commonplace that they seemed to emphasise his singularity. There was a peculiar lack of comfort, which suggested that he was indifferent to material things. The room was large, but so cumbered that it gave a cramped impression. Haddo dwelt there as if he were apart from any habitation that might be his. He moved cautiously among the heavy furniture, and his great obesity was somehow more remarkable. There was the acrid perfume which Margaret remembered a few days before in her vision of an Eastern city.

Asking her to sit down, he began to talk as if they were old acquaintances between whom nothing of moment had occurred. At last she took her courage in both hands.

"Why did you make me come here?" she asked suddenly.

"You give me credit now for very marvellous powers," he smiled.

"You knew I should come."

"I knew."

"What have I done to you that you should make me so unhappy? I want you to leave me alone."

"I shall not prevent you from going out if you choose to go. No harm has come to you. The door is open."

Her heart beat quickly, painfully almost, and she remained silent. She knew that she did not want to go. There was something that drew her strangely to him, and she was ceasing to resist. A strange feeling began to take hold of her, creeping stealthily through her limbs; and she was terrified, but unaccountably elated.

He began to talk with that low voice of his that thrilled her with a curious magic. He spoke not of pictures now, nor of books, but of life. He told her of strange Eastern places where no infidel had been, and her sensitive fancy was aflame with the honeyed fervour of his phrase. He spoke of the dawn upon sleeping desolate cities, and the moonlit nights of the desert, of the sunsets with their splendour, and of the crowded streets at noon. The beauty of the East rose before her. He told her of many-coloured webs and of silken carpets, the glittering steel of armour damascened, and of barbaric, priceless gems. The splendour of the East blinded her eyes. He spoke of frankincense and myrrh and aloes, of heavy perfumes of the scent-merchants, and drowsy odours of the Syrian gardens. The fragrance of the East filled her nostrils. And all these things were transformed by the power of his words till life itself seemed offered to her, a life of infinite vivacity, a life of freedom, a life of supernatural knowledge. It seemed to her that a comparison was drawn for her attention between the narrow round which awaited her as Arthur's wife and this fair, full existence. She shuddered to think of the dull house in Harley Street and the insignificance of its humdrum duties. But it was possible for her also to enjoy the wonder of the world. Her soul yearned for a beauty that the commonalty of men did not know. And what devil suggested, a warp as it were in the woof of Oliver's speech, that her exquisite loveliness gave her the right to devote herself to the great art of living? She felt a sudden desire for perilous adventures. As though fire passed through her, she sprang to her feet and stood with panting bosom, her flashing eyes bright with the multi-coloured pictures that his magic presented.

Oliver Haddo stood too, and they faced one another. Then, on a sudden, she knew what the passion was that consumed her. With a quick movement, his eyes more than ever strangely staring, he took her in his arms, and he kissed her lips. She surrendered herself to him voluptuously. Her whole body burned with the ecstasy of his embrace.

"I think I love you," she said, hoarsely.

She looked at him. She did not feel ashamed.

"Now you must go," he said.

He opened the door, and, without another word, she went. She walked through the streets as if nothing at all had happened. She felt neither remorse nor revulsion.

Then Margaret felt every day that uncontrollable desire to go to him; and, though she tried to persuade herself not to yield, she knew that her effort was only a pretence: she did not want anything to prevent her. When it seemed that some accident would do so, she could scarcely control her irritation. There was always that violent hunger of the soul which called her to him, and the only happy hours she had were those spent in his company. Day after day she felt that complete ecstasy when he took her in his huge arms, and kissed her with his heavy, sensual lips. But the ecstasy was extraordinarily mingled with loathing, and her physical attraction was allied with physical abhorrence.

Yet when he looked at her with those pale blue eyes, and threw into his voice those troubling accents, she forgot everything. He spoke of unhallowed things. Sometimes, as it were, he lifted a corner of the veil, and she caught a glimpse of terrible secrets. She understood how men had bartered their souls for infinite knowledge. She seemed to stand upon a pinnacle of the temple, and spiritual kingdoms of darkness, principalities of the unknown, were spread before her eyes to lure her to destruction. But of Haddo himself she learned nothing. She did not know if he loved her. She did not know if he had ever loved. He appeared to stand apart from human kind. Margaret discovered by chance that his mother lived, but he would not speak of her.

"Some day you shall see her," he said.

"When?"

"Very soon."

Meanwhile her life proceeded with all outward regularity. She found it easy to deceive her friends, because it occurred to neither that her frequent absence was not due to the plausible reasons she gave. The lies which at first seemed intolerable now tripped glibly off her tongue. But though they were so natural, she was seized often with a panic of fear lest they should be discovered; and sometimes, suffering agonies of remorse, she would lie in bed at night and think with utter shame of the way she was using Arthur. But things had gone too far now, and she must let them take their course. She scarcely knew why her feelings towards him had so completely changed. Oliver Haddo had scarcely mentioned his name and yet had poisoned her mind. The comparison between the two was to Arthur's disadvantage. She thought him a little dull now, and his commonplace way of looking at life contrasted with Haddo's fascinating boldness. She reproached Arthur in her heart because he had never understood what was in her. He narrowed her mind. And gradually she began to hate him because her debt of gratitude was so great. It seemed unfair that he should have done so much for her. He forced her to marry him by his beneficence. Yet Margaret continued to discuss with him the arrangement of their house, in Harley Street. It had been her wish to furnish the drawing-room in the style of Louis XV; and together they made long excursions to buy chairs or old pieces of silk with which to cover them. Everything should be perfect in its kind. The date of their marriage was fixed, and all the details were settled. Arthur was ridiculously happy. Margaret made no sign. She did not think of the future, and she spoke of it only to ward off suspicion. She was inwardly convinced now that the marriage would never take place, but what was to prevent it she did not know. She watched Susie and Arthur cunningly. But though she watched in order to conceal her own secret, it was another's that she discovered. Suddenly Margaret became aware that Susie was deeply in love with Arthur Burdon. The discovery was so astounding that at first it seemed absurd.

"You've never done that caricature of Arthur for me that you promised," she said, suddenly.

"I've tried, but he doesn't lend himself to it," laughed Susie.

"With that long nose and the gaunt figure I should have thought you could make something screamingly funny."

"How oddly you talk of him! Somehow I can only see his beautiful, kind eyes and his tender mouth. I would as soon do a caricature of him as write a parody on a poem I loved."

Margaret took the portfolio in which Susie kept her sketches. She caught the look of alarm that crossed her friend's face, but Susie had not the courage to prevent her from looking. She turned the drawings carelessly and presently came to a sheet upon which, in a more or less finished state, were half a dozen heads of Arthur. Pretending not to see it, she went on to the end. When she closed the portfolio Susie gave a sigh of relief.

"I wish you worked harder," said Margaret, as she put the sketches down. "I wonder you don't do a head of Arthur as you can't do a caricature."

"My dear, you mustn't expect everyone to take such an overpowering interest in that young man as you do."

The answer added a last certainty to Margaret's suspicion. She told herself bitterly that Susie was no less a liar than she. Next day, when the other was out, Margaret looked through the portfolio once more, but the sketches of Arthur had disappeared. She was seized on a sudden with anger because Susie dared to love the man who loved her.

The web in which Oliver Haddo enmeshed her was woven with skilful intricacy. He took each part of her character separately and fortified with consummate art his influence over her. There was something satanic in his deliberation, yet in actual time it was almost incredible that he could have changed the old abhorrence with which she regarded him into that hungry passion. Margaret could not now realise her life apart from his. At length he thought the time was ripe for the final step.

"It may interest you to know that I'm leaving Paris on Thursday," he said casually, one afternoon.

She started to her feet and stared at him with bewildered eyes.

"But what is to become of me?"

"You will marry the excellent Mr. Burdon."

"You know I cannot live without you. How can you be so cruel?"

"Then the only alternative is that you should accompany me."

Her blood ran cold, and her heart seemed pressed in an iron vise.

"What do you mean?"

"There is no need to be agitated. I am making you an eminently desirable offer of marriage."

She sank helplessly into her chair. Because she had refused to think of the future, it had never struck her that the time must come when it would be necessary to leave Haddo or to throw in her lot with his definitely. She was seized with revulsion. Margaret realised that, though an odious attraction bound her to the man, she loathed and feared him. The scales fell from her eyes. She remembered on a sudden Arthur's great love and all that he had done for her sake. She hated herself. Like a bird at its last gasp beating frantically against the bars of a cage, Margaret made a desperate effort to regain her freedom. She sprang up.

"Let me go from here. I wish I'd never seen you. I don't know what you've done with me."

"Go by all means if you choose," he answered.

He opened the door, so that she might see he used no compulsion, and stood lazily at the threshold, with a hateful smile on his face. There was something terrible in his excessive bulk. Rolls of fat descended from his chin and concealed his neck. His cheeks were huge, and the lack of beard added to the hideous nakedness of his face. Margaret stopped as she passed him, horribly repelled yet horribly fascinated. She had an immense desire that he should take her again in his arms and press her lips with that red voluptuous mouth. It was as though fiends of hell were taking revenge upon her loveliness by inspiring in her a passion for this monstrous creature. She trembled with the intensity of her desire. His eyes were hard and cruel.

"Go," he said.

She bent her head and fled from before him. To get home she passed through the gardens of the Luxembourg, but her legs failed her, and in exhaustion she sank upon a bench. The day was sultry. She tried to collect herself. Margaret knew well the part in which she sat, for in the enthusiastic days that seemed so long gone by she was accustomed to come there for the sake of a certain tree upon which her eyes now rested. It had all the slim delicacy of a Japanese print. The leaves were slender and fragile, half gold with autumn, half green, but so tenuous that the dark branches made a pattern of subtle beauty against the sky. The hand of a draughtsman could not have fashioned it with a more excellent skill. But now Margaret could take no pleasure in its grace. She felt a heartrending pang to think that thenceforward the consummate things of art would have no meaning for her. She had seen Arthur the evening before, and remembered with an agony of shame the lies to which she had been forced in order to explain why she could not see him till late that day. He had proposed that they should go to Versailles, and was bitterly disappointed when she told him they could not, as usual on Sundays, spend the whole day together. He accepted her excuse that she had to visit a sick friend. It would not have been so intolerable if he had suspected her of deceit, and his reproaches would have hardened her heart. It was his entire confidence which was so difficult to bear.

"Oh, if I could only make a clean breast of it all," she cried.

The bell of Saint Sulpice was ringing for vespers. Margaret walked slowly to the church, and sat down in the seats reserved in the transept for the needy. She hoped that the music she must hear there would rest her soul, and perhaps she might be able to pray. Of late she had not dared. There was a pleasant darkness in the place, and its large simplicity was soothing. In her exhaustion, she watched listlessly the people go to and fro. Behind her was a priest in the confessional. A little peasant girl, in a Breton *coiffe,* perhaps a maid-servant lately come from her native village to the great capital, passed in and knelt down. Margaret could hear her muttered words, and at intervals the deep voice of the priest. In three minutes she tripped neatly away. She looked so fresh in her plain black dress, so healthy and innocent, that Margaret could not restrain a sob of envy. The child had so little to confess, a few puny errors which must excite a smile on the lips of the gentle priest, and her candid spirit was like snow. Margaret would have given anything to kneel down and whisper in those passionless ears all that she suffered, but the priest's faith and hers were not the same. They spoke a different tongue, not of the lips but of the soul, and he would not listen to the words of an heretic.

A long procession of seminarists came in from the college which is under the shadow of that great church, two by two, in black cassocks and short white surplices. Many were tonsured already. Some were quite young. Margaret watched their faces, wondering if they were tormented by such agony as she. But they had a living faith to sustain them, and if some, as was plain, were narrow and obtuse, they had at least a fixed rule which prevented them from swerving into treacherous byways. One or two had a wan ascetic look, such as the saints may have had when the terror of life was known to them only in the imaginings of the cloister. The canons of the church followed in their more gorgeous vestments, and finally the officiating clergy.

The music was beautiful. There was about it a staid, sad dignity; and it seemed to Margaret fit thus to adore God. But it did not move her. She could not understand the words that the priests chanted; their gestures, their movements to and fro, were strange to her. For her that stately service had no meaning. And with a great cry in her heart she said that God had forsaken her. She was alone in an alien land. Evil was all about her, and in those ceremonies she could find no comfort. What could she expect when the God of her fathers left her to her fate? So that she might not weep in front of all those people, Margaret with down-turned face walked to the door. She felt utterly lost. As she walked along the interminable street that led to her own house, she was shaken with sobs.

"God has forsaken me," she repeated. "God has forsaken me."

Next day, her eyes red with weeping, she dragged herself to Haddo's door. When he opened it, she went in without a word. She sat down, and he watched her in silence.

"I am willing to marry you whenever you choose," she said at last.

"I have made all the necessary arrangements."

"You have spoken to me of your mother. Will you take me to her at once."

The shadow of a smile crossed his lips.

"If you wish it."

Haddo told her that they could be married before the Consul early enough on the Thursday morning to catch a train for England. She left everything in his hands.

"I'm desperately unhappy," she said dully.

Oliver laid his hands upon her shoulders and looked into her eyes.

"Go home, and you will forget your tears. I command you to be happy."

Then it seemed that the bitter struggle between the good and the evil in her was done, and the evil had conquered. She felt on a sudden curiously elated. It seemed no longer to matter that she deceived her faithful friends. She gave a bitter laugh, as she thought how easy it was to hoodwink them.

Wednesday happened to be Arthur's birthday, and he asked her to dine with him alone.

"We'll do ourselves proud, and hang the expense," he said.

They had arranged to eat at a fashionable restaurant on the other side of the river, and soon after seven he fetched her. Margaret was dressed with exceeding care. She stood in the middle of the room, waiting for Arthur's arrival, and surveyed herself in the glass. Susie thought she had never been more beautiful.

"I think you've grown more pleasing to look upon than you ever were," she said. "I don't know what it is that has come over you of late, but there's a depth in your eyes that is quite new. It gives you an odd mysteriousness which is very attractive."

Knowing Susie's love for Arthur, she wondered whether her friend was not heartbroken as she compared her own plainness with the radiant beauty that was before her. Arthur came in, and Margaret did not move. He stopped at the door to look at her. Their eyes met. His heart beat quickly, and yet he was seized with awe. His good fortune was too great to bear, when he thought that this priceless treasure was his.

He could have knelt down and worshipped as though a goddess of old Greece stood before him. And to him also her eyes had changed. They had acquired a burning passion which disturbed and yet enchanted him. It seemed that the lovely girl was changed already into a lovely woman. An enigmatic smile came to her lips.

"Are you pleased?" she asked.

Arthur came forward, and Margaret put her hands on his shoulders.

"You have scent on," he said.

He was surprised, for she had never used it before. It was a faint, almost acrid perfume that he did not know. It reminded him vaguely of those odours which he remembered in his childhood in the East. It was remote and strange. It gave Margaret a new and troubling charm. There had ever been something cold in her statuesque beauty, but this touch somehow curiously emphasied her sex. Arthur's lips twitched, and his gaunt face grew pale with passion. His emotion was so great that it was nearly pain. He was puzzled, for her eyes expressed things that he had never seen in them before.

"Why don't you kiss me?" she said.

She did not see Susie, but knew that a quick look of anguish crossed her face. Margaret drew Arthur towards her. His hands began to tremble. He had never ventured to express the passion that consumed him, and when he kissed her it was with a restraint that was almost brotherly. Now their lips met. Forgetting that anyone else was in the room, he flung his arms around Margaret. She had never kissed him in that way before, and the rapture was intolerable. Her lips were like living fire. He could not take his own away. He forgot everything. All his strength, all his self-control, deserted him. It crossed his mind that at this moment he would willingly die. But the delight of it was so great that he could scarcely withhold a cry of agony. At length Susie's voice reminded him of the world.

"You'd far better go out to dinner instead of behaving like a pair of complete idiots."

She tried to make her tone as flippant as the words, but her voice was cut by a pang of agony. With a little laugh, Margaret withdrew from Arthur's embrace and lightly looked at her friend. Susie's brave smile died away as she caught this glance, for there was in it a malicious hatred that startled her. It was so unexpected that she was terrified. What had she done? She was afraid, dreadfully afraid, that Margaret had guessed her secret. Arthur stood as if his senses had left him, quivering still with the extremity of passion.

"Susie says we must go," smiled Margaret.

He could not speak. He could not regain the conventional manner of polite society. Very pale, like a man suddenly awaked from deep sleep, he went out at Margaret's side. They walked along the passage. Though the door was closed behind them and they were out of earshot, Margaret seemed notwithstanding to hear Susie's passionate sobbing. It gave her a horrible delight.

The tavern to which they went was on the Boulevard des Italiens, and at this date the most frequented in Paris. It was crowded, but Arthur had reserved a table in the middle of the room. Her radiant loveliness made people stare at Margaret as she passed, and her consciousness of the admiration she excited increased her beauty. She was satisfied that amid that throng of the best-dressed women in the world she had cause to envy no one. The gaiety was charming. Shaded lights gave an opulent cosiness to the scene, and there were flowers everywhere. Innumerable mirrors reflected women of the world, admirably gowned, actresses of renown, and fashionable courtesans. The noise was very great. A Hungarian band played in a distant corner, but the music was drowned by the loud talking of excited men and the boisterous laughter of women. It was plain that people had come to spend their money with a lavish hand. The vivacious crowd was given over with all its heart to the pleasure of the fleeting moment. Everyone had put aside grave thoughts and sorrow.

Margaret had never been in better spirits. The champagne went quickly to her head, and she talked all manner of charming nonsense. Arthur was enchanted. He was very proud, very pleased, and very happy. They talked of all the things they would do when they were married. They talked of the places they must go to, of their home and of the beautiful things with which they would fill it. Margaret's animation was extraordinary. Arthur was amused at her delight with the brightness of the place, with the good things they ate, and with the wine. Her laughter was like a rippling brook. Everything tended to take him out of his usual reserve. Life was very pleasing, at that moment, and he felt singularly joyful.

"Let us drink to the happiness of our life," he said.

They touched glasses. He could not take his eyes away from her.

"You're simply wonderful to-night," he said. "I'm almost afraid of my good fortune."

"What is there to be afraid of?" she cried.

"I should like to lose something I valued in order to propitiate the fates. I am too happy now. Everything goes too well with me."

She gave a soft, low laugh and stretched out her hand on the table. No sculptor could have modelled its exquisite delicacy. She wore only one ring, a large emerald which Arthur had given her on their engagement. He could not resist taking her hand.

"Would you like to go on anywhere?" he said, when they had finished dinner and were drinking their coffee.

"No, let us stay here. I must go to bed early, as I have a tiring day before me to-morrow."

"What are you going to do?" he asked.

"Nothing of any importance," she laughed.

Presently the diners began to go in little groups, and Margaret suggested that they should saunter towards the Madeleine. The night was fine, but rather cold, and the broad avenue was crowded. Margaret watched the people. It was no less amusing than a play. In a little while, they took a cab and drove through the streets, silent already, that led to the quarter of the Montparnasse. They sat in silence, and Margaret nestled close to Arthur. He put his arm around her waist. In the shut cab that faint, oriental odour rose again to his nostrils, and his head reeled as it had before dinner.

"You've made me very happy, Margaret," he whispered. "I feel that, however long I live, I shall never have a happier day than this."

"Do you love me very much?" she asked, lightly.

He did not answer, but took her face in his hands and kissed her passionately. They arrived at Margaret's house, and she tripped up to the door. She held out her hand to him, smiling.

"Goodnight."

"It's dreadful to think that I must spend a dozen hours without seeing you. When may I come?"

"Not in the morning, because I shall be too busy. Come at twelve."

She remembered that her train started exactly at that hour. The door was opened, and with a little wave of the hand she disappeared.

X

Susie stared without comprehension at the note that announced Margaret's marriage. It was a *petit bleu* sent off from the Gare du Nord, and ran as follows:

"When you receive this I shall be on my way to London. I was married to Oliver Haddo this morning. I love him as I never loved Arthur. I have acted in this manner because I thought I had gone too far with Arthur to make an explanation possible. Please tell him.

"MARGARET"

Susie was filled with dismay. She did not know what to do nor what to think. There was a knock at the door, and she knew it must be Arthur, for he was expected at midday. She decided quickly that it was impossible to break the news to him then and there. It was needful first to find out all manner of things, and besides, it was incredible. Making up her mind, she opened the door.

"Oh, I'm so sorry Margaret isn't here," she said. "A friend of hers is ill and sent for her suddenly."

"What a bore!" answered Arthur. "Mrs. Bloomfield as usual, I suppose?"

"Oh, you know she's been ill?"

"Margaret has spent nearly every afternoon with her for some days."

Susie did not answer. This was the first she had heard of

Mrs. Bloomfield's illness, and it was news that Margaret was in the habit of visiting her. But her chief object at this moment was to get rid of Arthur.

"Won't you come back at five o'clock?" she said.

"But, look here, why shouldn't we lunch together, you and I?"

"I'm very sorry, but I'm expecting somebody in."

"Oh, all right. Then I'll come back at five."

He nodded and went out. Susie read the brief note once more, and asked herself if it could possibly be true. The callousness of it was appalling. She went to Margaret's room and saw that everything was in its place. It did not look as if the owner had gone on a journey. But then she noticed that a number of letters had been destroyed. She opened a drawer and found that Margaret's trinkets were gone. An idea struck her. Margaret had bought lately a number of clothes, and these she had insisted should be sent to her dressmaker, saying that it was needless to cumber their little apartment with them. They could stay there till she returned to England a few weeks later for her marriage, and it would be simpler to despatch them all from one place. Susie went out. At the door it occurred to her to ask the *concierge* if she knew where Margaret had gone that morning.

"*Parfaitement, Mademoiselle,*" answered the old woman. "I heard her tell the coachman to go to the British Consulate."

The last doubt was leaving Susie. She went to the dressmaker and there discovered that by Margaret's order the boxes containing her things had gone on the previous day to the luggage office of the Gare du Nord.

"I hope you didn't let them go till your bill was paid," said Susie lightly, as though in jest.

The dressmaker laughed.

"Mademoiselle paid for everything two or three days ago."

With indignation, Susie realised that Margaret had not only taken away the trousseau bought for her marriage with Arthur; but, since she was herself penniless, had paid for it with the money which he had generously given her. Susie drove then to Mrs. Bloomfield, who at once reproached her for not coming to see her.

"I'm sorry, but I've been exceedingly busy, and I knew that Margaret was looking after you."

"I've not seen Margaret for three weeks," said the invalid.

"Haven't you? I thought she dropped in quite often."

Susie spoke as though the matter were of no importance. She asked herself now where Margaret could have spent those afternoons. By a great effort she forced herself to speak of casual things with the garrulous old lady long enough to make her visit seem natural. On leaving her, she went to the Consulate, and her last doubt was dissipated. Then nothing remained but to go home and wait for Arthur. Her first impulse had been to see Dr. Porhoët and ask for his advice; but, even if he offered to come back with her to the studio, his presence would be useless. She must see Arthur by himself. Her heart was wrung as she thought of the man's agony when he knew the truth. She had confessed to herself long before that she loved him passionately, and it seemed intolerable that she of all persons must bear him this great blow.

She sat in the studio, counting the minutes, and thought with a bitter smile that his eagerness to see Margaret would make him punctual. She had eaten nothing since the *petit déjeuner* of the morning, and she was faint with hunger. But she had not the heart to make herself tea. At last he came. He entered joyfully and looked around.

"Is Margaret not here yet?" he asked, with surprise.

"Won't you sit down?"

He did not notice that her voice was strange, nor that she kept her eyes averted.

"How lazy you are," he cried. "You haven't got the tea."

"Mr. Burdon, I have something to say to you. It will cause you very great pain."

He observed now the hoarseness of her tone. He sprang to his feet, and a thousand fancies flashed across his brain. Something horrible had happened to Margaret. She was ill. His terror was so great that he could not speak. He put out his hands as does a blind man. Susie had to make an effort to go on. But she could not. Her voice was choked, and she began to cry. Arthur trembled as though he were seized with ague. She gave him the letter.

"What does it mean?"

He looked at her vacantly. Then she told him all that she had done that day and the places to which she had been.

"When you thought she was spending every afternoon with Mrs. Bloomfield, she was with that man. She made all the arrangements with the utmost care. It was quite premeditated."

Arthur sat down and leaned his head on his hand. He turned his back to her, so that she should not see his face. They remained in perfect silence. And it was so terrible that Susie began to cry quietly. She knew that the man she loved was suffering an agony greater than the agony of death, and she could not help him. Rage flared up in her heart, and hatred for Margaret.

"Oh, it's infamous!" she cried suddenly. "She's lied to you, she's been odiously deceitful. She must be vile and heartless. She must be rotten to the very soul."

He turned around sharply, and his voice was hard.

"I forbid you to say anything against her."

Susie gave a little gasp. He had never spoken to her before in anger. She flashed out bitterly.

"Can you love her still, when she's shown herself capable of such vile treachery? For nearly a month this man must have been making love to her, and she's listened to all we said of him. She's pretended to hate the sight of him, I've seen her cut him in the street. She's gone on with all the preparations for your marriage. She must have lived in a world of lies, and you never suspected anything because you had an unalterable belief in her love and truthfulness. She owes everything to you. For four years she's lived on your charity. She was only able to be here because you gave her money to carry out a foolish whim, and the very clothes on her back were paid for by you."

"I can't help it if she didn't love me," he cried desperately.

"You know just as well as I do that she pretended to love you. Oh, she's behaved shamefully. There can be no excuse for her."

He looked at Susie with haggard, miserable eyes.

"How can you be so cruel? For God's sake don't make it harder."

There was an indescribable agony in his voice. And as if his own words of pain overcame the last barrier of his self-control, he broke down. He hid his face in his hands and sobbed. Susie was horribly conscience-stricken.

"Oh, I'm so sorry," she said. "I didn't mean to say such hateful things. I didn't mean to be unkind. I ought to have remembered how passionately you love her."

It was very painful to see the effort he made to regain his self-command. Susie suffered as much as he did. Her impulse was to throw herself on her knees, and kiss his hands, and comfort him; but she knew that he was interested in her only because she was Margaret's friend. At last he got up and, taking his pipe from his pocket, filled it silently. She was terrified at the look on his face. The first time she had ever seen him, Susie wondered at the possibility of self-torture which was in that rough-hewn countenance; but she had never dreamed that it could express such unutterable suffering. Its lines were suddenly changed, and it was terrible to look upon.

"I can't believe it's true," he muttered. "I can't believe it."

There was a knock at the door, and Arthur gave a startled cry.

"Perhaps she's come back."

He opened it hurriedly, his face suddenly lit up by expectation; but it was Dr. Porhoët.

"How do you do?" said the Frenchman. "What is happening?"

He looked round and caught the dismay that was on the faces of Arthur and Susie.

"Where is Miss Margaret? I thought you must be giving a party."

There was something in his manner that made Susie ask why.

"I received a telegram from Mr. Haddo this morning."

He took it from his pocket and handed it to Susie. She read it and passed it to Arthur. It said:

"*Come to the studio at five. High jinks.*
"OLIVER HADDO"

"Margaret was married to Mr. Haddo this morning," said Arthur, quietly. "I understand they have gone to England."

Susie quickly told the doctor the few facts they knew. He was as surprised, as distressed, as they.

"But what is the explanation of it all?" he asked.

Arthur shrugged his shoulders wearily.

"She cared for Haddo more than she cared for me, I suppose. It is natural enough that she should go away in this fashion rather than offer explanations. I suppose she wanted to save herself a scene she thought might be rather painful."

"When did you see her last?"

"We spent yesterday evening together."

"And did she not show in any way that she contemplated such a step?"

Arthur shook his head.

"You had no quarrel?"

"We've never quarrelled. She was in the best of spirits. I've never seen her more gay. She talked the whole time of our house in London, and of the places we must visit when we were married."

Another contraction of pain passed over his face as he remembered that she had been more affectionate than she had ever been before. The fire of her kisses still burnt upon his lips. He had spent a night of almost sleepless ecstasy because he had been certain for the first time that the passion which consumed him burnt in her heart too. Words were dragged out of him against his will.

"Oh, I'm sure she loved me."

Meanwhile Susie's eyes were fixed on Haddo's cruel telegram. She seemed to hear his mocking laughter.

"Margaret loathed Oliver Haddo with a hatred that was almost unnatural. It was a physical repulsion like that which people sometimes have for certain animals. What can have happened to change it into so great a love that it has made her capable of such villainous acts?"

"We mustn't be unfair to him," said Arthur. "He put our backs up, and we were probably unjust. He has done some very remarkable things in his day, and he's no fool. It's possible that some people wouldn't mind the eccentricities which irritated us. He's certainly of very good family and he's rich. In many ways it's an excellent match for Margaret."

He was trying with all his might to find excuses for her. It would not make her treachery so intolerable if he could persuade himself that Haddo had qualities which might explain her infatuation. But as his enemy stood before his fancy, monstrously obese, vulgar, and overbearing, a shudder passed through him. The thought of Margaret in that man's arms tortured him as though his flesh were torn with iron hooks.

"Perhaps it's not true. Perhaps she'll return," he cried.

"Would you take her back if she came to you?" asked Susie.

"Do you think anything she can do has the power to make me love her less? There must be reasons of which we know nothing that caused her to do all she has done. I daresay it was inevitable from the beginning."

Dr. Porhoët got up and walked across the room.

"If a woman had done me such an injury that I wanted to take some horrible vengeance, I think I could devise nothing more subtly cruel than to let her be married to Oliver Haddo."

"Ah, poor thing, poor thing!" said Arthur. "If I could only suppose she would be happy! The future terrifies me."

"I wonder if she knew that Haddo had sent that telegram," said Susie.

"What can it matter?"

She turned to Arthur gravely.

"Do you remember that day, in this studio, when he kicked Margaret's dog, and you thrashed him? Well, afterwards, when he thought no one saw him, I happened to catch sight of his face. I never saw in my life such malignant hatred. It was the face of a fiend of wickedness. And when he tried to excuse himself, there was a cruel gleam in his eyes which terrified me. I warned you; I told you that he had made up his mind to revenge himself, but you laughed at me. And then he seemed to go out of our lives and I thought no more about it. I wonder why he sent Dr. Porhoët here today. He must have known that the doctor would hear of his humiliation, and he may have wished that he should be present at his triumph. I think that very moment he made up his mind to be even with you, and he devised this odious scheme."

"How could he know that it was possible to carry out such a horrible thing?" said Arthur.

"I wonder if Miss Boyd is right," murmured the doctor. "After all, if you come to think of it, he must have thought that he couldn't hurt you more. The whole thing is fiendish. He took away from you all your happiness. He must have known that you wanted nothing in the world more than to make Margaret your wife, and he has not only prevented that, but he has married her himself. And he can only have done it by poisoning her mind, by warping her very character. Her soul must be horribly besmirched; he must have entirely changed her personality."

"Ah, I feel that," cried Arthur. "If Margaret has broken her word to me, if she's gone to him so callously, it's because it's not the Margaret I know. Some devil must have taken possession of her body."

"You use a figure of speech. I wonder if it can possibly be a reality."

Arthur and Dr. Porhoët looked at Susie with astonishment.

"I can't believe that Margaret could have done such a thing," she went on. "The more I think of it, the more incredible it seems. I've known Margaret for years, and she was incapable of deceit. She was very kind-hearted. She was honest and truthful. In the first moment of horror, I was only indignant, but I don't want to think too badly of her. There is only one way to excuse her, and that is by supposing she acted under some strange compulsion."

Arthur clenched his hands.

"I'm not sure if that doesn't make it more awful than before. If he's married her, not because he cares, but in order to hurt me, what life will she lead with him? We know how heartless he is, and how vindictive, how horribly cruel."

"Dr. Porhoët knows more about these things than we do," said Susie. "Is it possible that Haddo can have cast some spell upon her that would make her unable to resist his will? Is is possible that he can have got such an influence over her that her whole character was changed?"

"How can I tell?" cried the doctor helplessly. "I have heard that such things may happen. I have read of them, but I have no proof. In these matters all is obscurity. The adepts in magic make strange claims. Arthur is a man of science, and he knows what the limits of hypnotism are."

"We know that Haddo had powers that other men have not," answered Susie. "Perhaps there was enough truth in his extravagant pretensions to enable him to do something that we can hardly imagine."

Arthur passed his hands wearily over his face.

"I'm so broken, so confused, that I cannot think sanely. At this moment everything seems possible. My faith in all the truths that have supported me is tottering."

For a while they remained silent. Arthur's eyes rested on the chair in which Margaret had so often sat. An unfinished canvas still stood upon the easel. It was Dr. Porhoët who spoke at last.

"But even if there were some truth in Miss Boyd's suppositions, I don't see how it can help you. You cannot do anything. You have no remedy, legal or otherwise. Margaret is apparently a free agent, and she has married this man. It is plain that many people will think she has done much better in marrying a country gentleman than in marrying a young surgeon. Her letter is perfectly lucid. There is no trace of compulsion. To all intents and purposes she has married him of her own free-will, and there is nothing to show that she desired to be released from him or from the passion which we may suppose enslaves her."

What he said was obviously true, and no reply was possible.

"The only thing is to grin and bear it," said Arthur, rising.

"Where are you going?" said Susie.

"I think I want to get away from Paris. Here everything will remind me of what I have lost. I must get back to my work."

He had regained command over himself, and except for the hopeless woe of his face, which he could not prevent from being visible, he was as calm as ever. He held out his hand to Susie.

"I can only hope that you'll forget," she said.

"I don't wish to forget," he answered, shaking his head. "It's possible that you will hear from Margaret. She'll want the things that she has left here, and I daresay will write to you. I should like you to tell her that I bear her no ill-will for anything she has done, and I will never venture to reproach her. I don't know if I shall be able to do anything for her, but I wish her to know that in any case and always I will do everything that she wants."

"If she writes to me, I will see that she is told," answered Susie gravely.

"And now good-bye."

"You can't go to London till to-morrow. Shan't I see you in the morning?"

"I think, if you don't mind, I won't come here again. The sight of all this rather disturbs me."

Again a contraction of pain passed across his eyes, and Susie saw that he was using a superhuman effort to preserve the appearance of composure. She hesitated a moment.

"Shall I never see you again?" she said. "I should be sorry to lose sight of you entirely."

"I should be sorry too," he answered. "I have learned how good and kind you are, and I shall never forget that you are Margaret's friend. When you come to London, I hope that you will let me know."

He went out. Dr. Porhoët, his hands behind his back, began to walk up and down the room. At last he turned to Susie.

"There is one thing that puzzles me," he said. "Why did he marry her?"

"You heard what Arthur said," answered Susie bitterly. "Whatever happened, he would have taken her back. The other man knew that he could only bind her to him securely by going through the ceremonies of marriage."

Dr. Porhoët shrugged his shoulders, and presently he left her. When Susie was alone she began to weep broken-heartedly, not for herself, but because Arthur suffered an agony that was hardly endurable.

XI

Arthur went back to London next day.

Susie felt it impossible any longer to stay in the deserted studio, and accepted a friend's invitation to spend the winter in Italy. The good Dr. Porhoët remained in Paris with his books and his occult studies.

Susie travelled slowly through Tuscany and Umbria. Margaret had not written to her, and Susie, on leaving Paris, had sent her friend's belongings to an address from which she knew they would eventually be forwarded. She could not bring herself to write. In answer to a note announcing her change of plans, Arthur wrote briefly that he had much work to do and was delivering a new course of lectures at St. Luke's; he had lately been appointed visiting surgeon to another hospital, and his private practice was increasing. He did not mention Margaret. His letter was abrupt, formal, and constrained. Susie, reading it for the tenth time, could make little of it. She saw that he wrote only from civility, without interest; and there was nothing to indicate his state of mind. Susie and her companion had made up their minds to pass some weeks in Rome; and here, to her astonishment, Susie had news of Haddo and his wife. It appeared that they had spent some time there, and the little English circle was talking still of their eccentricities. They travelled in some state, with a courier and a suite of servants; they had taken a carriage and were in the habit of driving every afternoon on the Pincio. Haddo had excited attention by the ex-

travagance of his costume, and Margaret by her beauty; she
was to be seen in her box at the opera every night, and her
diamonds were the envy of all beholders. Though people had
laughed a good deal at Haddo's pretentiousness, and been
exasperated by his arrogance, they could not fail to be impressed by his obvious wealth. But finally the pair had disappeared suddenly without saying a word to anybody. A good
many bills remained unpaid, but these, Susie learnt, had
been settled later. It was reported that they were now in
Monte Carlo.

"Did they seem happy?" Susie asked the gossiping friend
who gave her this scanty information.

"I think so. After all, Mrs. Haddo has almost everything
that a woman can want, riches, beauty, nice clothes, jewels.
She would be very unreasonable not to be happy."

Susie had meant to pass the later spring on the Riviera,
but when she heard that the Haddos were there, she hesitated. She did not want to run the risk of seeing them, and
yet she had a keen desire to find out exactly how things were
going. Curiosity and distaste struggled in her mind, but
curiosity won; and she persuaded her friend to go to Monte
Carlo instead of to Beaulieu. At first Susie did not see the
Haddos; but rumour was already much occupied with them,
and she had only to keep her ears open. In that strange place,
where all that is extravagant and evil, all that is morbid,
insane, and fantastic, is gathered together, the Haddos were
in fit company. They were notorious for their assiduity at the
tables and for their luck, for the dinners and suppers they
gave at places frequented by the very opulent, and for their
eccentric appearance. It was a complex picture that Susie put
together from the scraps of information she collected. After
two or three days she saw them at the tables, but they were

so absorbed in their game that she felt quite safe from discovery. Margaret was playing, but Haddo stood behind her
and directed her movements. Their faces were extraordinarily
intent. Susie fixed her attention on Margaret, for in what she
had heard of her she had been quite unable to recognise the
girl who had been her friend. And what struck her most now
was that there was in Margaret's expression a singular likeness to Haddo's. Notwithstanding her exquisite beauty, she
had a curiously vicious look, which suggested that somehow
she saw literally with Oliver's eyes. They had won great sums
that evening, and many persons watched them. It appeared
that they played always in this fashion, Margaret putting on
the stakes and Haddo telling her what to do and when to
stop. Susie heard two Frenchmen talking of them. She listened
with all her ears. She flushed as she heard one of them make
an observation about Margaret which was more than coarse.
The other laughed.

"It is incredible," he said.

"I assure you it's true. They have been married six months,
and she is still only his wife in name. The superstitious
through all the ages have believed in the power of virginity,
and the Church has made use of the idea for its own ends.
The man uses her simply as a mascot."

Then men laughed, and their conversation proceeded so
grossly that Susie's cheeks burned. But what she had heard
made her look at Margaret more closely still. She was radiant.
Susie could not deny that something had come to her that
gave a new, enigmatic savour to her beauty. She was dressed
more gorgeously than Susie's fastidious taste would have
permitted; and her diamonds, splendid in themselves, were
too magnificent for the occasion. At last, sweeping up the
money, Haddo touched her on the shoulder, and she rose.

Behind her was standing a painted woman of notorious dis-
reputability. Susie was astonished to see Margaret smile and
nod as she passed her.

Susie learnt that the Haddos had a suite of rooms at the
most expensive of the hotels. They lived in a whirl of gaiety.
They knew few English except those whose reputations were
damaged, but seemed to prefer the society of those foreigners
whose wealth and eccentricities made them the cynosure of
that little world. Afterwards, she often saw them, in company of Russian Grand-Dukes and their mistresses, of South
American women with prodigious diamonds, of noble gam-
blers and great ladies of doubtful fame, of strange men over-
dressed and scented. Rumour was increasingly busy with
them. Margaret moved among all those queer people with a
cold mysteriousness that excited the curiosity of the sated
idlers. The suggestion which Susie had overheard was repeated more circumstantially. But to this was joined presently
the report of orgies that were enacted in the darkened sitting-
room of the hotel, when all that was noble and vicious in
Monte Carlo was present. Oliver's eccentric imagination invented whimsical festivities. He had a passion for disguise,
and he gave a fancy-dress party of which fabulous stories
were told. He sought to revive the mystical ceremonies of
old religions, and it was reported that horrible rites had been
performed in the garden of the villa, under the shining moon,
in imitation of those he had seen in Eastern places. It was
said that Haddo had magical powers of extraordinary character, and the tired imagination of those pleasure-seekers was
tickled by his talk of black art. Some even asserted that the
blasphemous ceremonies of the Black Mass had been celebrated in the house of a Polish Prince. People babbled of
satanism and of necromancy. Haddo was thought to be im-

mersed in occult studies for the performance of a magical operation; and some said that he was occupied with the *Magnum Opus,* the greatest and most fantastic of alchemical experiments. Gradually these stories were narrowed down to the monstrous assertion that he was attempting to create living beings. He had explained at length to somebody that magical recipes existed for the manufacture of *homunculi.*

Haddo was known generally by the name he was pleased to give himself, The Brother of the Shadow; but most people used it in derision, for it contrasted absurdly with his astonishing bulk. They were amused or outraged by his vanity, but they could not help talking about him, and Susie knew well enough by now that nothing pleased him more. His exploits as a lion-hunter were well known, and it was reported that human blood was on his hands. It was soon discovered that he had a queer power over animals, so that in his presence they were seized with unaccountable terror. He succeeded in surrounding himself with an atmosphere of the fabulous, and nothing that was told of him was too extravagant for belief. But unpleasant stories were circulated also, and someone related that he had been turned out of a club in Vienna for cheating at cards. He played many games, but here, as at Oxford, it was found that he was an unscrupulous opponent. And those old rumours followed him that he took strange drugs. He was supposed to have odious vices, and people whispered to one another of scandals that had been with difficulty suppressed. No one quite understood on what terms he was with his wife, and it was vaguely asserted that he was at times brutally cruel to her. Susie's heart sank when she heard this; but on the few occasions upon which she caught sight of Margaret, she seemed in the highest spirits. One story inexpressibly shocked her. After lunching at some restaurant, Haddo gave a bad louis among the money with which he paid the bill, and there was a disgraceful altercation with the waiter. He refused to change the coin till a policeman was brought in. His guests were furious, and several took the first opportunity to cut him dead. One of those present narrated the scene to Susie, and she was told that Margaret laughed unconcernedly with her neighbour while the sordid quarrel was proceeding. The man's blood was as good as his fortune was substantial, but it seemed to please him to behave like an adventurer. The incident was soon common property, and gradually the Haddos found themselves cold-shouldered. The persons with whom they mostly consorted had reputations too delicate to stand the glare of publicity which shone upon all who were connected with him, and the suggestion of police had thrown a shudder down many a spine. What had happened in Rome happened here again: they suddenly disappeared.

Susie had not been in London for some time, and as the spring advanced she remembered that her friends would be glad to see her. It would be charming to spend a few weeks there with an adequate income; for its pleasures had hitherto been closed to her, and she looked forward to her visit as if it were to a foreign city. But though she would not confess it to herself, her desire to see Arthur was the strongest of her motives. Time and absence had deadened a little the intensity of her feelings, and she could afford to acknowledge that she regarded him with very great affection. She knew that he would never care for her, but she was content to be his friend. She could think of him without pain.

Susie stayed in Paris for three weeks to buy some of the

clothes which she asserted were now her only pleasure in life, and then went to London.

She wrote to Arthur, and he invited her at once to lunch with him at a restaurant. She was vexed, for she felt they could have spoken more freely in his own house; but as soon as she saw him, she realised that he had chosen their meeting-place deliberately. The crowd of people that surrounded them, the gaiety, the playing of the band, prevented any intimacy of conversation. They were forced to talk of commonplaces. Susie was positively terrified at the change that had taken place in him. He looked ten years older; he had lost flesh, and his hair was sprinkled with white. His face was extraordinarily drawn, and his eyes were weary from lack of sleep. But what most struck her was the change in his expression. The look of pain which she had seen on his face that last evening in the studio was now become settled, so that it altered the lines of his countenance. It was harrowing to look at him. He was more silent than ever, and when he spoke it was in a strange low voice that seemed to come from a long way off. To be with him made Susie curiously uneasy, for there was a strenuousness in him which deprived his manner of all repose. One of the things that had pleased her in him formerly was the tranquillity which gave one the impression that here was a man who could be relied on in difficulties. At first she could not understand exactly what had happened, but in a moment saw that he was making an unceasing effort at self-control. He was never free from suffering and he was constantly on the alert to prevent anyone from seeing it. The strain gave him a peculiar restlessness.

But he was gentler than he had ever been before. He seemed genuinely glad to see her and asked about her travels with interest. Susie led him to talk of himself, and he spoke willingly enough of his daily round. He was earning a good deal of money, and his professional reputation was making steady progress. He worked hard. Besides his duties at the two hospitals with which he was now connected, his teaching, and his private practice, he had read of late one or two papers before scientific bodies, and was editing a large work on surgery.

"How on earth can you find time to do so much?" asked Susie.

"I can do with less sleep than I used," he answered. "It almost doubles my working-day."

He stopped abruptly and looked down. His remark had given accidentally some hint at the inner life which he was striving to conceal. Susie knew that her suspicion was well-founded. She thought of the long hours he lay awake, trying in vain to drive from his mind the agony that tortured him, and the short intervals of troubled sleep. She knew that he delayed as long as possible the fatal moment of going to bed, and welcomed the first light of day, which gave him an excuse for getting up. And because he knew that he had divulged the truth he was embarrassed. They sat in awkward silence. To Susie, the tragic figure in front of her was singularly impressive amid that lighthearted throng: all about them happy persons were enjoying the good things of life, talking, laughing, and making merry. She wondered what refinement of self-torture had driven him to choose that place to come to. He must hate it.

When they finished luncheon, Susie took her courage in both hands.

"Won't you come back to my rooms for half an hour? We can't talk here."

He made an instinctive motion of withdrawal, as though

he sought to escape. He did not answer immediately, and she insisted.

"You have nothing to do for an hour, and there are many things I want to speak to you about."

"The only way to be strong is never to surrender to one's weakness," he said, almost in a whisper, as though ashamed to talk so intimately.

"Then you won't come?"

"No."

It was not necessary to specify the matter which it was proposed to discuss. Arthur knew perfectly that Susie wished to talk of Margaret, and he was too straight-forward to pretend otherwise. Susie paused for one moment.

"I was never able to give Margaret your message. She did not write to me."

A certain wildness came into his eyes, as if the effort he made was almost too much for him.

"I saw her in Monte Carlo," said Susie. "I thought you might like to hear about her."

"I don't see that it can do any good," he answered.

Susie made a little hopeless gesture. She was beaten.

"Shall we go?" she said.

"You are not angry with me?" he asked. "I know you mean to be kind. I'm very grateful to you."

"I shall never be angry with you," she smiled.

Arthur paid the bill, and they threaded their way among the tables. At the door she held out her hand.

"I think you do wrong in shutting yourself away from all human comradeship," she said, with that good-humoured smile of hers. "You must know that you will only grow absurdly morbid.

"I go out a great deal," he answered patiently, as though

he reasoned with a child. "I make a point of offering myself distractions from my work. I go to the opera two or three times a week."

"I thought you didn't care for music."

"I don't think I did," he answered. "But I find it rests me."

He spoke with a weariness that was appalling. Susie had never beheld so plainly the torment of a soul in pain.

"Wont you let me come to the opera with you one night?" she asked. "Or does it bore you to see me?"

"I should like it above all things," he smiled, quite brightly. "You're like a wonderful tonic. They're giving *Tristan* on Thursday. Shall we go together?"

"I should enjoy it enormously."

She shook hands with him and jumped into a cab.

"Oh, poor thing!" she murmured. "Poor thing! What can I do for him?"

She clenched her hands when she thought of Margaret. It was monstrous that she should have caused such havoc in that good, strong man.

"Oh, I hope she'll suffer for it," she whispered vindictively. "I hope she'll suffer all the agony that he has suffered."

Susie dressed herself for Covent Garden as only she could do. Her gown pleased her exceedingly, not only because it was admirably made, but because it had cost far more than she could afford. To dress well was her only extravagance. It was of taffeta silk, in that exquisite green which the learned in such matters call *Eau de Nil*; and its beauty was enhanced by the old lace which had formed not the least treasured part of her inheritance. In her hair she wore an ornament of Spanish paste, of exquisite workmanship, and round her neck a chain which had once adorned that of a madonna in an Andalusian church. Her individuality made even her

plainness attractive. She smiled at herself in the glass rue-
fully, because Arthur would never notice that she was perfectly dressed.

When she tripped down the stairs and across the pavement
to the cab with which he fetched her, Susie held up her skirt
with a grace she flattered herself was quite Parisian. As they
drove along, she flirted a little with her Spanish fan and
stole a glance at herself in the glass. Her gloves were so long
and so new and so expensive that she was really indifferent
to Arthur's inattention.

Her joyous temperament expanded like a spring flower
when she found herself in the Opera House. She put up her
glasses and examined the women as they came into the boxes
of the Grand Tier. Arthur pointed out a number of persons
whose names were familiar to her, but she felt the effort he
was making to be amiable. The weariness of his mouth that
evening was more noticeable because of the careless throng.
But when the music began he seemed to forget that any eye
was upon him; he relaxed the constant tension in which he
held himself; and Susie, watching him surreptitiously, saw
the emotions chase one another across his face. It was now
very mobile. The passionate sounds ate into his soul, mingling
with his own love and his own sorrow, till he was taken out
of himself; and sometimes he panted strangely. Through the
interval he remained absorbed in his emotion. He sat as
quietly as before and did not speak a word. Susie understood
why Arthur, notwithstanding his old indifference, now
showed such eager appreciation of music; it eased the pain
he suffered by transferring it to an ideal world, and his own
grievous sorrow made the music so real that it gave him an
enjoyment of extraordinary vehemence. When it was all

over and Isolde had given her last wail of sorrow, Arthur was so exhausted that he could hardly stir.

But they went out with the crowd, and while they were waiting in the vestibule for space to move in, a common friend came up to them. This was Arbuthnot, an eye-specialist, whom Susie had met on the Riviera and who, she presently discovered, was a colleague of Arthur's at St. Luke's. He was a prosperous bachelor with grey hair and a red, contented face, well-to-do, for his practice was large, and lavish with his money. He had taken Susie out to luncheon once or twice in Monte Carlo; for he liked women, pretty or plain, and she attracted him by her good-humour. He rushed up to them now and wrung their hands. He spoke in a jovial voice.

"The very people I wanted to see! Why haven't you been to see me, you wicked woman? I'm sure your eyes are in a deplorable condition."

"Do you think I would let a bold, bad man like you stare into them with an ophthalmoscope?" laughed Susie.

"Now look here, I want you both to do me a great favour. I'm giving a supper party at the Savoy, and two of my people have suddenly failed me. The table is ordered for eight, and you must come and take their places."

"I'm afraid I must get home," said Arthur. "I have a deuce of a lot of work to do."

"Nonsense," answered Arbuthnot. "You work much too hard, and a little relaxation will do you good." He turned to Susie: "I know you like curiosities in human nature; I'm having a man and his wife who will positively thrill you, they're so queer, and a lovely actress, and an awfully jolly American girl."

"I should love to come," said Susie, with an appealing look

at Arthur, "if only to show you how much more amusing I am than lovely actresses."

Arthur, forcing himself to smile, accepted the invitation. The specialist patted him cheerily on the back, and they agreed to meet at the Savoy.

"It's awfully good of you to come," said Susie, as they drove along. "Do you know, I've never been there in my life, and I'm palpitating with excitement."

"What a selfish brute I was to refuse!" he answered.

When Susie came out of the dressing-room, she found Arthur waiting for her. She was in the best of spirits.

"Now you must say you like my frock. I've seen six women turn green with envy at the sight of it. They think I must be French, and they're sure I'm not respectable."

"That is evidently a great compliment," he smiled.

At that moment Arbuthnot came up to them in his eager way and seized their arms.

"Come along. We're waiting for you. I'll just introduce you all round, and then we'll go in to supper."

They walked down the steps into the *foyer,* and he led them to a group of people. They found themselves face to face with Oliver Haddo and Margaret.

"Mr. Arthur Burdon—Mrs. Haddo. Mr. Burdon is a colleague of mine at St. Luke's; and he will cut out your appendix in a shorter time than any man alive."

Arbuthnot rattled on. He did not notice that Arthur had grown ghastly pale and that Margaret was blank with consternation. Haddo, his heavy face wreathed with smiles, stepped forward heartily. He seemed thoroughly to enjoy the situation.

"Mr. Burdon is an old friend of ours," he said. "In fact, it was he who introduced me to my wife. And Miss Boyd and I have discussed Art and the Immortality of the Soul with the gravity due to such topics."

He held out his hand, and Susie took it. She had a horror of scenes, and, though this encounter was as unexpected as it was disagreeable, she felt it needful to behave naturally. She shook hands with Margaret.

"How disappointing!" cried their host. "I was hoping to give Miss Boyd something quite new in the way of magicians, and behold! she knows all about him."

"If she did, I'm quite sure she wouldn't speak to me," said Oliver, with a bantering smile.

They went into the supper-room.

"Now, how shall we sit?" said Arbuthnot, glancing round the table.

Oliver looked at Arthur, and his eyes twinkled.

"You must really let my wife and Mr. Burdon be together. They haven't seen one another for so long that I'm sure they have no end of things to talk about." He chuckled to himself. "And pray give me Miss Boyd, so that she can abuse me to her heart's content."

This arrangement thoroughly suited the gay specialist, for he was able to put the beautiful actress on one side of him and the charming American on the other. He rubbed his hands.

"I feel that we're going to have a delightful supper."

Oliver laughed boisterously. He took, as was his habit, the whole conversation upon himself, and Susie was obliged to confess that he was at his best. There was a grotesque drollery about him that was very diverting, and it was almost impossible to resist him. He ate and drank with tremendous appetite. Susie thanked her stars at that moment that she was a woman who knew by long practice how to conceal her feelings, for Arthur, overcome with dismay at the meeting, sat in stony silence. But she talked gaily. She chaffed Oliver as though he were an old friend, and laughed vivaciously. She noticed meanwhile that Haddo, more extravagantly dressed than usual, had managed to get an odd fantasy into his evening clothes: he wore knee-breeches, which in itself was enough to excite attention; but his frilled shirt, his velvet collar, and oddly-cut satin waistcoat gave him the appearance of a comic Frenchman. Now that she was able to examine him more closely, she saw that in the last six months he was grown much balder; and the shiny whiteness of his naked crown contrasted oddly with the redness of his face. He was stouter, too, and the fat hung in heavy folds under his chin; his paunch was preposterous. The vivacity of his movements made his huge corpulence subtly alarming. He was growing indeed strangely terrible in appearance. His eyes had still that fixed, parallel look, but there was in them now at times a ferocious gleam. Margaret was as beautiful as ever, but Susie noticed that his influence was apparent in her dress; for there could be no doubt that it had crossed the line of individuality and had degenerated into the eccentric. Her gown was much too gorgeous. It told against the classical character of her beauty. Susie shuddered a little, for it reminded her of a courtesan's.

Margaret talked and laughed as much as her husband, but Susie could not tell whether this animation was affected or due to an utter callousness. Her voice seemed natural enough, yet it was inconceivable that she should be so lighthearted. Perhaps she was trying to show that she was happy. The supper proceeded, and the lights, the surrounding gaiety, the champagne, made everyone more lively. Their host was in uproarious spirits. He told a story or two at which everyone laughed. Oliver Haddo had an amusing anecdote handy. It was a little risky, but it was so funnily narrated that everyone roared but Arthur, who remained in perfect silence. Margaret had been drinking glass after glass of wine, and no sooner had her husband finished than she capped his story with another. But whereas his was wittily immoral, hers was simply gross. At first the other women could not understand to what she was tending, but when they saw, they looked down awkwardly at their plates. Arbuthnot, Haddo, and the other man who was there laughed very heartily; but Arthur flushed to the roots of his hair. He felt horribly uncomfortable. He was ashamed. He dared not look at Margaret. It was inconceivable that from her exquisite mouth such indecency should issue. Margaret, apparently quite unconscious of the effect she had produced, went on talking and laughing.

Soon the lights were put out, and Arthur's agony was ended. He wanted to rush away, to hide his face, to forget the sight of her and her gaiety, above all to forget that story. It was horrible, horrible.

She shook hands with him quite lightly.

"You must come and see us one day. We've got rooms at the Carlton."

He bowed and did not answer. Susie had gone to the dressing-room to get her cloak. She stood at the door when Margaret came out.

"Can we drop you anywhere?" said Margaret. "You must come and see us when you have nothing better to do."

Susie threw back her head. Arthur was standing just in front of them, looking down at the ground in complete abstraction.

"Do you see him?" she said, in a low voice quivering with indignation. "That is what you have made him."

He looked up at that moment and turned upon them his sunken, tormented yes. They saw his wan, pallied face with its look of hopeless woe.

"Do you know that he's killing himself on your account? He can't sleep at night. He's suffered the tortures of the damned. Oh, I hope you'll suffer as he's suffered!"

"I wonder that you blame me," said Margaret. "You ought to be rather grateful."

"Why?"

"You're not going to deny that you've loved him passionately from the first day you saw him? Do you think I didn't see that you cared for him in Paris? You care for him now more than ever."

Susie felt suddenly sick at heart. She had never dreamt that her secret was discovered. Margaret gave a bitter little laugh and walked past her.

XII

ARTHUR BURDON spent two or three days in a state of utter uncertainty, but at last the idea he had in mind grew so compelling as to overcome all objections. He went to the Carlton and asked for Margaret. He had learnt from the porter that Haddo was gone out and so counted on finding her alone. A simple device enabled him to avoid sending up his name. When he was shown into her private room Margaret was sitting down. She neither read nor worked.

"You told me I might call upon you," said Arthur.

She stood up without answering, and turned deathly pale. "May I sit down?" he asked.

She bowed her head. For a moment they looked at one another in silence. Arthur suddenly forgot all he had prepared to say. His intrusion seemed intolerable.

"Why have you come?" she said hoarsely.

They both felt that it was useless to attempt the conventionality of society. It was impossible to deal with the polite commonplaces that ease an awkward situation.

"I thought that I might be able to help you," he answered gravely.

"I want no help. I'm perfectly happy. I have nothing to say to you."

She spoke hurriedly, with a certain nervousness, and her eyes were fixed anxiously on the door as though she feared that someone would come in.

"I feel that we have much to say to one another," he insisted. "If it is inconvenient for us to talk here, will you not come and see me?"

"He'd know," she cried suddenly, as if the words were dragged out of her. "D'you think anything can be hidden from him?"

Arthur glanced at her. He was horrified by the terror that was in her eyes. In the full light of day a change was plain in her expression. Her face was strangely drawn, and pinched, and there was in it a constant look as of a person cowed. Arthur turned away.

"I want you to know that I do not blame you in the least for anything you did. No action of yours can ever lessen my affection for you."

"Oh, why did you come here? Why do you torture me by saying such things?"

She burst on a sudden into a flood of tears, and walked excitedly up and down the room.

"Oh, if you wanted me to be punished for the pain I've caused you, you can triumph now. Susie said she hoped I'd suffer all the agony that I've made you suffer. If she only knew!"

Margaret gave a hysterical laugh. She flung herself on her knees by Arthur's side and seized his hands.

"Did she think I didn't see? My heart bled when I looked at your poor wan face and your tortured eyes. Oh, you've changed. I could never have believed that a man could change so much in so few months, and it's I who've caused it all. Oh, Arthur, Arthur, you must forgive me. And you must pity me."

"But there's nothing to forgive, darling," he cried.

She looked at him steadily. Her eyes now were shining with a hard brightness.

"You say that, but you don't really think it. And yet, if you only knew, all that I have endured is on your account."

She made a great effort to be calm.

"What do you mean?" said Arthur.

"He never loved me, he would never have thought of me if he hadn't wanted to wound you in what you treasured most. He hated you, and he's made me what I am so that you might suffer. It isn't I who did all this, but a devil within me; it isn't I who lied to you and left you and caused you all this unhappiness."

She rose to her feet and sighed deeply.

"Once, I thought he was dying, and I helped him. I took him into the studio and gave him water. And he gained some dreadful power over me so that I've been like wax in his hands. All my will has disappeared, and I have to do his bidding. And if I try to resist . . ."

Her face twitched with pain and fear.

"I've found out everything since. I know that on that day when he seemed to be at the point of death, he was merely playing a trick on me, and he got Susie out of the way by sending a telegram from a girl whose name he had seen on a photograph. I've heard him roar with laughter at his cleverness."

She stopped suddenly, and a look of frightful agony crossed her face.

"And at this very minute, for all I know, it may be by his influence that I say this to you, so that he may cause you still greater suffering by allowing me to tell you that he never cared for me. You know now that my life is hell, and his vengeance is complete."

"Vengeance for what?"

"Don't you remember that you hit him once, and kicked

him unmercifully? I know him well now. He could have killed you, but he hated you too much. It pleased him a thousand times more to devise this torture for you and me."

Margaret's agitation was terrible to behold. This was the first time that she had ever spoken to a soul of all these things, and now the long restraint had burst as burst the waters of a dam. Arthur sought to calm her.

"You're ill and overwrought. You must try to compose yourself. After all, Haddo is a human being like the rest of us."

"Yes, you always laughed at his claims. You wouldn't listen to the things he said. But I *know*. Oh, I can't explain it; I daresay common sense and probability are all against it, but I've seen things with my own eyes that pass all comprehension. I tell you, he has powers of the most awful kind. That first day when I was alone with him, he seemed to take me to some kind of sabbath. I don't know what it was, but I saw horrors, vile horrors, that rankled for ever after like poison in my mind; and when we went up to his house in Staffordshire, I recognised the scene; I recognised the arid rocks, and the trees, and the lie of the land. I knew I'd been there before on that fatal afternoon. Oh, you must believe me! Sometimes I think I shall go mad with the terror of it all."

Arthur did not speak. Her words caused a ghastly suspicion to flash through his mind, and he could hardly contain himself. He thought that some dreadful shock had turned her brain. She buried her face in her hands.

"Look here," he said, "you must come away at once. You can't continue to live with him. You must never go back to Skene."

"I can't leave him. We're bound together inseparably."

"But it's monstrous. There can be nothing to keep you to

him. Come back to Susie. She'll be very kind to you; she'll help you to forget all you've endured."

"It's no use. You can do nothing for me."

"Why not?"

"Because, notwithstanding, I love him with all my soul."

"Margaret!"

"I hate him. He fills me with repulsion. And yet I do not know what there is in my blood that draws me to him against my will. My flesh cries out for him."

Arthur looked away in embarrassment. He could not help a slight, instinctive movement of withdrawal.

"Do I disgust you?" she said.

He flushed slightly, but scarcely knew how to answer. He made a vague gesture of denial.

"If you only knew," she said.

There was something so extraordinary in her tone that he gave her a quick glance of surprise. He saw that her cheeks were flaming. Her bosom was panting as though she were again on the point of breaking into a passion of tears.

"For God's sake, don't look at me!" she cried.

She turned away and hid her face. The words she uttered were in a shamed, unnatural voice.

"If you'd been at Monte Carlo you'd have heard them say, God knows how they knew it, that it was only through me he had his luck at the tables. He's contented himself with filling my soul with vice. I have no purity in me. I'm sullied through and through. I have made me into a sink of iniquity, and I loathe myself. I cannot look at myself without a shudder of disgust."

A cold sweat came over Arthur, and he grew more pale than ever. He realised now he was in the presence of a mystery that he could not unravel. She went on feverishly.

"The other night, at supper, I told a story, and I saw you wince with shame. It wasn't I that told it. The impulse came from him, and I knew it was vile, and yet I told it with gusto. I enjoyed the telling of it; I enjoyed the pain I gave you, and the dismay of those women. There seem to be two persons in me, and my real self, the old one that you knew and loved, is growing weaker day by day, and soon she will be dead entirely. And there will remain only the wanton soul in the virgin body."

Arthur tried to gather his wits together. He felt it an occasion on which it was essential to hold on to the normal view of things.

"But for God's sake leave him. What you've told me gives you every ground for divorce. It's all monstrous. The man must be so mad that he ought to be put in a lunatic asylum."

"You can do nothing for me," she said.

"But if he doesn't love you, what does he want you for?"

"I don't know, but I'm beginning to suspect."

She looked at Arthur steadily. She was now quite calm.

"I think he wishes to use me for a magical operation. I don't know if he's mad or not. But I think he means to try some horrible experiment, and I am needful for its success. That is my safeguard."

"Your safeguard?"

"He won't kill me because he needs me for that. Perhaps in the process I shall regain my freedom."

Arthur was shocked at the callousness with which she spoke. He went up to her and put his hands on her shoulders.

"Look here, you must pull yourself together, Margaret. This isn't sane. If you don't take care, your mind will give way altogether. You must come with me now. When you're out of his hands, you'll soon regain your calmness of mind.

You need never see him again. If you're afraid, you shall be hidden from him, and lawyers shall arrange everything between you."

"I daren't."

"But I promise you that you can come to no harm. Be reasonable. We're in London now, surrounded by people on every side. How do you think he can touch you while we drive through the crowded streets? I'll take you straight to Susie. In a week you'll laugh at the idle fears you had."

"How do you know that he is not in the room at this moment, listening to all you say?"

The question was so sudden, so unexpected, that Arthur was startled. He looked round quickly.

"You must be mad. You see that the room is empty."

"I tell you that you don't know what powers he has. Have you ever heard those old legends with which nurses used to frighten our childhood, of men who could turn themselves into wolves, and who scoured the country at night?" She looked at him with staring eyes. "Sometimes, when he's come in at Skene in the morning, with blood-shot eyes, exhausted with fatigue and strangely discomposed, I've imagined that he too . . ." She stopped and threw back her head. "You're right, Arthur, I think I shall go mad."

He watched her helplessly. He did not know what to do. Margaret went on, her voice quivering with anguish.

"When we were married, I reminded him that he'd promised to take me to his mother. He would never speak of her, but I felt I must see her. And one day, suddenly, he told me to get ready for a journey, and we went a long way, to a place I did not know, and we drove into the country. We seemed to go miles and miles, and we reached at last a large house, surrounded by a high wall, and the windows were heavily barred. We were shown into a great empty room. It was dismal and cold like the waiting-room at a station. A man came in to us, a tall man, in a frock-coat and gold spectacles. He was introduced to me as Dr. Taylor, and then, suddenly, I understood."

Margaret spoke in hurried gasps, and her eyes were staring wide, as though she saw still the scene which at the time had seemed the crowning horror of her experience.

"I knew it was an asylum, and Oliver hadn't told me a word. He took us up a broad flight of stairs, through a large dormitory—oh, if you only knew what I saw there! I was so horribly frightened, I'd never been in such a place before— to a cell. And the walls and the floor were padded."

Margaret passed her hand across her forehead to chase away the recollection of that awful sight.

"Oh, I see it still. I can never get it out of my mind."

She remembered with a morbid vividness the vast mis-shapen mass which she had seen heaped strangely in one corner. There was a slight movement in it as they entered, and she perceived that it was a human being. It was a woman, dressed in shapeless brown flannel; a woman of great stature and of a revolting, excessive corpulence. She turned upon them a huge, impassive face; and its unwrinkled smoothness gave it an appearance of aborted childishness. The hair was dishevelled, grey, and scanty. But what most terrified Margaret was that she saw in this creature an appalling likeness to Oliver.

"He told me it was his mother, and she'd been there for five-and-twenty years."

Arthur could hardly bear the terror that was in Margaret's eyes. He did not know what to say to her. In a little while she began to speak again, in a low voice and rapidly, as though to herself, and she wrung her hands.

"Oh, you don't know what I've endured! He used to spend long periods away from me, and I remained alone at Skene from morning till night, alone with my abject fear. Sometimes, it seemed that he was seized with a devouring lust for the gutter, and he would go to Liverpool or Manchester and throw himself among the very dregs of the people. He used to pass long days, drinking in filthy pot-houses. While the bout lasted, nothing was too depraved for him. He loved the company of all that was criminal and low. He used to smoke opium in fœtid dens—oh, you have no conception of his passion to degrade himself—and at last he would come back, dirty, with torn clothes, begrimed, sodden still with his long debauch; and his mouth was hot with the kisses of the vile women of the docks. Oh, he's so cruel when the fit takes him that I think he has a fiendish pleasure in the sight of suffering!"

It was more than Arthur could stand. His mind was made up to try a bold course. He saw on the table a whisky bottle and glasses. He poured some neat spirit into a tumbler and gave it to Margaret.

"Drink this," he said.

"What is it?"

"Never mind! Drink it at once."

Obediently she put it to her lips. He stood over her as she emptied the glass. A sudden glow filled her.

"Now come with me."

He took her arm and led her down the stairs. He passed through the hall quickly. There was a cab just drawn up at the door, and he told her to get in. One or two persons stared at seeing a woman come out of that hotel in a tea-gown and without a hat. He directed the driver to the house in which Susie lived and looked round at Margaret. She had fainted immediately she got into the cab.

When they arrived, he carried Margaret upstairs and laid her on a sofa. He told Susie what had happened and what he wanted of her. The dear woman forgot everything except that Margaret was very ill, and promised willingly to do all he wished.

For a week Margaret could not be moved. Arthur hired a little cottage in Hampshire, opposite the Isle of Wight, hoping that amid the most charming, restful scenery in England she would quickly regain her strength; and as soon as it was possible Susie took her down. But she was much altered. Her gaiety had disappeared and with it her determination. Although her illness had been neither long nor serious, she seemed as exhausted, physically and mentally, as if she had been for months at the point of death. She took no interest in her surroundings, and was indifferent to the shady lanes through which they drove and to the gracious trees and the meadows. Her old passion for beauty was gone, and she cared neither for the flowers which filled their little garden nor for the birds that sang continually. But at last it seemed necessary to discuss the future. Margaret acquiesced in all that was suggested to her, and agreed willingly that the needful steps should be taken to procure her release from Oliver Haddo. He made apparently no effort to trace her, and nothing had been heard of him. He did not know where Margaret was, but he might have guessed that Arthur was responsible for her flight, and Arthur was easily to be found. It made Susie vaguely uneasy that there was no sign of his existence. She wished that Arthur were not kept by his work in London.

At last a suit for divorce was instituted.

Two days after this, when Arthur was in his consulting-room, Haddo's card was brought to him. Arthur's jaw set more firmly.

"Show the gentleman in," he ordered.

When Haddo entered, Arthur, standing with his back to the fireplace, motioned him to sit down.

"What can I do for you?" he asked coldly.

"I have not come to avail myself of your surgical skill, my dear Burdon," smiled Haddo, as he fell ponderously into an armchair.

"So I imagined."

"Your perspicacity amazes me. I surmise that it is to you I owe this amusing citation which was served on me yesterday."

"I allowed you to come in so that I might tell you I will have no communication with you except through my solicitors."

"My dear fellow, why do you treat me with such discourtesy? It is true that you have deprived me of the wife of my bosom, but you might at least so far respect my marital rights as to use me civilly."

"My patience is not as good as it was," answered Arthur, "I venture to remind you that once before I lost my temper with you, and the result you must have found unpleasant."

"I should have thought you regretted that incident by now, O Burdon," answered Haddo, entirely unabashed.

"My time is very short," said Arthur.

"Then I will get to my business without delay. I thought it might interest you to know that I propose to bring a counter-petition against my wife, and I shall make you co-respondent."

"You infamous blackguard!" cried Arthur furiously. "You know as well as I do that your wife is above suspicion."

"I know that she left my hotel in your company, and has been living since under your protection."

Arthur grew livid with rage. He could hardly restrain himself from knocking the man down. He gave a short laugh.

"You can do what you like. I'm really not frightened."

"The innocent are so very incautious. I assure you that I can make a good enough story to ruin your career and force you to resign your appointments at the various hospitals you honour with your attention."

"You forget that the case will not be tried in open court," said Arthur.

Haddo looked at him steadily. He did not answer for a moment.

"You're quite right," he said at last, with a little smile. "I had forgotten that."

"Then I need not detain you longer."

Oliver Haddo got up. He passed his hand reflectively over his huge face. Arthur watched him with scornful eyes. He touched a bell, and the servant at once appeared.

"Show this gentleman out."

Not in the least disconcerted, Haddo strolled calmly to the door.

Arthur gave a sigh of relief, for he concluded that Haddo would not show fight. His solicitor indeed had already assured him that Oliver would not venture to defend the case.

Margaret seemed gradually to take more interest in the proceedings, and she was full of eagerness to be set free. She did not shrink from the unpleasant ordeal of a trial. She could talk of Haddo with composure. Her friends were able to persuade themselves that in a little while she would be her old self again, for she was growing stronger and more cheerful; her charming laughter rang through the little house as it had been used to do in the Paris studio. The case was to come on at the end of July, before the long vacation, and Susie had agreed to take Margaret abroad as soon as it was done.

But presently a change came over her. As the day of the trial drew nearer, Margaret became excited and disturbed; her gaiety deserted her, and she fell into long, moody silences. To some extent this was comprehensible, for she would have to disclose to callous ears the most intimate details of her married life; but at last her nervousness grew so marked that Susie could no longer ascribe it to natural causes. She thought it necessary to write to Arthur about it.

"My dear Arthur:

"I don't know what to make of Margaret, and I wish you would come down and see her. The good-humour which I have noticed in her of late has given way to a curious irritability. She is so restless that she cannot keep still for a moment. Even when she is sitting down her body moves in a manner that is almost convulsive. I am beginning to think that the strain from which she suffered is bringing on some nervous disease, and I am really alarmed. She walks about the house in a peculiarly aimless manner, up and down the stairs, in and out of the garden. She has grown suddenly much more silent, and the look has come back to her eyes which they had when first we brought her down here. When I beg her to tell me what is troubling her, she says: 'I'm afraid that something is going to happen.' She will not or cannot explain what she means. The last few weeks have set my own nerves on edge, so that I do not know how much of what I observe is real, and how much is due to my fancy; but I wish you would come and put a little courage into me. The oddness of it

all is making me uneasy, and I am seized with preposterous terrors. I don't know what there is in Haddo that inspires me with
this unaccountable dread. He is always present to my thoughts.
I seem to see his dreadful eyes and his cold, sensual smile. I wake
up at night, my heart beating furiously, with the consciousness
that something quite awful has happened.

"Oh, I wish the trial were over, and that we were happy in
Germany.

"Yours ever
"SUSAN BOYD"

Susie took a certain pride in her common sense, and it
was humiliating to find that her nerves could be so dis-
traught. She was worried and unhappy. It had not been easy
to take Margaret back to her bosom as if nothing had happened. Susie was human; and, though she did ten times more
than could be expected of her, she could not resist a feeling
of irritation that Arthur sacrificed her so calmly. He had no
room for other thoughts, and it seemed quite natural to him
that she should devote herself entirely to Margaret's welfare.

Susie walked some way along the road to post this letter
and then went to her room. It was a wonderful night, starry
and calm, and the silence was like balm to her troubles. She
sat at the window for a long time, and at last, feeling more
tranquil, went to bed. She slept more soundly than she had
done for many days. When she awoke the sun was streaming
into her room, and she gave a deep sigh of delight. She could
see trees from her bed, and blue sky. All her troubles seemed
easy to bear when the world was so beautiful, and she was
ready to laugh at the fears that had so affected her.

She got up, put on a dressing-gown, and went to Margaret's room. It was empty. The bed had not been slept in.
On the pillow was a note.

"It's no good; I can't help myself. I've gone back to him. Don't trouble about me any more. It's quite hopeless and useless.

"M."

Susie gave a little gasp. Her first thought was for Arthur, and she uttered a wail of sorrow because he must be cast again into the agony of desolation. Once more she had to break the dreadful news. She dressed hurriedly and ate some breakfast. There was no train till nearly eleven, and she had to bear her impatience as best she could. At last it was time to start, and she put on her gloves. At that moment the door was opened, and Arthur came in.

She gave a cry of terror and turned pale.

"I was just coming to London to see you," she faltered. "How did you find out?"

"Haddo sent me a box of chocolates early this morning with a card on which was written: *I think the odd trick is mine.*"

The cruel vindictiveness, joined with a schoolboy love of taunting the vanquished foe, was very characteristic. Susie gave Arthur Burdon the note which she had found in Margaret's room. He read it and then thought for a long time.

"I'm afraid she's right," he said at length. "It seems quite hopeless. The man has some power over her which we can't counteract."

Susie wondered whether his strong scepticism was failing at last. She could not withstand her own feeling that there was something preternatural about the hold that Oliver had over Margaret. She had no shadow of a doubt that he was able to affect his wife even at a distance, and was convinced now that the restlessness of the last few days was due to this mysterious power. He had been at work in some strange way, and Margaret had been aware of it. At length she could not resist and had gone to him instinctively: her will was as little concerned as when a chip of steel flies to a magnet.

"I cannot find it in my heart now to blame her for anything she has done," said Susie. "I think she is the victim of a most lamentable fate. I can't help it. I must believe that he was able to cast a spell on her; and to that is due all that has happened. I have only pity for her great misfortunes."

"Has it occurred to you what will happen when she is back in Haddo's hands?" cried Arthur. "You know as well as I do how revengeful he is and how hatefully cruel. My heart bleeds when I think of the tortures, sheer physical tortures, which she may suffer."

He walked up and down in desperation.

"And yet there's nothing whatever that one can do. One can't go to the police and say that a man has cast a magic spell on his wife."

"Then you believe it too?" said Susie.

"I don't know what I believe now," he cried. "After all, we can't do anything if she chooses to go back to her husband. She's apparently her own mistress." He wrung his hands. "And I'm imprisoned in London! I can't leave it for a day. I ought not to be here now, and I must get back in a couple of hours. I can do nothing, and yet I'm convinced that Margaret is utterly wretched."

Susie paused for a minute or two. She wondered how he would accept the suggestion that was in her mind.

"Do you know, it seems to me that common methods are useless. The only chance is to fight him with his own weapons. Would you mind if I went over to Paris to consult Dr. Porhoët? You know that he is learned in every branch of the occult, and perhaps he might help us."

But Arthur pulled himself together.

"It's absurd. We mustn't give way to superstition. Haddo is merely a scoundrel and a charlatan. He's worked on our nerves as he's worked on poor Margaret's. It's impossible to suppose that he has any powers greater than the common run of mankind."

"Even after all you've seen with your own eyes?"

"If my eyes show me what all my training assures me is impossible, I can only conclude that my eyes deceive me."

"Well, I shall run over to Paris."

XIII

SOME WEEKS later Dr. Porhoët was sitting among his books in the quiet, low room that overlooked the Seine. He had given himself over to a pleasing melancholy. The heat beat down upon the noisy streets of Paris, and the din of the great city penetrated even to his fastness in the Île Saint Louis. He remembered the cloud-laden sky of the country where he was born, and the south-west wind that blew with a salt freshness. The long streets of Brest, present to his fancy always in a drizzle of rain, with the lights of cafés reflected on the wet pavements, had a familiar charm. Even in foul weather the sailor-men who trudged along them gave one a curious sense of comfort. There was delight in the smell of the sea and in the freedom of the great Atlantic. And then he thought of the green lanes and of the waste places with their scented heather, the fair broad roads that led from one old sweet town to another, of the *Pardons* and their gentle, sad crowds. Dr. Porhoët gave a sigh.

"It is good to be born in the land of Brittany," he smiled.

But his *bonne* showed Susie in, and he rose with a smile to greet her. She had been in Paris for some time, and they had seen much of one another. He basked in the gentle sympathy with which she interested herself in all the abstruse, quaint matters on which he spent his time; and, divining her love for Arthur, he admired the courage with which she effaced herself. They had got into the habit of eating many of their meals together in a quiet house opposite the Cluny called La Reine Blanche, and here they had talked of so many things that their acquaintance was grown into a charming friendship.

"I'm ashamed to come here so often," said Susie, as she entered. "Matilde is beginning to look at me with a suspicious eye."

"It is very good for you to entertain a tiresome old man," he smiled, as he held her hand. "But I should have been disappointed if you had forgotten your promise to come this afternoon, for I have much to tell you."

"Tell me at once," she said, sitting down.

"I have discovered an MS. at the library of the Arsenal this morning that no one knew anything about."

He said this with an air of triumph, as though the achievement were of national importance. Susie had a tenderness for his innocent mania; and, though she knew the work in question was occult and incomprehensible, congratulated him heartily.

"It is the original version of a book by Paracelsus. I have not read it yet, for the writing is most difficult to decipher, but one point caught my eye on turning over the pages. That is the gruesome fact that Paracelsus fed the *homunculi* he manufactured on human blood. One wonders how he came by it."

Susie gave a little start, which Dr. Porhoët noticed.

"What is the matter with you?"

"Nothing," she said quickly.

He looked at her for a moment, then proceeded with the subject that strangely fascinated him.

"You must let me take you one day to the library of the Arsenal. There is no richer collection in the world of books dealing with the occult sciences. And of course you know that it was at the Arsenal that the tribunal sat, under the suggestive name of *chambre ardente,* to deal with cases of sorcery and magic?"

"I didn't," smiled Susie.

"I always think that these manuscripts and queer old books, which are the pride of our library, served in many an old trial. There are volumes there of innocent appearance that have hanged wretched men and sent others to the stake. You would not believe how many persons of fortune, rank, and intelligence, during the great reign of Louis XIV, immersed themselves in these satanic undertakings."

Susie did not answer. She could not now deal with these matters in an indifferent spirit. Everything she heard might have some bearing on the circumstances which she had discussed with Dr. Porhoët times out of number. She had never been able to pin him down to an affirmation of faith. Certain strange things had manifestly happened, but what the explanation of them was, no man could say. He offered analogies from his well-stored memory. He gave her books to read till she was saturated with occult science. At one moment, she was inclined to throw them all aside impatiently, and, at another, was ready to believe that everything was possible.

Dr. Porhoët stood up and stretched out a meditative finger. He spoke in that agreeably academic manner which, at the beginning of their acquaintance, had always entertained Susie, because it contrasted so absurdly with his fantastic utterances.

"It was a strange dream that these wizards cherished. They sought to make themselves beloved of those they cared for and to revenge themselves on those they hated; but, above all, they sought to become greater than the common run of men and to wield the power of the gods. They hesitated at nothing to gain their ends. But Nature with difficulty allows her secrets to be wrested from her. In vain they lit their furnaces, and in vain they studied their crabbed books, called up the dead, and conjured ghastly spirits. Their reward was disappointment and wretchedness, poverty, the scorn of men, torture, imprisonment, and shameful death. And yet, perhaps after all, there may be some particle of truth hidden away in these dark places."

"You never go further than the cautious perhaps," said Susie. "You never give me any definite opinion."

"In these matters it is discreet to have no definte opinion," he smiled, with a shrug of the shoulders. "If a wise man studies the science of the occult, his duty is not to laugh at everything, but to seek patiently, slowly, perseveringly, the truth that may be concealed in the night of these illusions."

The words were hardly spoken when Matilde, the ancient *bonne,* opened the door to let a visitor come in. It was Arthur Burdon. Susie gave a cry of surprise, for she had received a brief note from him two days before, and he had said nothing of crossing the Channel.

"I'm glad to find you both here," said Arthur, as he shook hands with them.

"Has anything happened?" cried Susie.

His manner was curiously distressing, and there was a nervousness about his movements that was very unexpected in so restrained a person.

"I've seen Margaret again," he said.

"Well?"

He seemed unable to go on, and yet both knew that he had something important to tell them. He looked at them vacantly, as though all he had to say was suddenly gone out of his mind.

"I've come straight here," he said, in a dull, bewildered

fashion. "I went to your hotel, Susie, in the hope of finding you; but when they told me you were out, I felt certain you would be here."

"You seem worn out, *cher ami*," said Dr. Porhoët, looking at him. "Will you let Matilde make you a cup of coffee?"

"I should like something," he answered, with a look of utter weariness.

"Sit still for a minute or two, and you shall tell us what you want to when you are a little rested."

Dr. Porhoët had not seen Arthur since the afternoon in the previous year when, in answer to Haddo's telegram, he had gone to the studio in the Rue Campagne Première. He watched him anxiously while Arthur drank his coffee. The change in him was extraordinary; there was a cadaverous exhaustion about his face, and his eyes were sunken in their sockets. But what alarmed the good doctor most was that Arthur's personality seemed thoroughly thrown out of gear. All that he had endured during these nine months had robbed him of the strength of purpose, the matter-of-fact sureness, which had distinguished him. He was now unbalanced and neurotic.

Arthur did not speak. With his eyes fixed moodily on the ground, he wondered how much he could bring himself to tell them. It revolted him to disclose his inmost thoughts, yet he was come to the end of his tether and needed the doctor's advice. He found himself obliged to deal with circumstances that might have existed in a world of nightmare, and he was driven at last to take advantage of his friend's peculiar knowledge.

Returning to London after Margaret's flight, Arthur Burdon had thrown himself again into the work which for so long had been his only solace. It had lost its savour; but he would not take this into account, and he slaved away mechanically, by perpetual toil seeking to deaden his anguish. But as the time passed he was seized on a sudden with a curious feeling of foreboding, which he could in no way resist; it grew in strength till it had all the power of an obsession, and he could not reason himself out of it. He was sure that a great danger threatened Margaret. He could not tell what it was, nor why the fear of it was so persistent, but the idea was there always, night and day; it haunted him like a shadow and pursued him like remorse. His anxiety increased continually, and the vagueness of his terror made it more tormenting. He felt quite certain that Margaret was in imminent peril, but he did not know how to help her. Arthur supposed that Haddo had taken her back to Skene; but, even if he went there, he had no chance of seeing her. What made it more difficult still, was that his chief at St. Luke's was away, and he was obliged to be in London in case he should be suddenly called upon to do some operation. But he could think of nothing else. He felt it urgently needful to see Margaret. Night after night he dreamed that she was at the point of death, and heavy fetters prevented him from stretching out a hand to help her. At last he could stand it no more. He told a brother surgeon that private business forced him to leave London, and put the work into his hands. With no plan in his head, merely urged by an obscure impulse, he set out for the village of Venning, which was about three miles from Skene.

It was a tiny place, with one public-house serving as a hotel to the rare travellers who found it needful to stop there, and Arthur felt that some explanation of his presence was necessary. Having seen at the station an advertisement of a large farm to let, he told the inquisitive landlady that he had come to see it. He arrived late at night. Nothing could be done then, so he occupied the time by trying to find out something about the Haddos.

Oliver was the local magnate, and his wealth would have made him an easy topic of conversation even without his eccentricity. The landlady roundly called him insane, and as an instance of his queerness told Arthur, to his great dismay, that Haddo would have no servants to sleep in the house: after dinner everyone was sent away to the various cottages in the park, and he remained alone with his wife. It was an awful thought that Margaret might be in the hands of a raving madman, with not a soul to protect her. But if he learnt no more than this of solid fact, Arthur heard much that was significant. To his amazement the old fear of the wizard had grown up again in that lonely place, and the garrulous woman gravely told him of Haddo's evil influence on the crops and cattle of farmers who had aroused his anger. He had had an altercation with his bailiff, and the man had died within a year. A small freeholder in the neighbourhood had refused to sell the land which would have rounded off the estate of Skene, and a disease had attacked every animal on his farm so that he was ruined. Arthur was impressed because, though she reported these rumours with mock scepticism as the stories of ignorant yokels and old women, the innkeeper had evidently a terrified belief in their truth. No one could deny that Haddo had got possession of the land he wanted; for, when it was put to auction, no one would bid against him, and he bought it for a song.

As soon as he could do so naturally, Arthur asked after Margaret. The woman shrugged her shoulders. No one knew anything about her. She never came out of the park gates, but sometimes you could see her wandering about inside by herself. She saw no one. Haddo had long since quarrelled with the surrounding gentry; and though one old lady, the mother of a neighbouring landowner, had called when Margaret first came, she had not been admitted, and the visit was never returned.

"She'll come to no good, poor lady," said the hostess of the inn. "And they do say she's a perfect picture to look at."

Arthur went to his room. He longed for the day to come. There was no certain means of seeing Margaret. It was useless to go to the park gates, since even the tradesmen were obliged to leave their goods at the lodge; but it appeared that she walked alone, morning and afternoon, and it might be possible to see her then. He decided to climb into the park and wait till he came upon her in some spot where they were not likely to be observed.

Next day the great heat of the last week was gone, and the melancholy sky was dark with lowering clouds. Arthur inquired for the road which led to Skene, and set out to walk the three miles which separated him from it. The country was grey and barren. There was a broad waste of heath, with gigantic boulders strewn as though in prehistoric times Titans had waged there a mighty battle. Here and there were trees, but they seemed hardly to withstand the fierce winds of winter; they were old and bowed before the storm. One of them attracted his attention. It had been struck by lightning and was riven asunder, leafless; but the maimed branches were curiously set on the trunk so that they gave it the appearance of a human being writhing in the torture of infernal agony. The wind whistled strangely. Arthur's heart sank as he walked on. He had never seen a country so desolate.

He came to the park gates at last and stood for some time in front of them. At the end of a long avenue, among the trees, he could see part of a splendid house. He walked along the wooden palisade that surrounded the park. Suddenly he came to a spot where a board had been broken down. He looked up and down the road. No one was in sight. He climbed up the low, steep bank, wrenched down a piece more of the fence, and slipped in.

He found himself in a dense wood. There was no sign of a path, and he advanced cautiously. The bracken was so thick and high that it easily concealed him. Dead owners had plainly spent much care upon the place, for here alone in the neighbourhood were trees in abundance; but of late it had been utterly neglected. It had run so wild that there were no traces now of its early formal arrangement; and it was so hard to make one's way, the vegetation was so thick, that it might almost have been some remnant of primeval forest. But at last he came to a grassy path and walked along it slowly. He stopped on a sudden, for he heard a sound. But it was only a pheasant that flew heavily through the low trees. He wondered what he should do if he came face to face with Oliver. The innkeeper had assured him that the squire seldom came out, but spent his days locked in the great attics at the top of the house. Smoke came from the chimneys of them, even in hottest days of summer, and weird tales were told of the devilries there committed.

Arthur went on, hoping in the end to catch sight of Margaret, but he saw no one. In that grey, chilly day the woods, notwithstanding their greenery, were desolate and sad. A sombre mystery seemed to hang over them. At last he came to a stone bench at a cross-way among the trees, and, since it was the only resting-place he had seen, it struck him that Margaret might come there to sit down. He hid himself in the bracken. He had forgotten his watch and did not know how the time passed; he seemed to be there for hours.

But at length his heart gave a great beat against his ribs, for all at once, so silently that he had not heard her approach, Margaret came into view. She sat on the stone bench. For a moment he dared not move in case the sound frightened her. He could not tell how to make his presence known. But it was necessary to do something to attract her attention, and he could only hope that she would not cry out.

"Margaret," he called softly.

She did not move, and he repeated her name more loudly. But still she made no sign that she had heard. He came forward and stood in front of her.

"Margaret."

She looked at him quietly. He might have been someone she had never set eyes on, and yet from her composure she might have expected him to be standing there.

"Margaret, don't you know me?"

"What do you want?" she answered placidly.

He was so taken aback that he did not know what to say. She kept gazing at him steadfastly. On a sudden her calmness vanished, and she sprang to her feet.

"Is it you really?" she cried, terribly agitated. "I thought it was only a shape that mimicked you."

"Margaret, what do you mean? What has come over you?"

She stretched out her hand and touched him.

"I'm flesh and blood all right," he said, trying to smile.

She shut her eyes for a moment, as though in an effort to collect herself.

"I've had hallucinations lately," she muttered. "I thought it was some trick played upon me."

Suddenly she shook herself.

"But what are you doing here? You must go. How did you come? Oh, why won't you leave me alone?"

"I've been haunted by a feeling that something horrible was going to happen to you. I was obliged to come."

"For God's sake, go. You can do me no good. If he finds out you've been here——"

She stopped, and her eyes were dilated with terror. Arthur seized her hands.

"Margaret, I can't go—I can't leave you like this. For Heaven's sake, tell me what is the matter. I'm so dreadfully frightened."

He was aghast at the difference wrought in her during the two months since he had seen her last. Her colour was gone, and her face had the greyness of the dead. There were strange lines on her forehead, and her eyes had an unnatural glitter. Her youth had suddenly left her. She looked as if she were struck down by mortal illness.

"What is the matter with you?" he asked.

"Nothing." She looked about her anxiously. "Oh, why don't you go? How can you be so cruel?"

"I must do something for you," he insisted.

She shook her head.

"It's too late. Nothing can help me now." She paused; and when she spoke again it was with a voice so ghastly that it might have come from the lips of a corpse. "I've found out at last what he's going to do with me. He wants me for his great experiment, and the time is growing shorter."

"What do you mean by saying he wants you?"

"He wants—my life."

Arthur gave a cry of dismay, but she put up her hand.

"It's no use resisting. It can't do any good—I think I shall be glad when the moment comes. I shall at least cease to suffer."

"But you must be mad."

"I don't know. I know that he is."

"But if your life is in danger, come away for God's sake. After all, you're free. He can't stop you."

"I should have to go back to him, as I did last time," she answered, shaking her head. "I thought I was free then, but gradually I knew that he was calling me. I tried to resist, but I couldn't. I simply had to go to him."

"But it's awful to think that you are alone with a man who's practically raving mad."

"I'm safe for to-day," she said quietly. "It can only be done in the very hot weather. If there's no more this year, I shall live till next summer."

"Oh, Margaret, for God's sake don't talk like that. I love you—I want to have you with me always. Won't you come away with me and let me take care of you? I promise you that no harm shall come to you."

"You don't love me any more; you're only sorry for me now."

"It's not true."

"Oh yes it is. I saw it when we were in the country. Oh, I don't blame you. I'm a different woman from the one you loved. I'm not the Margaret you knew."

"I can never care for anyone but you."

She put her hand on his arm.

"If you ever loved me, I implore you to go. You don't know what you expose me to. And when I'm dead, you must marry Susie. She loves you with all her heart, and she deserves your love."

"Margaret, don't go. Come with me."

"And take care. He will never forgive you for what you did. If he can, he will kill you."

She started violently, as though she heard a sound. Her face was convulsed with sudden fear.

"For God's sake go, go!"

She turned from him quickly, and, before he could prevent her, had vanished. With heavy heart he plunged again into the bracken.

When Arthur had given his friends some account of this meeting, he stopped and looked at Dr. Porhoët. The doctor went thoughtfully to his bookcase.

"What is it you want me to tell you?" he asked.

"I think the man is mad," said Arthur. "I found out at what asylum his mother was, and by good luck was able to see the superintendent on my way through London. He told me that he had grave doubts about Haddo's sanity, but it was impossible at present to take any steps. I came straight here because I wanted your advice. Granting that the man is out of his mind, is it possible that he may be trying some experiment that entails a sacrifice of human life?"

"Nothing is more probable," said Dr. Porhoët gravely.

Susie shuddered. She remembered the rumour that had reached her ears in Monte Carlo.

"They said there that he was attempting to make living creatures by a magical operation." She glanced at the doctor, but spoke to Arthur. "Just before you came in, our friend was talking of that book of Paracelsus in which he speaks of feeding the monsters he had made on human blood."

Arthur gave a horrified cry.

"The most significant thing to my mind is that fact about Margaret which we are certain of," said Dr. Porhoët. "All works that deal with the Black Arts are unanimous upon the supreme efficacy of the virginal condition."

"But what is to be done?" asked Arthur in desperation. "We can't leave her in the hands of a raving madman." He turned on a sudden deathly white. "For all we know she may be dead now."

"Have you ever heard of Gilles de Rais?" said Dr. Porhoët, continuing his reflections. "That is the classic instance of human sacrifice. I know the country in which he lived; and the peasants to this day dare not pass at night in the neighbourhood of the ruined castle which was the scene of his horrible crimes."

"It's awful to know that this dreadful danger hangs over her, and to be able to do nothing."

"We can only wait," said Dr. Porhoët.

"And if we wait too long, we may be faced by a terrible catastrophe."

"Fortunately we live in a civilised age. Haddo has a great care of his neck. I hope we are frightened unduly."

It seemed to Susie that the chief thing was to distract Arthur, and she turned over in her mind some means of directing his attention to other matters.

"I was thinking of going down to Chartres for two days with Mrs. Bloomfield," she said. "Won't you come with me? It is the most lovely cathedral in the world, and I think you will find it restful to wander about it for a little while. You can do no good, here or in London. Perhaps when you are calm, you will be able to think of something practical."

Dr. Porhoët saw what her plan was, and joined his entreaties to hers that Arthur should spend a day or two in a place that had no associations for him. Arthur was too exhausted to argue, and from sheer weariness consented. Next day Susie took him to Chartres. Mrs. Bloomfield was no trouble to them, and Susie induced him to linger for a week

in that pleasant, quiet town. They passed many hours in the
stately cathedral, and they wandered about the surrounding
country. Arthur was obliged to confess that the change had
done him good, and a certain apathy succeeded the agitation
from which he had suffered so long. Finally Susie persuaded
him to spend three or four weeks in Brittany with Dr. Porhoët, who was proposing to revisit the scenes of his childhood. They returned to Paris. When Arthur left her at the
station, promising to meet her again in an hour at the restaurant where they were going to dine with Dr. Porhoët, he
thanked her for all she had done.

"I was in an absurdly hysterical condition," he said, holding her hand. "You've been quite angelic. I knew that nothing could be done, and yet I was tormented with the desire to
do something. Now I've got myself in hand once more. I
think my common sense was deserting me, and I was on the
point of believing in the farrago of nonsense which they call
magic. After all, it's absurd to think that Haddo is going to do
any harm to Margaret. As soon as I get back to London, I'll
see my lawyers, and I daresay something can be done. If he's
really mad, we'll have him put under restraint, and Margaret
will be free. I shall never forget your kindness."

Susie smiled and shrugged her shoulders.

She was convinced that he would forget everything if Margaret came back to him. But she chid herself for the bitterness
of the thought. She loved him, and she was glad to be able
to do anything for him.

She returned to the hotel, changed her frock, and walked
slowly to the Chien Noir. It always exhilarated her to come
back to Paris; and she looked with happy, affectionate eyes
at the plane trees, the yellow trams that rumbled along incessantly, and the lounging people. When she arrived, Dr.

Porhoët was waiting, and his delight at seeing her again was flattering and pleasant. They talked of Arthur. They wondered why he was late.

In a moment he came in. They saw at once that something quite extraordinary had taken place.

"Thank God, I've found you at last!" he cried.

His face was moving strangely. They had never seen him so discomposed.

"I've been round to your hotel, but I just missed you. Oh, why did you insist on my going away?"

"What on earth's the matter?" cried Susie.

"Something awful has happened to Margaret."

Susie started to her feet with a sudden cry of dismay.

"How do you know?" she asked quickly.

He looked at them for a moment and flushed. He kept his eyes upon them, as though actually to force his listeners into believing what he was about to say.

"I feel it," he answered hoarsely.

"What do you mean?"

"It came upon me quite suddenly, I can't explain why or how. I only know that something has happened."

He began again to walk up and down, prey to an agitation that was frightful to behold. Susie and Dr. Porhoët stared at him helplessly. They tried to think of something to say that would calm him.

"Surely if anything had occurred, we should have been informed."

He turned to Susie angrily.

"How do you suppose we could know anything? She was quite helpless. She was imprisoned like a rat in a trap."

"But, my dear friend, you mustn't give way in this fashion," said the doctor. "What would you say of a patient who came to you with such a story?"

Arthur answered the question with a shrug of the shoulders.

"I should say he was absurdly hysterical."

"Well?"

"I can't help it, the feeling's there. If you try all night you'll never be able to argue me out of it. I feel it in every bone of my body. I couldn't be more certain if I saw Margaret lying dead in front of me."

Susie saw that it was indeed useless to reason with him. The only course was to accept his conviction and make the best of it.

"What do you want us to do?" she asked.

"I want you both to come to England with me at once. If we start now we can catch the evening train."

Susie did not answer, but she got up. She touched the doctor on the arm.

"Please come," she whispered.

He nodded and untucked the napkin he had already arranged over his waistcoat.

"I've got a cab at the door," said Arthur.

"And what about clothes for Miss Susie?" said the doctor.

"Oh, we can't wait for that," cried Arthur. "For God's sake, come quickly."

Susie knew that there was plenty of time to fetch a few necessary things before the train started, but Arthur's impatience was too great to be withstood.

"It doesn't matter," she said. "I can get all I want in England."

He hurried them to the door and told the cabman to drive to the station as quickly as ever he could.

"For Heaven's sake, calm down a little," said Susie. "You'll be no good to anyone in that state."

"I feel certain we're too late."

"Nonsense! I'm convinced that you'll find Margaret safe and sound."

He did not answer. He gave a sigh of relief as they drove into the courtyard of the station.

XIV

Susie never forgot the horror of that journey to England. They arrived in London early in the morning and, without stopping, drove to Euston. For three or four days there had been unusual heat, and even at that hour the streets were sultry and airless. The train north was crowded, and it seemed impossible to get a breath of air. Her head ached, but she was obliged to keep a cheerful demeanour in the effort to allay Arthur's increasing anxiety. Dr. Porhoët sat in front of her. After the sleepless night his eyes were heavy and his face deeply lined. He was exhausted. At length, after much tiresome changing, they reached Venning. She had expected a greater coolness in that northern country; but there was a hot blight over the place, and, as they walked to the inn from the little station, they could hardly drag their limbs along.

Arthur had telegraphed from London that they must have rooms ready, and the landlady expected them. She recognised Arthur. He passionately desired to ask her whether anything had happened since he went away, but forced himself to be silent for a while. He greeted her with cheerfulness.

"Well, Mrs. Smithers, what has been going on since I left you?" he cried.

"Of course you wouldn't have heard, sir," she answered gravely.

He began to tremble, but with an almost superhuman effort controlled his voice.

"Has the squire hanged himself?" he asked lightly.

"No, sir—but the poor lady's dead."

He did not answer. He seemed turned to stone. He stared with ghastly eyes.

"Poor thing!" said Susie, forcing herself to speak. "Was it—very sudden?"

The woman turned to Susie, glad to have someone with whom to discuss the event. She took no notice of Arthur's agony.

"Yes, mum; no one expected it. She died quite sudden like. She was only buried this morning."

"What did she die of?" asked Susie, her eyes on Arthur.

She feared that he would faint. She wanted enormously to get him away, but did not know how to manage it.

"They say it was heart disease," answered the landlady. "Poor thing! It's a happy release for her."

"Won't you get us some tea, Mrs. Smithers? We're very tired, and we should like something immediately."

"Yes, miss. I'll get it at once."

The good woman bustled away. Susie quickly locked the door. She seized Arthur's arm.

"Arthur, Arthur."

She expected him to break down. She looked with agony at Dr. Porhoët, who stood helplessly by.

"You couldn't have done anything if you'd been here. You heard what the woman said. If Margaret died of heart disease, your suspicions were quite without ground."

He shook her away, almost violently.

"For God's sake, speak to us," cried Susie.

His silence terrified her more than would have done any outburst of grief. Dr. Porhoët went up to him gently.

"Don't try to be too brave, my friend. You will not suffer so much if you allow yourself a little weakness."

"For Heaven's sake leave me alone!" said Arthur, hoarsely.

They drew back and watched him silently. Susie heard their hostess come along to the sitting-room with tea, and she unlocked the door. The landlady brought in the things. She was on the point of leaving them when Arthur stopped her.

"How do you know that Mrs. Haddo died of heart disease?" he asked suddenly.

His voice was hard and stern. He spoke with a peculiar abruptness that made the poor woman look at him in amazement.

"Dr. Richardson told me so."

"Had he been attending her?"

"Yes, sir. Mr. Haddo had called him in several times to see his lady."

"Where does Dr. Richardson live?"

"Why, sir, he lives at the white house near the station." She could not make out why Arthur asked these questions.

"Did Mr. Haddo go to the funeral?"

"Oh yes, sir. I've never seen anyone so upset."

"That'll do. You can go."

Susie poured out the tea and handed a cup to Arthur. To her surprise, he drank the tea and ate some bread and butter. She could not understand him. The expression of strain, and the restlessness which had been so painful, were both gone from his face, and it was set now to a look of grim determination. At last he spoke to them.

"I'm going to see this doctor. Margaret's heart was as sound as mine."

"What are you going to do?"

"Do?"

He turned on her with a peculiar fierceness.

"I'm going to put a rope round that man's neck, and if the law won't help me, by God, I'll kill him myself."

"*Mais, mon ami, vous êtes fou*," cried Dr. Porhoët, springing up.

Arthur put out his hand angrily, as though to keep him back. The frown on his face grew darker.

"You *must* leave me alone. Good Heavens, the time has gone by for tears and lamentation. After all I've gone through for months, I can't weep because Margaret is dead. My heart is dried up. But I know that she didn't die naturally, and I'll never rest so long as that fellow lives."

He stretched out his hands and with clenched jaws prayed that one day he might hold the man's neck between them, and see his face turn livid and purple as he died.

"I am going to this fool of a doctor, and then I shall go to Skene."

"You must let us come with you," said Susie.

"You need not be frightened," he answered. "I shall not take any steps of my own till I find the law is powerless."

"I want to come with you all the same."

"As you like."

Susie went out and ordered a trap to be got ready. But since Arthur would not wait, she arranged that it should be sent for them to the doctor's door. They went there at once, on foot.

Dr. Richardson was a little man of five-and-fifty, with a fair beard that was now nearly white, and prominent blue eyes. He spoke with a broad Staffordshire accent. There was in him something of the farmer, something of the well-to-do tradesman, and at the first glance his intelligence did not impress one.

Arthur was shewn with his two friends into the consulting-room, and after a short interval the doctor came in. He was dressed in flannels and had an old-fashioned racket in his hand.

"I'm sorry to have kept you waiting, but Mrs. Richardson has got a few lady-friends to tea, and I was just in the middle of a set."

His effusiveness jarred upon Arthur, whose manner by contrast became more than usually abrupt.

"I have just learnt of the death of Mrs. Haddo. I was her guardian and her oldest friend. I came to you in the hope that you would be able to tell me something about it."

Dr. Richardson gave him at once the suspicious glance of a stupid man.

"I don't know why you come to me instead of to her husband. He will be able to tell you all that you wish to know."

"I came to you as a fellow-practitioner," answered Arthur. "I am at St. Luke's Hospital." He pointed to his card, which Dr. Richardson still held. "And my friend is Dr. Porhoët, whose name will be familiar to you with respect to his studies in Malta Fever."

"I think I read an article of yours in the *B.M.J.*," said the country doctor.

His manner assumed a singular hostility. He had no sympathy with London specialists, whose attitude towards the general practitioner he resented. He was pleased to sneer at their pretensions to omniscience, and quite willing to pit himself against them.

"What can I do for you, Mr. Burdon?"

"I should be very much obliged if you would tell me as exactly as possible how Mrs. Haddo died."

"It was a very simple case of endocarditis."

"May I ask how long before death you were called in."

The doctor hesitated. He reddened a little.

"I'm not inclined to be cross-examined," he burst out, suddenly making up his mind to be angry. "As a surgeon I daresay your knowledge of cardiac diseases is neither extensive nor peculiar. But this was a very simple case, and everything was done that was possible. I don't think there's anything I can tell you."

Arthur took no notice of the outburst.

"How many times did you see her?"

"Really, sir, I don't understand your attitude. I can't see that you have any right to question me."

"Did you have a post-mortem?"

"Certainly not. In the first place there was no need, as the cause of death was perfectly clear, and secondly you must know as well as I do that the relatives are very averse to anything of the sort. You gentlemen in Harley Street don't understand the conditions of private practice. We haven't the time to do post-mortems to gratify a needless curiosity."

Arthur was silent for a woment. The little man was evidently convinced that there was nothing odd about Margaret's death, but his foolishness was as great as his obstinacy. It was clear that several motives would induce him to put every obstacle in Arthur's way, and chief of these was the harm it would do him if it were discovered that he had given a certificate of death carelessly. He would naturally do anything to avoid scandal. Still Arthur was obliged to speak.

"I think I'd better tell you frankly that I'm not satisfied, Dr. Richardson. I can't persuade myself that this lady's death was due to natural causes."

"Stuff and nonsense!" cried the other angrily. "I've been in practice for hard upon thirty-five years, and I'm willing to stake my professional reputation on it."

"I have reason to think you are mistaken."

"And to what do you ascribe death, pray?" asked the doctor.

"I don't know yet."

"Upon my soul, I think you must be out of your senses. Really, sir, your behaviour is childish. You tell me that you are a surgeon of some eminence . . ."

"I surely told you nothing of the sort."

"Anyhow, you read papers before learned bodies and have them printed. And you come with as silly a story as a Staffordshire peasant who thinks someone has been trying to poison him because he's got a stomach-ache. You may be a very admirable surgeon, but I venture to think I am more capable than you of judging in a case which I attended and you know nothing about."

"I mean to take the steps necessary to get an order for exhumation, Dr. Richardson, and I cannot help thinking it will be worth your while to assist me in every possible way."

"I shall do nothing of the kind. I think you very impertinent, sir. There is no need for exhumation, and I shall do everything in my power to prevent it. And I tell you as chairman of the board of magistrates, my opinion will have as great value as any specialist's in Harley Street."

He flounced to the door and held it open. Susie and Dr. Porhoët walked out; and Arthur, looking down thoughtfully, followed on their heels. Dr. Richardson slammed the street-door angrily.

Dr. Porhoët slipped his arm in Arthur's.

"You must be reasonable, my friend," he said. "From his own point of view this doctor has all the rights on his side. You have nothing to justify your demands. It is monstrous to expect that for a vague suspicion you will be able to get an order for exhumation."

Arthur did not answer. The trap was waiting for them.

"Why do you want to see Haddo?" insisted the doctor. "You will do no more good than you have with Dr. Richardson."

"I have made up my mind to see him," answered Arthur shortly. "But there is no need that either of you should accompany me."

"If you go, we will come with you," said Susie.

Without a word Arthur jumped into the dog-cart, and Susie took a seat by his side. Dr. Porhoët, with a shrug of the shoulders, mounted behind. Arthur whipped up the pony, and at a smart trot they traversed the three miles across the barren heath that lay between Venning and Skene.

When they reached the park gates, the lodgekeeper, as luck would have it, was standing just inside, and she held one of them open for her little boy to come in. He was playing in the road and showed no inclination to do so. Arthur jumped down.

"I want to see Mr. Haddo," he said.

"Mr. Haddo's not in," she answered roughly.

She tried to close the gate, but Arthur quickly put his foot inside.

"Nonsense! I have to see him on a matter of great importance."

"Mr. Haddo's orders are that no one is to be admitted."

"I can't help that, I'm proposing to come in, all the same."

Susie and Dr. Porhoët came forward. They promised the small boy a shilling to hold their horse.

"Now then, get out of here," cried the woman. "You're not coming in, whatever you say."

She tried to push the gate to, but Arthur's foot prevented her. Paying no heed to her angry expostulations, he forced his way in. He walked quickly up the drive. The lodge-keeper accompanied him, with shrill abuse. The gate was left unguarded, and the others were able to follow without difficulty.

"You can go to the door, but you won't see Mr. Haddo," the woman cried angrily. "You'll get me sacked for letting you come."

Susie saw the house. It was a fine old building in the Elizabethan style, but much in need of repair; and it had the desolate look of a place that has been long uninhabited. The garden that surrounded it had been allowed to run wild, and the avenue up which they walked was green with rank weeds. Here and there a fallen tree, which none had troubled to remove, marked the owner's negligence. Arthur went to the door and rang a bell. They heard it clang through the house as though not a soul lived there. A man came to the door, and as soon as he opened it, Arthur, expecting to be refused admission, pushed in. The fellow was as angry as the virago, his wife, who explained noisily how the three strangers had got into the park.

"You can't see the squire, so you'd better be off. He's up in the attics, and no one's allowed to go to him."

The man tried to push Arthur away.

"Be off with you, or I'll send for the police."

"Don't be a fool," said Arthur. "I mean to find Mr. Haddo."

The housekeeper and his wife broke out with abuse, to which Arthur listened in silence. Susie and Dr. Porhoët stood by anxiously. They did not know what to do. Suddenly a voice at their elbows made them start, and the two servants were immediately silent.

"What can I do for you?"

Oliver Haddo was standing motionless behind them. It

startled Susie that he should have come upon them so suddenly, without a sound. Dr. Porhoët, who had not seen him for some time, was astounded at the change which had taken place in him. The corpulence which had been his before was become now a positive disease. He was enormous. His chin was a mass of heavy folds distended with fat, and his cheeks were puffed up so that his eyes were preternaturally small. He peered at you from between the swollen lids. All his features had sunk into that hideous obesity. His ears were horribly bloated, and the lobes were large and swelled. He had apparently a difficulty in breathing, for his large mouth, with its scarlet, shining lips, was constantly open. He had grown much balder and now there was only a crescent of long hair stretching across the back of his head from ear to ear. There was something terrible about that great shining scalp. His paunch was huge; he was a very tall man and held himself erect, so that it protruded like a vast barrel. His hands were infinitely repulsive; they were red and soft and moist. He was sweating freely, and beads of perspiration stood on his forehead and on his shaven lip.

For a moment they all looked at one another in silence. Then Haddo turned to his servants.

"Go," he said.

As though frightened out of their wits, they made for the door and with a bustling hurry flung themselves out. A torpid smile crossed his face as he watched them go. Then he moved a step nearer his visitors. His manner had still the insolent urbanity which was customary to him.

"And now, my friends, will you tell me how I can be of service to you?"

"I have come about Margaret's death," said Arthur.

Haddo, as was his habit, did not immediately answer. He

looked slowly from Arthur to Dr. Porhoët, and from Dr. Porhoët to Susie. His eyes rested on her hat, and she felt uncomfortably that he was inventing some gibe about it.

"I should have thought this hardly the moment to intrude upon my sorrow," he said at last. "If you have condolences to offer, I venture to suggest that you might conveniently send them by means of the penny post."

Arthur frowned.

"Why did you not let me know that she was ill?" he asked.

"Strange as it may seem to you, my worthy friend, it never occurred to me that my wife's health could be any business of yours."

A faint smile flickered once more on Haddo's lips, but his eyes had still the peculiar hardness which was so uncanny. Arthur looked at him steadily.

"I have every reason to believe that you killed her," he said.

Haddo's face did not for an instant change its expression.

"And have you communicated your suspicions to the police?"

"I propose to."

"And, if I am not indiscreet, may I inquire upon what you base them?"

"I saw Margaret three weeks ago, and she told me that she went in terror of her life."

"Poor Margaret! She had always the romantic temperament. I think it was that which first brought us together."

"You damned scoundrel!" cried Arthur.

"My dear fellow, pray moderate your language. This is surely not an occasion when you should give way to your lamentable taste for abuse. You outrage all Miss Boyd's susceptibilities." He turned to her with an airy wave of his fat hand. "You must forgive me if I do not offer you the hospitality of Skene, but the loss I have so lately sustained does not permit me to indulge in the levity of entertaining."

He gave her an ironical, low bow; then looked once more at Arthur.

"If I can be of no further use to you, perhaps you would leave me to my own reflections. The lodgekeeper will give you the exact address of the village constable."

Arthur did not answer. He stared into vacancy, as if he were turning over things in his mind. Then he turned sharply on his heel and walked towards the gate. Susie and Dr. Porhoët, taken completely aback, did not know what to do; and Haddo's little eyes twinkled as he watched this discomfiture.

"I always thought that your friend had deplorable manners," he murmured.

Susie, feeling very ridiculous, flushed, and Dr. Porhoët awkwardly took off his hat. As they walked away, they felt Haddo's mocking gaze fixed upon them, and they were heartily thankful to reach the gate. They found Arthur waiting for them.

"I beg your pardon," he said, "I forgot that I was not alone."

The three of them drove slowly back to the inn.

"What are you going to do now?" asked Susie.

For a long time Arthur made no reply, and Susie thought he could not have heard her. At last he broke the silence.

"I see that I can do nothing by ordinary methods. I realise that it is useless to make a public outcry. There is only my own conviction that Margaret came to a violent end, and I cannot expect anyone to pay heed to that."

"After all, it's just possible that she really died of heart disease."

Arthur gave Susie a long look. He seemed to consider her words deliberately.

"Perhaps there are means to decide that conclusively," he replied at length, thoughtfully, as though he were talking to himself.

"What are they?"

Arthur did not answer. When they came to the door of the inn, he stopped.

"Will you go in? I wish to take a walk by myself," he said.

Susie looked at him anxiously.

"You're not going to do anything rash?"

"I will do nothing till I have made quite sure that Margaret was foully murdered."

He turned on his heel and walked quickly away. It was late now, and they found a frugal meal waiting for them in the little sitting-room. It seemed no use to delay it till Arthur came back, and silently, sorrowfully, they ate. Afterwards, the doctor smoked cigarettes, while Susie sat at the open window and looked at the stars. She thought of Margaret, of her beauty and her charming frankness, of her fall and of her miserable end; and she began to cry quietly. She knew enough of the facts now to be aware that the wretched girl was not to blame for anything that had happened. A cruel fate had fallen upon her, and she had been as powerless as in the old tales Phædra, the daughter of Minos, or Myrrha of the beautiful hair. The hours passed, and still Arthur did not return. Susie thought now only of him, and she was frightfully anxious.

But at last he came in. The night was far advanced. He put down his hat and sat down. For a long while he looked silently at Dr. Porhoët.

"What is it, my friend?" asked the good doctor at length.

"Do you remember that you told us once of an experiment you made in Alexandria?" he said, after some hesitation.

He spoke in a curious voice.

"You told us that you took a boy, and when he looked in a magic mirror, he saw things which he could not possibly have known."

"I remember very well," said the doctor.

"I was much inclined to laugh at you at the time. I was convinced that the boy was a knave who deceived you."

"Yes?"

"Of late I've thought of that story often. Some hidden recess of my memory has been opened, and I seem to remember strange things. Was I the boy who looked in the ink?"

"Yes," said the doctor quietly.

Arthur did not say anything. A profound silence fell upon them, while Susie and the doctor watched him intently. They wondered what was in his mind.

"There is a side of my character which I did not know till lately," Arthur said at last. "When first it dawned upon me, I fought against it. I said to myself that deep down in all of us, a relic from the long past, is the remains of the superstition that blinded our fathers; and it is needful for the man of science to fight against it with all his might. And yet it was stronger than I. Perhaps my birth, my early years, in those Eastern lands where everyone believes in the supernatural, affected me although I did not know it. I began to remember vague, mysterious things, which I never knew had been part of my knowledge. And at last one day it seemed that a new window was opened on to my soul, and I saw with extraordinary clearness the incident which you had described. I knew suddenly it was part of my own experience. I saw you take me by the hand and pour the ink on my palm and bid me look at it. I felt again the strange glow that thrilled me, and with an indescribable distinctness I saw things in the mirror which were not there before. I saw people whom I had never seen. I saw them perform certain actions. And some force I knew not, obliged me to speak. And at length everything grew dim, and I was as exhausted as if I had not eaten all day."

He went over to the open window and looked out. Neither of the others spoke. The look on Arthur's face, curiously outlined by the light of the lamp, was very stern. He seemed to undergo some mental struggle of extraordinary violence. His breath came quickly. At last he turned and faced them. He spoke hoarsely, quickly.

"I *must* see Margaret again."

"Arthur, you're mad!" cried Susie.

He went up to Dr. Porhoët and, putting his hands on his shoulders, looked fixedly into his eyes.

"You have studied this science. You know all that can be known of it. I want you to show her to me."

The doctor gave an exclamation of alarm.

"My dear fellow, how can I? I have read many books, but I have never practised anything. I have only studied these matters for my amusement."

"Do you believe it can be done?"

"I don't understand what you want."

"I want you to bring her to me so that I may speak with her, so that I may find out the truth."

"Do you think I am God that I can raise men from the dead?"

Arthur's hands pressed him down in the chair from which he sought to rise. His fingers were clenched on the old man's shoulders so that he could hardly bear the pain.

"You told us how once Eliphas Levi raised a spirit. Do you believe that was true?"

"I don't know. I have always kept an open mind. There was much to be said on both sides."

"Well, now you *must* believe. You must do what he did."

"You must be mad, Arthur."

"I want you to come to that spot where I saw her last. If her spirit can be brought back anywhere, it must be in that place where she sat and wept. You know all the ceremonies and all the words that are necessary."

But Susie came forward and laid her hand on his arm. He looked at her with a frown.

"Arthur, you know in your heart that nothing can come of it. You're only increasing your unhappiness. And even if you could bring her from the grave for a moment, why can you not let her troubled soul rest in peace?"

"If she died a natural death we shall have no power over her, but if her death was violent perhaps her spirit is earthbound still. I tell you I must be certain. I want to see her once more, and afterwards I shall know what to do."

"I cannot, I cannot," said the doctor.

"Give me the books and I will do it alone."

"You know that I have nothing here."

"Then you must help me," said Arthur. "After all, why should you mind? We perform a certain operation, and if nothing happens we are no worse off than before. On the other hand, if we succeed. . . . Oh, for God's sake, help me! If you have any care for my happiness do this one thing for me."

He stepped back and looked at the doctor. The Frenchman's eyes were fixed upon the ground.

"It's madness," he muttered.

He was intensely moved by Arthur's appeal. At last he shrugged his shoulders.

"After all, if it is but a foolish mummery it can do no harm."

"You will help me?" cried Arthur.

"If it can give you any peace or any satisfaction, I am willing to do what I can. But I warn you to be prepared for a great disappointment."

XV

ARTHUR wished to set about the invocation then and there, but Dr. Porhoët said it was impossible. They were all exhausted after the long journey, and it was necessary to get certain things together without which nothing could be done. In his heart he thought that a night's rest would bring Arthur to a more reasonable mind. When the light of day shone upon the earth he would be ashamed of the desire which ran counter to all his prepossessions. But Arthur remembered that on the next day it would be exactly a week since Margaret's death, and it seemed to him that then their spells might have a greater efficacy.

When they came down in the morning and greeted one another, it was plain that none of them had slept.

"Are you still of the same purpose as last night?" asked Dr. Porhoët gravely.

"I am."

The doctor hesitated nervously.

"It will be necessary, if you wish to follow out the rules of the old necromancers, to fast through the whole day."

"I am ready to do anything."

"It will be no hardship to me," said Susie, with a little hysterical laugh. "I feel I couldn't eat a thing if I tried."

"I think the whole affair is sheer folly," said Dr. Porhoët.

"You promised me you would try."

The day, the long summer day, passed slowly. There was a hard brilliancy in the sky that reminded the Frenchman of

214

those Egyptian heavens when the earth seemed crushed beneath a bowl of molten fire. Arthur was too restless to remain
indoors and left the others to their own devices. He walked
without aim, as fast as he could go; he felt no weariness. The
burning sun beat down upon him, but he did not know it.
The hours passed with lagging feet. Susie lay on her bed and
tried to read. Her nerves were so taut that, when there was
a sound in the courtyard of a pail falling on the cobbles, she
cried out in terror. The sun rose, and presently her window
was flooded with quivering rays of gold. It was midday. The
day passed, and it was afternoon. The evening came, but it
brought no freshness. Meanwhile Dr. Porhoët sat in the little
parlour, with his head between his hands, trying by a great
mental effort to bring back to his memory all that he had
read. His heart began to beat more quickly. Then the night
fell, and one by one the stars shone out. There was no wind.
The air was heavy. Susie came downstairs and began to talk
with Dr. Porhoët. But they spoke in a low tone, as if they
were afraid that someone would overhear. They were faint
now with want of food. The hours went one by one, and
the striking of a clock filled them each time with a mysterious
apprehension. The lights in the village were put out little by
little, and everybody slept. Susie had lighted the lamp, and
they watched beside it. A cold shiver passed through her.

"I feel as though someone were lying dead in the room,"
she said.

"Why does not Arthur come?"

They spoke inconsequently, and neither heeded what the
other said. The window was wide open, but the air was
difficult to breathe. And now the silence was so unusual that
Susie grew strangely nervous. She tried to think of the noisy
streets in Paris, the constant roar of traffic, and the shuffling

of the crowds toward evening as the work people returned to their homes. She stood up.

"There's no air to-night. Look at the trees. Not a leaf is moving."

"Why does not Arthur come?" repeated the doctor.

"There's no moon to-night. It will be very dark at Skene."

"He's walked all day. He should be here by now."

Susie felt an extraordinary oppression, and she panted for breath. At last they heard a step on the road outside, and Arthur stood at the window.

"Are you ready to come?" he said.

"We've been waiting for you."

They joined him, bringing the few things that Dr. Porhoët had said were necessary, and they walked along the solitary road that led to Skene. On each side the heather stretched into the dark night, and there was a blackness about it that was ominous. There was no sound save that of their own steps. Dimly, under the stars, they saw the desolation with which they were surrounded. The way seemed very long. They were utterly exhausted, and they could hardly drag one foot after the other.

"You must let me rest for a minute," said Susie.

They did not answer, but stopped, and she sat on a boulder by the wayside. They stood motionless in front of her, waiting patiently till she was ready. After a little while she forced herself to get up.

"Now I can go," she said.

Still they did not speak, but walked on. They moved like figures in a dream, with a stealthy directness, as though they acted under the influence of another's will. Suddenly the road stopped, and they found themselves at the gates of Skene.

"Follow me very closely," said Arthur.

He turned on one side, and they followed a paling. Susie could feel that they walked along a narrow path. She could see hardly two steps in front of her. At last he stood still.

"I came here earlier in the night and made the opening easier to get through."

He turned back a broken piece of railing and slipped in. Susie followed, and Dr. Porhoët entered after her.

"I can see nothing," said Susie.

"Give me your hand, and I will lead you."

They walked with difficulty through the tangled bracken, among closely planted trees. They stumbled, and once Dr. Porhoët fell. It seemed that they went a long way. Susie's heart beat fast with anxiety. All her weariness was forgotten.

Then Arthur stopped them, and he pointed in front of him. Through an opening in the trees, they saw the house. All the windows were dark except those just under the roof, and from them came bright lights.

"Those are the attics which he uses as a laboratory. You see, he is working now. There is no one else in the house."

Susie was curiously fascinated by the flaming lights. There was an awful mystery in those unknown labours which absorbed Oliver Haddo night after night till the sun rose. What horrible things were done there, hidden from the eyes of men? By himself in that vast house the madman performed ghastly experiments; and who could tell what dark secrets he trafficked in?

"There is no danger that he will come out," said Arthur. "He remains there till the break of day."

He took her hand again and led her on. Back they went among the trees, and presently they were on a pathway. They walked along with greater safety.

"Are you all right, Porhoët?" asked Arthur.

"Yes."

But the trees grew thicker and the night more sombre. Now the stars were shut out, and they could hardly see in front of them.

"Here we are," said Arthur.

They stopped, and found that there was in front of them a green space formed by four cross-ways. In the middle a stone bench gleamed vaguely against the darkness.

"This is where Margaret sat when last I saw her."

"I can see to do nothing here," said the doctor.

They had brought two flat bowls of brass to serve as censers, and these Arthur gave to Dr. Porhoët. He stood by Susie's side while the doctor busied himself with his preparations. They saw him move to and fro. They saw him bend to the ground. Presently there was a crackling of wood, and from the brazen bowls red flames shot up. They did not know what he burnt, but there were heavy clouds of smoke, and a strong, aromatic odour filled the air. Now and again the doctor was sharply silhouetted against the light. His slight, bowed figure was singularly mysterious. When Susie caught sight of his face, she saw that it was touched with a strong emotion. The work he was at affected him so that his doubts, his fears, had vanished. He looked like some old alchemist busied with unnatural things. Susie's heart began to beat painfully. She was growing desperately frightened and stretched out her hand so that she might touch Arthur. Silently he put his arm through hers. And now the doctor was tracing strange signs upon the ground. The flames died down and only a glow remained, but he seemed to have no difficulty in seeing what he was about. Susie could not discern what figures he drew. Then he put more twigs upon the braziers, and the flames

THE MAGICIAN   219

sprang up once more, cutting the darkness sharply as with
a sword.

"Now come," he said .

But, inexplicably, a sudden terror seized Susie. She felt that
the hairs of her head stood up, and a cold sweat broke out
on her body. Her limbs had grown on an instant inconceiv-
ably heavy, so that she could not move. A panic such as she
had never known came upon her, and, except that her legs
would not carry her, she would have fled blindly. She began
to tremble. She tried to speak, but her tongue clave to her
throat.

"I can't, I'm afraid," she muttered hoarsely.

"You must. Without you we can do nothing," said Arthur.

She could not reason with herself. She had forgotten everything except that she was frightened to death. Her heart was
beating so quickly that she almost fainted. And now Arthur
held her, so firmly that she winced.

"Let me go," she whispered. "I won't help you. I'm afraid."

"You must," he said. "You must.

"No.

"I tell you, you must come."

"Why?"

Her deadly fear expressed itself in a passion of sudden
anger.

"Because you love me, and it's the only way to give me
peace."

She uttered a low wail of pain, and her terror gave way
to shame. She blushed to the roots of her hair because he
too knew her secret. And then she was seized again with
anger because he had the cruelty to taunt her with it. She
had recovered her courage now, and she stepped forward.

Dr. Porhoët told her where to stand. Arthur took his place in front of her.

"You must not move till I give you leave. If you go outside the figure I have drawn, I cannot protect you."

For a moment Dr. Porhoët stood in perfect silence. Then he began to recite strange words in Latin. Susie heard him but vaguely. She did not know the sense, and his voice was so low that she could not have distinguished the words. But his intonation had lost that gentle irony which was habitual to him, and he spoke with a trembling gravity that was extraordinarily impressive. Arthur stood immobile as a rock. The flames died away, and they saw one another only by the glow of the ashes, dimly, like persons in a vision of death. There was silence. Then the necromancer spoke again, and now his voice was louder. He seemed to utter weired invocations, but they were in a tongue that the others knew not. And while he spoke the light from the burning cinders on a sudden went out.

It did not die, but was sharply extinguished, as though by invisible hands. And now the darkness was more sombre than that of the blackest night. The trees that surrounded them were hidden from their eyes, and the whiteness of the stone bench was seen no longer. They stood but a little way one from the other, but each might have stood alone. Susie strained her eyes, but she could see nothing. She looked up quickly; the stars were gone out, and she could see no further over her head than round about. The darkness was terrifying. And from it, Dr. Porhoët's voice had a ghastly effect. It seemed to come, wonderfully changed, from the void of bottomless chaos. Susie clenched her hands so that she might not faint.

All at once she started, for the old man's voice was cut

by a sudden gust of wind. A moment before, the utter silence had been almost intolerable, and now a storm seemed to have fallen upon them. The trees all around them rocked in the wind; they heard the branches creak; and they heard the hissing of the leaves. They were in the midst of a hurricane. And they felt the earth sway as it resisted the straining roots of great trees, which seemed to be dragged up by the force of the furious gale. Whistling and roaring, the wind stormed all about them, and the doctor, raising his voice, tried in vain to command it. But the strangest thing of all was that, where they stood, there was no sign of the raging blast. The air immediately about them was as still as it had been before, and not a hair on Susie's head was moved. And it was terrible to hear the tumult, and yet to be in a calm that was almost unnatural.

On a sudden, Dr. Porhoët raised his voice, and with a sternness they had never heard in it before, cried out in that unknown language. Then he called upon Margaret. He called her name three times. In the uproar Susie could scarcely hear. Terror had seized her again, but in her confusion she remembered his command, and she dared not move.

"Margaret, Margaret, Margaret."

Without a pause between, as quickly as a stone falls to the ground, the din which was all about them ceased. There was no gradual diminution. But at one moment there was a roaring hurricane and at the next a silence so complete that it might have been the silence of death.

And then, seeming to come out of nothingness, extraordinarily, they heard with a curious distinctness the sound of a woman weeping. Susie's heart stood still. They heard the sound of a woman weeping, and they recognised the voice of Margaret. A groan of anguish burst from Arthur's lips, and he was on the point of starting forward. But quickly Dr. Porhoët put out his hand to prevent him. The sound was heartrending, the sobbing of a woman who had lost all hope, the sobbing of a woman terrified. If Susie had been able to stir, she would have put her hands to her ears to shut out the ghastly agony of it.

And in a moment, notwithstanding the heavy darkness of the starless night, Arthur saw her. She was seated on the stone bench as when last he had spoken with her. In her anguish she sought not to hide her face. She looked at the ground, and the tears fell down her cheeks. Her bosom heaved with the pain of her weeping.

Then Arthur knew that all his suspicions were justified.

XVI

ARTHUR would not leave the little village of Venning. Neither Susie nor the doctor could get him to make any decision. None of them spoke of the night which they had spent in the woods of Skene; but it coloured all their thoughts, and they were not free for a single moment from the ghastly memory of it. They seemed still to hear the sound of that passionate weeping. Arthur was moody. When he was with them, he spoke little; he opposed a stubborn resistance to their efforts at diverting his mind. He spent long hours by himself, in the country, and they had no idea what he did. Susie was terribly anxious. He had lost his balance so completely that she was prepared for any rashness. She divined that his hatred of Haddo was no longer within the bounds of reason. The desire for vengeance filled him entirely, so that he was capable of any violence.

Several days went by.

At last, in concert with Dr. Porhoët, she determined to make one more attempt. It was late at night, and they sat with open windows in the sitting-room of the inn. There was a singular oppressiveness in the air which suggested that a thunderstorm was at hand. Susie prayed for it; for she ascribed to the peculiar heat of the last few days much of Arthur's sullen irritability.

"Arthur, you *must* tell us what you are going to do," she said. "It is useless to stay here. We are all so ill and nervous that we cannot consider anything rationally. We want you to come away with us to-morrow."

"You can go if you choose," he said. "I shall remain till that man is dead."

"It is madness to talk like that. You can do nothing. You are only making yourself worse by staying here."

"I have quite made up my mind."

"The law can offer you no help, and what else can you do?"

She asked the question, meaning if possible to get from him some hint of his intentions; but the grimness of his answer, though it only confirmed her vague suspicions, startled her.

"If I can do nothing else, I shall shoot him like a dog."

She could think of nothing to say, and for a while they remained in silence. Then he got up.

"I think I should prefer it if you went," he said. "You can only hamper me."

"I shall stay here as long as you do."

"Why?"

"Because if you do anything, I shall be compromised. I may be arrested. I think the fear of that may restrain you."

He looked at her steadily. She met his eyes with a calmness which showed that she meant exactly what she said, and he turned uneasily away. A silence even greater than before fell upon them. They did not move. It was so still in the room that it might have been empty. The breathlessness of the air increased, so that it was horribly oppressive. Suddenly there was a loud rattle of thunder, and a flash of lightning tore across the heavy clouds. Susie thanked Heaven for the storm which would give presently a welcome freshness. She felt excessively ill at ease, and it was a relief to ascribe her sensation to a state of the atmosphere. Again the thunder rolled. It was so loud that it seemed to be immediately above their heads. And the wind rose suddenly and swept with a long moan through the trees that surrounded the house. It was a sound so human that it might have come from the souls of dead men suffering hopeless torments of regret.

The lamp went out, so suddenly that Susie was vaguely frightened. It gave one flicker, and they were in total darkness. It seemed as though someone had leaned over the chimney and blown it out. The night was very black, and they could not see the window which opened on to the country. The darkness was so peculiar that for a moment no one stirred.

Then Susie heard Dr. Porhoët slip his hand across the table to find matches, but it seemed that they were not there. Again a loud peal of thunder startled them, but the rain would not fall. They panted for fresh air. On a sudden Susie's heart gave a bound, and she sprang up.

"There's someone in the room."

The words were no sooner out of her mouth than she heard Arthur fling himself upon the intruder. She knew at once, with the certainty of an intuition, that it was Haddo. But how had he come in? What did he want? She tried to cry out, but no sound came from her throat. Dr. Porhoët seemed bound to his chair. He did not move. He made no sound. She knew that an awful struggle was proceeding. It was a struggle to the death between two men who hated one another, but the most terrible part of it was that nothing was heard. They were perfectly noiseless. She tried to do something, but she could not stir. And Arthur's heart exulted, for his enemy was in his grasp, under his hands, and he would not let him go while life was in him. He clenched his teeth and tightened his straining muscles. Susie heard his laboured breathing, but she only heard the breathing of one man. She wondered in abject terror what that could mean. They struggled silently, hand to hand, and Arthur knew that his strength was greater. He had made up his mind what to do and directed all his energy to a definite end. His enemy was extraordinarily powerful, but Arthur appeared to create strength from the sheer force of his will. It seemed for hours that they struggled. He could not bear him down.

Suddenly, he knew that the other was frightened and sought to escape from him. Arthur tightened his grasp; for nothing in the world now would he ever loosen his hold. He took a deep, quick breath, and then put out all his strength in a tremendous effort. They swayed from side to side. Arthur felt as if his muscles were being torn from the bones, he could not continue for more than a moment longer; but the agony that flashed across his mind at the thought of failure braced him to a sudden angry jerk. All at once Haddo collapsed, and they fell heavily to the ground. Arthur was breathing more quickly now. He thought that if he could keep on for one instant longer, he would be safe. He threw all his weight on the form that rolled beneath him, and bore down furiously on the man's arm. He twisted it sharply, with all his might, and felt it give way. He gave a low cry of triumph; the arm was broken. And now his enemy was seized with panic; he struggled madly, he wanted only to get away from those long hands that were killing him. They seemed to be of iron. Arthur seized the huge bullock throat and dug his fingers into it, and they sunk into the heavy rolls of fat; and he flung the whole weight of his body into them. He exulted, for he knew that his enemy was in his power at last; he was strangling him, strangling the life out of him. He wanted light so that he might see the horror of that vast face, and the deadly fear, and the staring eyes. And still he pressed with those iron hands. And now the movements were strangely convulsive. His victim writhed in the agony of death. His struggles were desperate, but the avenging hands held him as in a vice. And then the movements grew spasmodic, and then they grew weaker. Still the hands pressed upon the gigantic throat, and Arthur forgot everything. He was mad with rage and fury and hate and sorrow. He thought of Margaret's anguish and of her fiendish torture, and he wished the man had ten lives so that he might take them one by one. And at last all was still, and that vast mass of flesh was motionless, and he knew that his enemy was dead. He loosened his grasp and slipped one hand over the heart. It would never beat again. The man was stone dead. Arthur got up and straightened himself. The darkness was intense still, and he could see nothing. Susie heard him, and at length she was able to speak.

"Arthur what have you done?"

"I've killed him," he said hoarsely.

"O God, what shall we do?"

Arthur began to laugh aloud, hysterically, and in the darkness his hilarity was terrifying.

"For God's sake let us have some light."

"I've found the matches," said Dr. Porhoët.

He seemed to awake suddenly from his long stupor. He struck one, and it would not light. He struck another, and Susie took off the globe and the chimney as he kindled the wick. Then he held up the lamp, and they saw Arthur looking at them. His face was ghastly. The sweat ran off his forehead in great beads, and his eyes were bloodshot. He trembled in every limb. Then Dr. Porhoët advanced with the lamp and held it forward. They looked down on the floor for the man who lay there dead. Susie gave a sudden cry of horror.

There was no one there.

Arthur stepped back in terrified surprise. There was no one in the room, living or dead, but the three friends. The ground sank under Susie's feet, she felt horribly ill, and she fainted. When she awoke, seeming difficultly to emerge from an eternal night, Arthur was holding down her head.

"Bend down," he said. "Bend down."

All that had happened came back to her, and she burst into tears. Her self-control deserted her, and, clinging to him for protection, she sobbed as though her heart would break. She was shaken from head to foot. The strangeness of this last horror had overcome her, and she could have shrieked with fright.

"It's all right," he said. "You need not be afraid."

"Oh, what does it mean?"

"You must pluck up courage. We're going now to Skene."

She sprang to her feet, as though to get away from him; her heart beat wildly.

"No, I can't; I'm frightened."

"We must see what it means. We have no time to lose, or the morning will be upon us before we get back."

Then she sought to prevent him.

"Oh, for God's sake, don't go, Arthur. Something awful may await you there. Don't risk your life."

"There is no danger. I tell you the man is dead."

"If anything happened to you . . ."

She stopped, trying to restrain her sobs; she dared not go on. But he seemed to know what was in her mind.

"I will take no risks, because of you. I know that whether I live or dies is not a—matter of indifference to you."

She looked up and saw that his eyes were fixed upon her gravely. She reddened. A curious feeling came into her heart.

"I will go with you wherever you choose," she said humbly.

"Come, then."

They stepped out into the night. And now, without rain, the storm had passed away, and the stars were shining. They walked quickly. Arthur went in front of them. Dr. Porhoët and Susie followed him, side by side, and they had to hasten their steps in order not to be left behind. It seemed to them that the horror of the night was passed, and there was a fragrancy in the air which was wonderfully refreshing. The sky was beautiful. And at last they came to Skene. Arthur led them again to the opening in the palisade, and he took Susie's hand. Presently they stood in the place from which a few days before they had seen the house. As then, it stood in massive blackness against the night and, as then, the attic windows shone out with brilliant lights. Susie started, for she had expected that the whole place would be in darkness.

"There is no danger, I promise you," said Arthur gently. "We are going to find out the meaning of all this mystery."

He began to walk towards the house.

"Have you a weapon of some sort?" asked the doctor.

Arthur handed him a revolver.

"Take this. It will reassure you, but you will have no need of it. I bought it the other day when—I had other plans."

Susie gave a little shudder. They reached the drive and walked to the great portico which adorned the façade of the house. Arthur tried the handle, but it would not open.

"Will you wait here?" he said. "I can get through one of the windows, and I will let you in."

He left them. They stood quietly there, with anxious hearts; they could not guess what they would see. They were afraid that something would happen to Arthur, and Susie regretted that she had not insisted on going with him. Suddenly she remembered that awful moment when the light of the lamp had been thrown where all expected to see a body, and there was nothing.

"What do you think it meant?" she cried suddenly. "What is the explanation?"

"Perhaps we shall see now," answered the doctor.

Arthur still lingered, and she could not imagine what had become of him. All sorts of horrible fancies passed through her mind, and she dreaded she knew not what. At last they heard a footstep inside the house, and the door was opened.

"I was convinced that nobody slept here, but I was obliged to make sure. I had some difficulty in getting in."

Susie hesitated to enter. She did not know what horrors awaited her, and the darkness was terrifying.

"I cannot see," she said.

"I've brought a torch," said Arthur.

He pressed a button, and a narrow ray of bright light was cast upon the floor. Dr. Porhoët and Susie went in. Arthur carefully closed the door, and flashed the light of his torch all round them. They stood in a large hall, the floor of which was scattered with the skins of lions that Haddo on his celebrated expedition had killed in Africa. There were perhaps a dozen, and their number gave a wild, barbaric note. A great oak staircase led to the upper floors.

"We must go through all the rooms," said Arthur.

He did not expect to find Haddo till they came to the lighted attics, but it seemed needful nevertheless to pass right through the house on their way. A flash of his torch had shown him that the walls of the hall were decorated with all manner of armour, ancient swords of Eastern handiwork, barbaric weapons from central Africa, savage implements of mediæval warfare; and an idea came to him. He took down a huge battle-axe and swung it in his hand.

"Now come."

Silently, holding their breath as though they feared to wake the dead, they went into the first room. They saw it difficultly with their scant light, since the thin shaft of brilliancy, emphasising acutely the surrounding darkness, revealed it only piece by piece. It was a large room, evidently unused, for the furniture was covered with holland, and there was a mustiness about it which suggested that the windows were seldom opened. As in many old houses, the rooms led not from a passage but into one another, and they walked through many till they came back into the hall. They had all a desolate, uninhabited air. Their sombreness was increased by the oak with which they were panelled. There was panelling in the hall too, and on the stairs that led broadly to the top of the house. As they ascended, Arthur stopped for one moment and passed his hand over the polished wood.

"It would burn like tinder," he said.

They went through the rooms on the first floor, and they were as empty and as cheerless. Presently they came to that which had been Margaret's. In a bowl were dead flowers. Her brushes were still on the toilet table. But it was a gloomy chamber, with its dark oak, and so comfortless that Susie shuddered. Arthur stood for a time and looked at it, but he said nothing. They found themselves again on the stairs and they went to the second storey. But here they seemed to be at the top of the house.

"How does one get up to the attics?" said Arthur, looking about him with surprise.

He paused for a while to think. Then he nodded his head.

"There must be some steps leading out of one of the rooms."

They went on. And now the ceilings were much lower, with heavy beams, and there was no furniture at all. The emptiness seemed to make everything more terrifying. They felt that they were on the threshold of a great mystery, and Susie's heart began to beat fast. Arthur conducted his examination with the greatest method; he walked round each room carefully, looking for a door that might lead to a staircase; but there was no sign of one.

"What will you do if you can't find the way up?" asked Susie.

"I shall find the way up," he answered.

They came to the staircase once more and had discovered nothing. They looked at one another helplessly.

"It's quite clear there is a way," said Arthur, with impatience. "There must be something in the nature of a hidden door somewhere or other."

He leaned against the balustrade and meditated. The light of his lantern threw a narrow ray upon the opposite wall.

"I feel certain it must be in one of the rooms at the end of the house. That seems the most natural place to put a means of ascent to the attics."

They went back, and again he examined the panelling of a small room that had outside walls on three sides of it. It was the only one that did not lead into another.

"It must be here," he said.

Presently he gave a little laugh, for he saw that a small door was concealed by the woodwork. He pressed it where he thought there might be a spring, and it flew open. Their torch showed them a narrow wooden staircase. They walked up and found themselves in front of a door Arthur tried it, but it was locked. He smiled grimly.

"Will you get back a little," he said.

He lifted his axe and swung it down upon the latch. The handle was shattered, but the lock did not yield. He shook his head. As he paused for a moment, and there was a complete silence, Susie distinctly heard a slight noise. She put her hand on Arthur's arm to call his attention to it, and with strained ears they listened. There was something alive on the other side of that door. They heard its curious sound: it was not that of a human voice, it was not the crying of an animal, it was extraordinary.

It was a sort of gibber, hoarse and rapid, and it filled them with an icy terror because it was so weird and so unnatural.

"Come away, Arthur," said Susie. "Come away."

"There's some living thing in there," he answered.

He did not know why the sound horrified him. The sweat broke out on his forehead.

"Something awful will happen to us," whispered Susie, shaking with uncontrollable fear.

"The only thing is to break the door down."

The horrid gibbering was drowned by the noise he made. Quickly, without pausing, he began to hack at the oak door with all his might. In rapid succession his heavy blows rained down, and the sound echoed through the empty house. There was a crash, and the door swung back. They had been so long in almost total darkness that they were blinded for an instant by the dazzling light. And then instinctively they started back, for, as the door opened, a wave of heat came out upon them so that they could hardly breathe. The place was like an oven.

They entered. It was lit by enormous lamps, the light of

which was increased by reflectors, and warmed by a great furnace. They could not understand why so intense a heat was necessary. The narrow windows were closed. Dr. Porhoët caught sight of a thermometer and was astounded at the temperature it indicated. The room was used evidently as a laboratory. On broad tables were test-tubes, basins and baths of white porcelain, measuring-glasses, and utensils of all sorts; but the surprising thing was the great scale upon which everything was. Neither Arthur nor Dr. Porhoët had ever seen such gigantic measures nor such large test-tubes. There were rows of bottles, like those in the dispensary of a hospital, each containing great quantities of a different chemical. The three friends stood in silence. The emptiness of the room contrasted so oddly with its appearance of being in immediate use that it was uncanny. Susie felt that he who worked there was in the midst of his labours, and might return at any moment; he could have only gone for an instant into another chamber in order to see the progress of some experiment. It was quite silent. Whatever had made those vague, unearthly noises was hushed by their approach.

The door was closed between this room and the next. Arthur opened it, and they found themselves in a long, low attic, ceiled with great rafters, as brilliantly lit and as hot as the first. Here too were broad tables laden with retorts, instruments for heating, huge test-tubes, and all manner of vessels. The furnace that warmed it gave a steady heat. Arthur's gaze travelled slowly from table to table, and he wondered what Haddo's experiments had really been. The air was heavy with an extraordinary odour; it was not musty, like that of the closed rooms through which they had passed, but singularly pungent, disagreeable and sickly. He asked himself what it could spring from. Then his eyes fell upon a huge receptable that stood on the table nearest to the furnace. It was covered with a white cloth. He took it off. The vessel was about four feet high, round, and shaped somewhat like a washing tub, but it was made of glass more than an inch thick. In it was a spherical mass, a little larger than a football, of a peculiar, livid colour. The surface was smooth, but rather coarsely grained, and over it ran a dense system of blood-vessels. It reminded the two medical men of those huge tumours which are preserved in spirit in hospital museums. Susie looked at it with an incomprehensible disgust. Suddenly she gave a cry.

"Good God, it's moving!"

Arthur put his hand on her arm quickly to quieten her and bent down with irresistible curiosity. They saw that it was a mass of flesh unlike that of any human being; and it pulsated regularly. The movement was quite distinct, up and down, like the delicate heaving of a woman's breast when she is asleep. Arthur touched the thing with one finger and it shrank slightly.

"It's quite warm," he said.

He turned it over, and it remained in the position in which he had placed it, as if there were neither top nor bottom to it. But they could see now, irregularly placed on one side, a few short hairs. They were just like human hairs.

"Is it alive?" whispered Susie, struck with horror and amazement.

"Yes!"

Arthur seemed fascinated. He could not take his eyes off the loathsome thing. He watched it slowly heave with even motion.

"What can it mean?" he asked.

He looked at Dr. Porhoët with pale and startled face. A

thought was coming to him, but a thought so unnatural, extravagant, and terrible that he pushed it from him with a movement of both hands, as though it were a material thing. Then all three turned around abruptly with a start, for they heard again the wild gibbering which had first shocked their ears. In the wonder of this revolting object they had forgotten all the rest. The sound seemed extraordinarily near, and Susie drew back instinctively, for it appeared to come from her very side.

"There's nothing here," said Arthur. "It must be in the next room."

"Oh, Arthur, let us go," cried Susie. "I'm afraid to see what may be in store for us. It is nothing to us, and what we see may poison our sleep for ever."

She looked appealingly at Dr. Porhoët. He was white and anxious. The heat of that place had made the sweat break out on his forehead.

"I have seen enough. I want to see no more," he said.

"Then you may go, both of you," answered Arthur. "I do not wish to force you to see anything. But I shall go on. Whatever it is, I wish to find out."

"But Haddo? Supposing he is there, waiting? Perhaps you are only walking into a trap that he has set for you."

"I am convinced that Haddo is dead."

Again that unintelligible jargon, unhuman and shrill, fell upon their ears, and Arthur stepped forward. Susie did not hesitate. She was prepared to follow him anywhere. He opened the door, and there was a sudden quiet. Whatever made those sounds were there. It was a larger room than any of the others and much higher, for it ran along the whole front of the house. The powerful lamps showed every corner of it at once, but, above, the beams of the open ceiling were dark with shadow. And here the nauseous odour, which had struck them before, was so overpowering that for a while they could not go in. It was indescribably foul. Even Arthur thought it would make him sick, and he looked at the windows to see if it was possible to open them; but it seemed they were hermetically closed. The extreme warmth made the air more overpowering. There were four furnaces here, and they were all alight. In order to give out more heat and to burn slowly, the fronts of them were open, and one could see that they were filled with glowing coke.

The room was furnished no differently from the others, but to the various instruments for chemical operations on a large scale were added all manner of electrical appliances. Several books were lying about, and one had been left open face downwards on the edge of a table. But what immediately attracted their attention was a row of those large glass vessels like that which they had seen in the adjoining room. Each was covered with a white cloth. They hesitated a moment, for they knew that here they were face to face with the great enigma. At last Arthur pulled away the cloth from one. None of them spoke. They stared with astonished eyes. For here, too, was a strange mass of flesh, almost as large as a new-born child, but there was in it the beginnings of something ghastly human. It was shaped vaguely like an infant, but the legs were joined together so that it looked like a mummy rolled up in its coverings. There were neither feet nor knees. The trunk was formless, but there was a curious thickening on each side; it was as if a modeller had meant to make a figure with the arms loosely bent, but had left the work unfinished so that they were still one with the body. There was something that resembled a human head, covered with long golden hair, but it was horrible; it was an uncouth mass, without eyes or nose or mouth. The colour was a kind of sickly pink, and it was almost transparent. There was a very slight movement in it, rhythmical and slow. It was living too.

Then quickly Arthur removed the covering from all the other jars but one; and in a flash of the eyes they saw abominations so awful that Susie had to clench her fists in order not to scream. There was one monstrous thing in which the limbs approached nearly to the human. It was extraordinarily heaped up, with fat tiny arms, little bloated legs, and an absurd squat body, so that it looked like a Chinese mandarin in porcelain. In another the trunk was almost like that of a human child, except that it was patched strangely with red and grey. But the terror of it was that at the neck it branched hideously, and there were two distinct heads, monstrously large, but duly provided with all their features. The features were a caricature of humanity so shameful that one could hardly bear to look. And as the light fell on it, the eyes of each head opened slowly. They had no pigment in them, but were pink, like the eyes of white rabbits; and they stared for a moment with an odd, unseeing glance. Then they were shut again, and what was curiously terrifying was that the movements were not quite simultaneous; the eyelids of one head fell slowly just before those of the other. And in another place was a ghastly monster in which it seemed that two bodies had been dreadfully entangled with one another. It was a creature of nightmare, with four arms and four legs, and this one actually moved. With a peculiar motion it crawled along the bottom of the great receptable in which it was kept, towards the three persons who looked at it. It seemed to wonder what they did. Susie started back with fright, as it raised itself on its four legs and tried to reach up to them.

Susie turned away and hid her face. She could not look at

those ghastly counterfeits of humanity. She was terrified and ashamed.

"Do you understand what this means?" said Dr. Porhoët to Arthur, in an awed voice. "It means that he has discovered the secret of life."

"Was it for these vile monstrosities that Margaret was sacrificed in all her loveliness?"

The two men looked at one another with sad, wondering eyes.

"Don't you remember that he talked of the manufacture of human beings? It's these misshapen things that he's succeeding in producing," said the doctor.

"There is one more that we haven't seen," said Arthur.

He pointed to the covering which still hid the largest of the vases. He had a feeling that it contained the most fearful of all these monsters; and it was not without an effort that he drew the cloth away. But no sooner had he done this than something sprang up, so that instinctively he started back, and it began to gibber in piercing tones. These were the unearthly sounds that they had heard. It was not a voice, it was a kind of raucous crying, hoarse yet shrill, uneven like the barking of a dog, and appalling. The sounds came forth in rapid succession, angrily, as though the being that uttered them sought to express itself in furious words. It was mad with passion and beat against the glass walls of its prison with clenched fists. For the hands were human hands, and the body, though much larger, was of the shape of a new-born child. The creature must have stood about four feet high. The head was horribly misshapen. The skull was enormous, smooth and distended like that of a hydrocephalic, and the forehead protruded over the face hideously. The features were almost unformed, preternaturally small under the great, overhanging brow; and they had an expression of fiendish malignity. The tiny, misshapen countenance writhed with convulsive fury, and from the mouth poured out a foaming spume. It raised its voice higher and higher, shrieking senseless gibberish in its rage. Then it began to hurl its whole body madly against the glass walls and to beat its head. It appeared to have a sudden incomprehensible hatred for the three strangers. It was trying to fly at them, the toothless gums moved spasmodically, and it threw its face into horrible grimaces. That nameless, loathsome abortion was the nearest that Oliver Haddo had come to the human form.

"Come away," said Arthur. "We must not look at this."

He quickly flung the covering over the jar.

"Yes, for God's sake let us go," said Susie.

"We haven't done yet," answered Arthur. "We haven't found the author of all this."

He looked at the room in which they were, but there was no door except that by which they had entered. Then he uttered a startled cry, and stepping forward fell on his knee.

On the other side of the long tables heaped up with instruments, hidden so that at first they had not seen him, Oliver Haddo lay on the floor, dead. His blue eyes were staring wide, and they seemed larger than they had ever been. They kept still the expression of terror which they had worn in the moment of his agony, and his heavy face was distorted with deadly fear. It was purple and dark, and the eyes were injected with blood.

"He died of suffocation," whispered Dr. Porhoët.

Arthur pointed to the neck. There could be seen on it distinctly the marks of the avenging fingers that had strangled the life out of him. It was impossible to hesitate.

"I told you that I had killed him," said Arthur.

Then he remembered something more. He took hold of the right arm. He was convinced that it had been broken during that desperate struggle in the darkness. He felt it carefully and listened. He heard plainly the two parts of the bone rub against one another. The dead man's arm was broken just in the place where he had broken it. Arthur stood up. He took one last look at his enemy. That vast mass of flesh lay heaped up on the floor in horrible disorder.

"Now that you have seen, will you come away?" said Susie, interrupting him.

The words seemed to bring him suddenly to himself.

"Yes, we must go quickly."

They turned away and with hurried steps walked through those bright attics till they came to the stairs.

"Now go down and wait for me at the door," said Arthur. "I will follow you immediately."

"What are you going to do?" asked Susie.

"Never mind. Do as I tell you. I have not finished here yet."

They went down the great oak staircase and waited in the hall. They wondered what Arthur was about. Presently he came running down.

"Be quick!" he cried. "We have no time to lose."

"What have you done, Arthur?"

"There's no time to tell you now."

He hurried them out and slammed the door behind him. He took Susie's hand.

"Now we must run. Come."

She did not know what his haste signified, but her heart beat furiously. He dragged her along. Dr. Porhoët hurried on behind them. Arthur plunged into the wood. He would not leave them time to breathe.

"You must be quick," he said.

At last they came to the opening in the fence, and he helped them to get through. Then he carefully replaced the wooden paling and, taking Susie's arm, began to walk rapidly towards their inn.

"I'm frightfully tired," she said. "I simply can't go so fast."

"You must. Presently you can rest as long as you like."

They walked very quickly for a while. Now and then Arthur looked back. The night was still quite dark, and the stars shone out in their myriads. At last he slackened their pace.

"Now you can go more slowly,' he said.

Susie saw the smiling glance that he gave her. His eyes were full of tenderness. He put his arm affectionately round her shoulders to support her.

"I'm afraid you're quite exhausted, poor thing," he said. "I'm sorry to have had to hustle you so much."

"It doesn't matter at all."

She leaned against him comfortably. With that protecting arm about her, she felt capable of any fatigue. Dr. Porhoët stopped.

"You must really let me roll myself a cigarette," he said.

"You may do whatever you like," answered Arthur.

There was a different ring in his voice now, and it was soft with a good-humour that they had not heard in it for many months. He appeared singularly relieved. Susie was ready to forget the terrible past and give herself over to the happiness that seemed at last in store for her. They began to saunter slowly on. And now they could take pleasure in the exquisite night. The air was very suave, odorous with the heather that was all about them, and there was an enchanting peace in that scene which wonderfully soothed their weariness. It was

dark still, but they knew the dawn was at hand, and Susie rejoiced in the approaching day. In the east the azure of the
night began to thin away into pale amethyst, and the trees
seemed gradually to stand out from the darkness in a ghostly
beauty. Suddenly birds began to sing all around them in a
splendid chorus. From their feet a lark sprang up with a
rustle of wings and, mounting proudly upon the air, chanted
blithe canticles to greet the morning. They stood upon a little
hill.

"Let us wait here and see the sun rise," said Susie.

"As you will."

They stood all three of them, and Susie took in deep, joyful breaths of the sweet air of dawn. The whole land, spread
at her feet, was clothed in the purple dimness that heralds day,
and she exulted in its beauty. But she noticed that Arthur,
unlike herself and Dr. Porhoët, did not look toward the east.
His eyes were fixed steadily upon the place from which they
had come. What did he look for in the darkness of the west?
She turned round, and a cry broke from her lips, for the
shadows there were lurid with a deep red glow.

"It looks like a fire," she said

"It is. Skene is burning like tinder."

And as he spoke it seemed that the roof fell in, for suddenly vast flames sprang up, rising high into the still night
air; and they saw that the house they had just left was blazing
furiously. It was a magnificent sight from the distant hill on
which they stood to watch the fire as it soared and sank, as it
shot scarlet tongues along like strange Titanic monsters, as it
raged from room to room. Skene was burning. It was beyond
the reach of human help. In a little while there would be no
trace of all those crimes and all those horrors. Now it was one

mass of flame. It looked like some primeval furnace, where the gods might work unheard-of miracles.

"Arthur, what have you done?" asked Susie, in a tone that was hardly audible.

He did not answer directly. He put his arm about her shoulder again, so that she was obliged to turn round.

"Look, the sun is rising."

In the east, a long ray of light climbed up the sky, and the sun, yellow and round, appeared upon the face of the earth.

THE WORKS OF
W. SOMERSET MAUGHAM

An Arno Press Collection

NOVELS

Ashenden: Or, The British Agent. 1941
The Bishop's Apron. 1906
Cakes and Ale. 1935
Catalina: A Romance. 1948
Christmas Holiday. 1939
The Explorer. With Four Illustrations by F. Graham Cootes. 1909
The Hero. 1901
The Hour Before the Dawn. 1942
Liza of Lambeth. 1936
The Magician: Together with a Fragment of Autobiography. 1957
The Making of a Saint: A Romance of Mediaeval Italy. 1966
The Moon and Sixpence. 1919
Mrs. Craddock. 1903
The Narrow Corner. 1932
Of Human Bondage. 1915
The Painted Veil. 1925
The Razor's Edge. 1943
Then and Now. 1946
Theatre. 1937
Up at the Villa. 1941

ESSAYS

The Art of Fiction: An Introduction to Ten Novels and Their
    Authors. 1955
Books and You. 1940
Points of View: Five Essays. 1959
Selected Prefaces and Introductions. 1963
Strictly Personal. 1941
The Summing Up. 1938
The Vagrant Mood: Six Essays. 1953
A Writer's Notebook. 1949

TRAVEL

Andalusia: The Land of the Blessed Virgin. 1935
Don Fernando: Or Variations on Some Spanish Themes. 1935
France at War. 1940
The Gentleman in the Parlour: A Record of a Journey from
  Rangoon to Haiphong. 1930
On a Chinese Screen. 1942

PLAYS

East of Suez: A Play in Seven Scenes. 1922
For Services Rendered: A Play in Three Acts. 1933
The Letter: A Play in Three Acts. 1925
The Sacred Flame: A Play in Three Acts. 1928
Sheppey: A Play in Three Acts. 1933
Six Comedies. 1939

SHORT STORIES

Ah King. 1933
Casuarina Tree. 1926
Cosmopolitans. 1938
Creatures of Circumstance. 1947
First Person Singular. 1931
The Mixture as Before. 1940
The Trembling of a Leaf. 1934
Seventeen Lost Stories. Compiled and with an Introduction by
  Craig V. Showalter. 1969